Home for Christmas

Home for Christmas

STORIES FROM THE MARITIMES AND NEWFOUNDLAND

Edited by
SABINE CAMPBELL

Cover illustration ©Judi Pennanen, 1999. Reproduced with permission.
Book design by Julie Scriver.
Printed in Canada by Transcontinental Printing.
10 9 8 7 6 5 4 3 2 1

Canadian Cataloguing in Publication Data

Home for Christmas
ISBN 0-86492-269-8

1. Christmas stories, Canadian (English) — Atlantic Provinces.*
I. Campbell, Sabine.

PS8329.5.M37H65 1999   C813'.0108334   C99-950177-1
PR9198.2.M32H65 1999

Published with the financial support of the Canada Council for the Arts, the Government of Canada through the Book Publishing Industry Development Program, and the New Brunswick Department of Economic Development, Tourism and Culture.
Canadä

Goose Lane Editions
469 King Street
Fredericton, New Brunswick
CANADA E3B 1E5

Contents

Gifts

SABINE CAMPBELL

Christmas. A time of warmth in the winter cold, a time of green in the winter white. An emotional time, full of hope as well as sadness, love as well as anger. Christmas brings us memories of home, of childhood, of things lost. We remember and long for the scents of Christmas: the warm smells of baking, roasting, cooking, the wonderfully evocative smell of fir, spruce or pine, and the crisp cold smell of winter. It is a time of contrasts.

I love it! Christmas for me combines what was best about my childhood and also about my own young and now grown-up family. I love the bustle of the preparations and the still-for-me breathless excitement of Christmas Eve and morning. It means I've been lucky; the great disappointments of my life didn't hit at Christmastime, perhaps, and I am always aware that the long winter nights will give way to ever-lengthening days bringing us again to spring.

We celebrate the last Christmas of this millennium, welcome the year 2000 with its magical three fat zeros, and hope that the new century will be a more gentle one than the last. Mixed with the excitement of the dawn are the memories of just how grim the dusk and darkness of the old century were. The state of our planet — so many wars; the depleted resources of an abused environment, from dead rain forests to dying oceans — influences us all, and so it has the writers of the Christmas stories in *Home for Christmas*.

Although the stories reflect mainly on the happy times of Christmas, they include fear, hopelessness, hunger and lost love. The death of love is perhaps more sad than love lost, and saddest of all is the death of a loved one. Mark Tunney writes about a child not living to see another Christmas; Lynn Coady's story includes a baby given away, while Kelly Cooper talks about yearning for a baby; Herb Curtis's Hilda Porter finds and gives affection on Christmas Eve; Anne Simpson weaves an ancient myth into her family Christmas. Many of the stories deal with the memories of childhood, when hardship can be transformed at the last moment. Magic is found in the lighted candles on a tree, as Bob Gibbs recollects, or in the surprise of a red sleigh under Ephie Carrier's tree.

Always at Christmas we think of children: babies already born, yet to come or longed for. Christmas is a bit like having a baby. When it finally arrives, it is so wonderful and we are so happy to see it that we forget all the trouble it has created beforehand. There always seems to be that moment, shortly before the baby is born or a few days before Christmas, when we ask why on earth we have let ourselves in for this yet again — how could we have forgotten the trouble and pain that's always involved? But the feeling lasts only for a moment. When we see the tree lighted for the first time or hug the new baby, when we smell a favourite Christmas food or hear the first knock of visitors at the door, then all the pain, work and worry dissolve, and we can open our hearts and welcome the festive season.

Merry Christmas!

A Christmas Story

RAY GUY

A youngster angel by the name of Clarence — four foot, seven inches tall and no odds now how many years old — was out for a walk along the Golden Strand one day in company with a grandfather angel.

The weather was fair to middlin' as it generally always is in the Land Beyond the Blue.

The grandfather angel dodged along puffing on an imaginary pipe stuffed with imaginary Beaver tobacco of very best light-leaf plug.

It was imaginary because this part of the Kingdom of Heaven is plastered fore and aft with "No Smoking" signs.

The grandfather angel, who had been a Salvationer in life although many times a backslider, trailed along the beach behind the livelier youngster angel, Clarence, and from time to time broke out in a Chorus.

He had a "wonderful throat" as many of the womankind Army goers used to remark admiringly after Barracks down there Below.

Whenever the Young People's Sergeant Major put out the call to "Rise Her! All Over the Building!" on the chorus of "Oh, Boundless Salvation," the Founder's song, he could fairly drown out the old soldier putting the blocks to the big bass drum — even though he was sitting two seats from the back.

And now, up here at last in the Glory Land, as he dodged along that Celestial Landwash, anyone with half an ear could easily hear him above the waves of the wide Ocean of Mercy as they rolled in on the Golden Strand:

Oh, we'll walk and talk on the Golden Strand,
We'll walk on the Golden Shore . . .

Horrrk! Ptwew! Here he took out his imaginary pipe and launched an imaginary spit to leeward.

We'll sing of His love in the Realms Above,
And we won't come back anymore.

Little did he ever think as he sang that self-same chorus Down Below that he'd ever live to see the day when he really would be walking on the Golden Strand on the Other Side.

Baiting up in Golden Bay off Cape St. Mary's in the later part of a civil June, with the glory of the morning on the wave and three letters of a plug of Beaver still left in his Guernsey pocket, was the closest he used to think he'd ever come to it.

But here he was. The Kingdom of Heaven was a pretty fair place indeed. He never ceased to marvel at the wideness and depth of the Ocean of Mercy, at the never failing favourable tides on the Golden Strand or at the hills behind with no dark valleys and from whence came the Light.

There was only one thing he really missed up here in That Land where the sun will never set and the leaves will never fade, and that was a bit of fog.

Oh, not all the time, mind you. And not a cold, black troublesome fog with the wind southeast. But a white and luminous caplin-scull fog in a stark calm now and then just for remembrances sake.

Although never one to find much fault with Almighty God — even when the old Acadia broke down and put him in jeopardy of a broadside swell for the tenth time running — he did think that the occasional bit of fog would really touch off the Kingdom of Heaven to perfection.

"Hello, then! Hello, then! Hello, then!" sang out the youngster angel, Clarence, of a sudden.

He snatched something out of the water and skipped backwards out of the lop so as not to get the tail of his robe of purest white wet or overrun the tops of his long rubbers.

"What's this, granda?" he said. "What's this?"

"What old trash and rubbitch there do be washin' up on the beaches these days, at all, at all," said the grandfather angel. "Whenever they get a unseasonable high breeze Down Below it drives in shockin'. Show here."

Clarence handed the dripping wet stuff to the grandfather angel.

"That's what they calls paper Down Below," said the grandfather angel, for he was wonderful sagacious and had sailed on foreign-going vessels.

"'Pears to me to be part of a newspaper of some description. Can't hardly make it out without me eyeglasses. 'Tis not a leaf out of the *War Cry* and that's for certain.

"Hold on. Hold on. I can bare make out that part. 'St. John's' it says here, and 'Newfoundland.'"

Clarence was puzzled by all this, for he was more or less an Innocent Lamb and had not much knowledge, let alone remembrance, of the world.

"What's newspaper, granda?" he asked. "What's St. John's? What's Newfoundland?"

"Newfoundland is a poor country badly used by traitors and slaves!" said the grandfather angel, suddenly rising to the rolling heights of oratory he had often achieved while giving his Testimony before the Penitent Form Down Below. "But one which, by the Grace of He Who is Higher Than All, will always muddle along through the rough and the smooth and find a safe harbour at the last!"

This really didn't give Clarence much of a clue because, although he was doing fairly well with his lessons at the St. Stephen's Upgrading School for Cherubim and Seraphim, he was still of tender years and his child's mind couldn't grasp these matters.

"But, now," said the grandfather angel, now his more usual and tranquil self once again, "this'll be St. John's city, which is named after the old skipper down the shore.

"A untidy place, an unruly place, where much riotous living goes ahead and where you got to watch 'em like a hawk or they'll rob the coppers off your eyes in the transaction of a box of 'baccy or a jug of brandy for your stomach's sake.

"And a newspaper, Mr. Quiz-Box, is where they cuts down trees and squats them out flat for to make paper and then prints stuff on them. It is a sinful, sinful practice. Them fellers what puts out the newspapers Down Below should be on their knees night and day, beggin' forgiveness for destroyin' the handiwork of Our Blessed Lord in the forests and turnin' it to such a low and useless purpose."

Although Clarence was nothing if not curious, he quickly lodged the piece of wicked soggy newspaper down on the rock they were sitting on in case his fingers started to burn.

"Granda, what is them fellers Down Below like?"

"Accordin' to the best authorities," replied the grandfather angel, spitting again to leeward, "they're a little lower than the angels, which is us. Now, how much lower 'a little lower' is, I don't know."

"Can't you mind anything at all about before you Crossed Over?" persisted the youngster angel, who was always and forever asking questions about this and that.

"A bit, here and there," replied the grandfather, gazing out over the wide Ocean of Mercy and smoking his imaginary pipe, "but only the very best bits. When you commences to get along in life and your time is nearly come, your memory is not what it used to be. You can only mind the very best bits. That's the way it is all figured out."

"Oh," said Clarence pensively. "I see. Granda? All hands is alike up here in the Glory Land and there is no difference with regards to race, country, colour, religion, creed or politics. But do you remember . . . do you think . . . that me and you . . . I mean to say, yourself and myself . . . mightn't be Newfoundland angels?"

"What," said the grandfather angel, amazed, "in the devil put a notion like that into your head!"

"Well," said Clarence, "them two fellers sittin' back of me at the St. Stephen's Upgradin' School for Cherubim and Seraphim said the other day that I must be a Newfoundlander because I talks quare."

"You're old enough to know better," said the grandfather angel. "When you comes through the Pearly Gate it is like joining on to another country. All hands is alike when they passes out the citizenship papers. Yes and no. We might or might not be Newfoundland angels. I can't clearly remember. But if you thinks so, keep it to yourself, as talk like that will only cause a fuss. And the Kingdom of Heaven is the last place in the world that we wants to stir up a fuss."

Clarence seemed satisfied on this point and then skipped off to have a bit of a fly-around for himself. The grandfather angel continued to sit on a rock on the Golden Strand and look out over the Ocean of Mercy. He wasn't much of a one for flying. Whenever he got ten feet off the ground he commenced to get giddy-headed. It was all right as a novelty, he thought, but he wouldn't like to make a practice of it.

"Clarence!" he called out sharply. "Come down here and pick up that harp of yours. Lodge it up above high-water mark. The tide is risin'!"

"Oh, shag that bloody harp," cried Clarence petulantly. "Harp, harp, harp is all I hears. I'm sick of harp practice. I can play by ear already but they says you got to play by note."

"Keep a civil tongue in your head, sir," said the grandfather angel sternly, "or them long rubbers will be took away from you and put up back of the stove for a week, not to be touched."

This awful threat caused immediate repentance on the part of the youngster angel Clarence, and he did as he was told.

"Granda," he said, as they continued their walk along the Golden Strand, "what kinds of people is it gets in through them Pearly Gates?"

"All kinds," said the grandfather angel, keeping an eye out for a glass ball or a nice piece of BC var drove ashore, for old habits, good and bad, are hard to break.

"There's your little Chinee, and there's your little black boy from other countries up here so well as yourself. In our Father's house there is many mansions . . . a damn sight more than some fellers Down Below could ever credit."

"Yes, but what about that other place," said Clarence. "Some goes there when they gets turned down from coming in here."

"There's some gets their applications turned down, yes," said the grandfather angel, "but that's a matter of court work at the last Trump. I never had no head for court work. Never had the education. I 'low it would take all the lawyers in St. John's to figure it out."

"Do even RCs and the Church of Englanders get in through the Pearly Gates if their applications are in order?" asked Clarence.

"Oh, yes, yes, indeed," said the grandfather angel in tones of awe, for the flexibility and stretch of the very outer boundaries of Salvation never ceased to amaze him.

"Is it hot over in the other place?" asked Clarence, "with them all the time heaving on the coal and sticking fish prongs into you?"

"Well, now," said the grandfather angel as they paused to take another spell, "I minds that the Young People's Sergeant Major Down Below — who was no slouch, mind you, for knowing the Scriptures from cover to cover and inside out — always said the Other Place was a bit on the sultry side with fire and brimstone and gnashin' of teeth. But from talkin' to one and the other since I come up Yonder, I hear that the other place is just about the same as this place here. The only difference bein' that the fellers who goes to the other place is never content, not even for one day or one hour, and they can never figure out why it is they isn't content. Arrrr, nobody Below ever dreamed that Hell could be that terrible."

To get the awful picture out of his head the grandfather angel looked out again over the boundless Ocean of Mercy and took some comfort in the fact that its limits were more than the mind of man could fathom.

"No, no, no," he said reflectively as the youngster angel Clarence picked up his harp and they moved on. "The Glory Land is not near so far away as the moon, and it is not near so complicated as some fellers thinks."

The day grew late — as days in the Kingdom of Heaven go — and they turned toward home.

Soon every angel in the Kingdom would be sweeping through the gates of the New Jerusalem, and the Herald Angels would blow their silver trumpets and all hands would rise her all over the building at the birthday of the Prince of Peace.

Clarence knew that he would never get that bloody harp down pat in time. Playing by ear was all very well for informal occasions, but you really needed to be able to play by note at the birthday of the Fairest of Ten Thousand, the Lily of the Valley, the Bright and Morning Star.

"Don't trouble yourself," said the grandfather angel, knowing Clarence's worry. "Don't trouble yourself so long as you always do the very best you can."

They hadn't noticed it happening, but there it was. The wide Ocean of Mercy had become stark staring calm. A white, luminous fog rolled in across the Golden Strand and encompassed them round about, and the purple flowers of a clump of flagroot on the beach were beaded with dew.

Another Christmas

ANN COPELAND

Silence.

All Advent, an absence of noise and talk, a silence deepening and enfolding, weaving an expectant cocoon about us as we moved through daily tasks domestic and unnoteworthy: cleaning the house, memorizing the vow catechism, learning church history, studying the Ignatian way of prayer, trying to practise it. We were postulants — knocking, as the word itself suggests, at the door of the Order we'd chosen, asking for admission. The initial trial period of six months was almost over. In less than a month, if all went well, we'd be admitted to become novices, to wear the habit and white veil. For now, we had the sense, the seven of us left, that trial time, our first trial, was coming to an end.

For me the Advent silence had held one notable interruption. Each day, for half an hour, while others were busy with extra Christmas preparation, I'd been permitted to enter the small novitiate chapel and practise on the pipe organ. It was a permission not easily given, but in view of the important feast coming, I, as the one keyboard person then at the novitiate, was permitted to prepare.

Every afternoon I'd slip into chapel, remove my white celluloid postulant cuffs, set them on the bench beside me, lift the rolltop cover of the organ, click on the motor, touch again the smooth ivory keys. Sometimes Sister Henry, the sacristan, would be working in the sanctuary at the far end of chapel. Black skirt hooked up beneath a special white sacristan's apron, white veil pinned back, she'd glide about her privileged domain with feline efficiency, dusting the pale green marble sanctuary steps, polishing to full lustre the gold and sapphire mosaic lamb on the altar front, draping spotless white across the sacrificial table. A short three years later, before she ever stepped into the classroom, she would die of leukemia, mourned by parents bewildered that God should take so early a daughter they'd already given him. In her memory they donated a bronze virgin to a new chapel in Delaware.

Flipping through the hymnal I would consider possible pieces, play them softly, tentatively, experimenting with stops — the mellow flutes, the throatier reeds — seeking sounds suitable for what I imagined Christmas Eve would be. Trumpet? Too brash. Celeste? Too schmaltzy. I was flying blind, choosing by ear and by instinct. I'd never spent a Christmas here. Nor had I ever been at an organ, responsible for Christmas music. For twenty-one years I'd spent Christmas Eve at home, immersed in the domestic tensions of family Yuletide. I didn't miss that.

I chose my hymns with care. I knew it was taboo to enjoy Christmas carols ahead of time. That the whole point of Advent was penance (three Sundays purple, one rose), that it was a time of preparing, hollowing out, making crooked ways straight. That to burst into "Hark the Herald Angels Sing" when, so to speak, the child was still on his way to our hearts, would hardly be appropriate. Nonetheless, I did have to practise them. I hadn't practised seriously on a keyboard in over four years. Now I discovered how totally I must give myself to this demanding instrument — feet, ankles, heels, trunk, arms, wrists, fingers, mind always focused, ears open, listening. "You play the piano," our novice mistress had told me. "Surely you could learn the organ." Frustrated by slack ankles, I drilled my wayward feet to gain a sense of intervals, retrained my fingers to precision as they released air so magically turned to music. Closing the swell box, I barely whispered the forbidden carols in the empty chapel, Mary and Joseph sculptured and impervious in their distant niches. Some selections seemed less objectionable, more properly liturgical. For those I luxuriated in the organ's full palette, boldly displaying the sensuous harmonies of Palestrina, urging aloft with a single one foot principal the ancient cry: "O come, O come, Emmanuel." "Drop down dew, ye heavens, from above, and let the clouds rain the just one," sang mellow flutes in limpid legato, as afternoon sun slanted gold and purple through the high stained glass and the single red sanctuary lamp continued to flicker. Unashamedly, I boomed the mighty O Antiphons we began to sing on December 17, each with its final stirring plea: *Veni ad docendum nos . . . veni ad liberandum nos . . . veni et illumina sedentes in tenebris mortis.* A single golden harp sang "The First Noel," jubilant silver trumpets "Joy to the World," the *Gloria in Excelsis Deo* became a revolving prism of bells splintering into shards of opalescent joy, praise transparent as crystal.

As Christmas drew nearer, buoyed up by the possibilities my fingers were uncovering, I decided to risk a simplified version of "Jesu, Joy of Man's Desiring" I'd found in the organ bench.

Aside from those few hours at the keyboard, the weeks before Christmas grew stark. Bleak. Rations diminished. I hated the dry toast put out for collation each afternoon beside our required glass of milk. Scrubbing intensified. The sweet astringent smell of lemon oil pervaded the visitors' parlour; ammonia gassed us as we rubbed imaginary spots from already gleaming windows. We were to wax and polish the entire old rambling two-storey timbered country house, once the home of Margaret Sanger. By what process it had become the nest where consecrated virgins were hatched I never did learn.

Years later, beset by the need to link my own offspring with that harbour of my spirit, I would bring them to visit the novitiate, only to discover loosestrife blossoming among the rubble, buttercups and violets winking where once I'd tackled arsis and thesis, daisies rampant in the sacristy. The whole building had been gutted by fire. Only the stone frame of the chapel remained.

We picked our way over debris, stepped through the hint of a doorway. Inside — nothing. No altar. No windows. No communion railing. No choir stalls. No organ. Had the chapel died on a grander scale, had there been time for moss to grow and sparrows to nest, had my children been more attuned to invisible angelic hosts — we might have stood within that transformed temple and imagined monks chanting, our spirits refreshed by the echoes of their strenuous piety. Bare ruined choirs. But no. Nothing like that. No sweet birds sang. A bat swooped. The iron sun beat upon our uncovered heads. Weary from hours of travel in a hot car, the children were thirsty and irritable.

Farther down the road we came upon a large square concrete building. Sterile. We pulled up to the front door. I got out and rang the bell.

A grim-faced modernized nun with whiskers answered, opening the door suspiciously. Feeling grimy and vaguely suspect (how had this woman and her children found their way to this spot so carefully hidden from the world?) I asked politely if we might have a glass of water.

"Wait here," she said and disappeared, closing the door behind her.

A few moments later she returned with one Styrofoam cup full of tepid water.

I could have quoted her chapter and verse: "Whatsoever you do unto the least of these . . ." Instead, we drove away.

That abortive trip begot in me only the urge to get on with life, leave the past where it belonged, to the bats in that particular belfry.

Afternoons, after Vespers, we gathered for an hour of choir practise, twenty postulants and novices sitting erect on straight chairs in the room we called the library. Sister Dolores, choir mistress that year, drilled, persuaded, cajoled, entreated.

"Follow the line of the notation, make your voices soar, then dip. Listen!" Behind her round horn-rimmed glasses, her soft brown eyes shone as her sweet soprano voice caressed those Latin vowels, belling forth pure desire. Twelve years later she would be carted away to a mental hospital, fed to the electric shock system, transformed into a frightened husk of tremulous docility.

We tried to imitate her, holding our backs ramrod straight, eager to miss no chance for bodily mortification even as we aspired to the condition of angels.

"Now, Sister. The Introit for Midnight Mass on Christmas Eve. *Dominus dixit ad me, filius meus es tu, ego hodie genui te.* Imagine you are singing from the bosom of the Trinity. Put into your voices the quiet, the hush, the mystery. This is a song from the other side, from eternity."

Day after day, as pale sun fingered frost on the casement windows, we drilled, vowelling our way toward the empyrean. Staring intently at the square notations on the tissue-thin pages of our libers (held high above our knees) we fought aching bones, tin ears, raised our voices in hope, linked in a communal fugue of the spirit. Everything was an opportunity.

For Matins on Christmas Eve, the two senior novices with the best voices, Sister Thomas and Sister Dolores, would intone the great invitatory. Though it would be sung in Latin that night, each of us was set to translate it ahead of time. ". . . in the year, from the creation of the world, when in the beginning God created heaven and earth, five thousand one hundred and ninety-nine; from the flood, two thousand nine hundred and fifty-seven; from the birth of Abraham, two thousand and fifteen; from Moses . . ." All history divided into Before and After. We rejoiced to live in the After.

The week before Christmas, at odd moments, you might come upon the two choristers practising in the most unlikely places. One afternoon, on my way to a starching session in the laundry, I met them out back near the garbage pails, their white veils fluttering in wind, blue and white gingham aprons covering their black skirts, thin shawls about their shoulders, their voices calling out across the bluelighted landscape of dead alders and denuded oaks. ". . . from Moses and the coming of the Israelites out of Egypt, one thousand five hundred and ten; from the anointing of King David, one thousand and thirty-two; in the sixty-fifth week, according to the prophecy of Daniel . . ." It might have been a clip from Ingmar Bergman.

Another day, as I carried slop to the pigs who rooted in their hardened mud enclosure at the far side of our immense vegetable

ANN COPELAND

garden, I came upon the choristers standing at the entrance to that snow-covered wasteland. Sister Thomas eyed me, then looked quickly down at her liber. She was my angel, an earnest, oppressively conscientious soul, charged with encouraging me through the first difficult six months of learning a new life. Those humourless eyes, that ruddy face. Later, she would leave, run off with the chaplain in her convent, a tall gaunt Jesuit with ancient-mariner eyes and a greying beard. We would not be told for days. First — her empty place in chapel, refectory. Her classes discreetly covered. Then the square typed notice on the community room bulletin board. Surrounding it all, ominous silence, the kind of silence one dreaded. In those days we all prayed daily for perseverance.

As I approached our rambunctious piglets and leaden sow that December afternoon, emptied the two heavy pails and watched the animals wriggle and snort, I heard behind me the two voices again calling across the dead landscape. ". . . in the year seven hundred and fifty-two from the founding of the city of Rome; in the forty-second year of the empire of Octavian Augustus, when the whole world was at peace . . ."

Pigs notwithstanding, it seemed to me eerily beautiful.

Peace. And starkness.

Our Advent meditations focused on John the Baptist, on deep and simple virtues — penance, contrition, poverty, purity, humility — old fashioned words, almost an embarrassment to utter now without a tinge of irony. We avoided exuberance. We had no touch with the outside world. Advent mail would be held until Christmas Day. The house felt emptier and emptier. There was, of course, no Christmas tree, though we were surrounded by acres of evergreens. No wreaths. No presents. No candles. No tinsel.

The world outside bleached cold and grey. Snow came early that year, intensifying the sense of isolation. Isolation, separation: these were necessary. These were the sword. He had come to bring the sword. His promised peace would follow. For one half hour a day I turned air into silver and gold, lute and reed, charmed from pipe and bellows the promise of a saviour. Ah, sweet alchemy of music, strange liturgy of air. What more did I want, expect, of Christmas? Surely not the boredom of watching a lonely uncle open yet another gift-wrapped tie. Not the tedium of vacuuming Styrofoam, refolding wrapping paper, organizing thank you notes. Not the catatonic post-turkey doze of geriatric relatives. No, not that.

What, then?

A week before Christmas, Sister Thomas, looking secretive and smug, surprised us postulants.

"You are permitted to make cards for your families," she said, smiling as if we'd been offered the moon. "Meet me in the novitiate room at four o'clock."

I could practise until four fifteen and did not intend to sacrifice one minute of it. By the time I got to the novitiate room, the others were already busy.

A square room on the second floor above the refectory, the novitiate room had windows along two sides, blackboards along the inside wall, and two long pine tables with chairs stretching the length of the room. Here we survived the weekly chapter of faults, absorbed conferences from Mother Theodore, and here only were we permitted, in rare moments, to study. On Visiting Sundays, whatever goodies our families brought us were set out on the long pine table to be collected by the senior novice and put away for sharing or distribution, when needed. In this room, also, each of us had a cubbyhole in the corner, a shelf which held our reading book, a notebook, pencils, various small items like that.

Now, spread out in colourful disarray along the table, were strips of coloured construction paper, pencils, coloured ink, brand new crayons, a calligraphy set, shiny silver foil, stars — the kind the nuns stuck to our papers in grammar school. Even a pile of cotton wads and varied pieces of coloured felt. In six months I had not seen such litter, such colour — except in my musical imagination.

When I entered the room Sheila glanced up with a wink that said *imagine this,* then bent quickly over her work.

Still in the afterglow of "Jesu, Joy of Man's Desiring," I found a place, tried to think what would mean anything to my parents after the long drive up on Christmas Day to see me. I leafed through my liber, my office book, came to the three Masses of Christmas, then the Vespers. The *Magnificat* Antiphon. *Hodie Christus natus est; hodie Salvator apparuit; hodie in terra canunt Angeli, laetantur Archangeli; hodie exsultant justi, dicentes Gloria in excelsis Deo, alleluia.*

That was it. I would make a card that said simply: *Hodie Christus natus est.* Like an ancient monk, I would illuminate it. Something in gold and silver, with touches of red. First I'd outline the whole thing in black.

I began to work.

By Christmas Eve we'd finished our cards. The house shone. My back ached. I'd done what I could at the organ. Sister Angelica went over the whole service with me, checking cues. I was nervous.

After choir rehearsal we went, as usual, to the novitiate room. Here our superior wrote on the blackboard what we were to do next, setting the hours out before us like jugs. Into them we poured what we could, turning the water of time into the wine of eternity. Every minute counted.

On the blackboard in her perfect Palmer Method, she'd written: *Postulants, with Sister Thomas, go to Our Lady's Garden at 2:30.*

Our Lady's Garden? In December?

Too well trained to indulge in questioning glances, we turned and headed downstairs to the cupboards near the laundry where we kept aprons, shawls, boots. It was bitter cold, below zero. In winter we wore only a narrow crocheted shawl when we went outside, a balance to the opposite perversity that required us in ninety-degree heat to be swathed from head to toe in ten pounds of serge and plastic. In any case, that day, without a word, we gathered shawls, donned boots and aprons, and followed Sister Thomas. She carried a pail in one hand, several small knives in the other.

She headed with us out across the long front lawn, covered then with several inches of snow, toward the overgrown garden at the end of the lawn. Our Lady's Garden. Here, in summer, surrounded by nodding delphinium and iris, a wilderness of sprightly daisies and robust wild pea, I'd sit for afternoon meditation in a pool of sun watching ants, bees, mosquitoes, frogs — life moving and jumping around me as I tried to still my spirit to attention. Now, in late December, the garden was a frozen tangle of choked bushes and dead roots, presided over by a glazed virgin with chipped hands and a stare as blankly cold as the pale eye of sun above us.

"We need moss," said Sister Thomas. Her full cheeks were already raw from the wind that bit at us as we crossed the long lawn. Her eyes, sharp blue, had begun to water. She pointed to the pail. "I've got a few knives. Once you've loosened the moss with a knife, it'll just pull up in strips. We need all you can get and we have only about an hour."

We didn't look at each other. This was modesty of the eyes. We didn't ask questions. This was restraint of curiosity. We separated and tried to imagine where, when no snow covered it, we could remember seeing moss. We knelt in the snow, felt wet go through out habits, our stockings, striking our callused knees. No matter. We found moss.

I pulled and yanked, got my quota. Kneeling low behind a mess of what would again be forsythia, come spring, I was somewhat protected from the wind. Nonetheless, cold fingered my bones, coated my lungs, dried my throat. My face burned, or was it numb? After a while pain began to pound at my temples. I remembered Dante's hell, a frozen pit. Judas there. Frozen. I couldn't feel my feet.

I tried not to focus on my misery. It was only body. Sister Sheila, kneeling near me, sat back on her heels and looked at me. She let out a long sigh of disgust as she crossed her arms and held her hands beneath her armpits. I returned her look. No words necessary.

I bent back over my task, my little plot, scrabbling at frozen earth, jabbing a dull knife with all my might into the crusty surface. It was Christmas Eve. *"Consolamini, consolamini, popule meus,"* we would sing in a few hours at Matins, Isaiah promising a redeemer. Impudent hope. . . . But still, I did love the liturgy, its empowering faith that by joining in a prayer so ancient and timeless one broke apart the bonds of time and, in some mysterious way, entered the stream of salvific history. *Consolamini.* I said the word over and over, desperate incantation against the railing of my mind. I knew all about the third degree of humility, even then. And already doubted my capacity to practise it. That day, however, in the Advent spirit, I tried. I went on digging. *Veni ad liberandum nos.*

After an hour, Sister Thomas nodded appreciatively, gestured toward her nearly full pail, gathered the knives from our raw hands, wiped the tears from her cheeks, and led us back up the front lawn — cold, tired, our cheeks like chopped meat, our hands numb and bleeding.

Merry Christmas.

That night we were put to bed early. "Put to bed" sounds odd for a group of college graduates in their early twenties. It is accurate. We were told to retire by eight-thirty since we would be rising at eleven for Matins and Lauds and then midnight Mass.

I went to my cell and hung out my special Sunday postulant's veil to put on later. I prepared for bed as quietly as possible, spreading a thin white washcloth in my basin to mute the sound of the cold water I poured from my pitcher, lifting each hook of my cell curtain carefully so as not to make a zing. The dormitory was very quiet that night, each of us no doubt trying to maintain the maximum inner silence to prepare for His coming. My hands still ached from battling earth in the quest for moss. I worked at my nails, digging out dirt, but traces of it resisted. Finally I lay down on the narrow bed, turned on my side, put my hands under my pillow, and barely remembering to think of the points for my next morning's meditation, fell into a deep sleep.

Something jarred. Tearing ragged edges of sleep. Slitting dreams. Some sound. Angels? A sound unlike any I'd heard. Close by. Just outside the cell curtain. High above their blending voices rang a pure clear soprano, full and round. Sister Dolores, surely. No one else could sing like that.

"O little town of Bethlehem, how still we see thee lie, Above thy deep and dreamless streets . . ." Their voices moved away, out of the dormitory, into the hallway. Joy rang through the large silent house. I could hear them in the other dormitory, then back out in the hall, then fading down the hallway at the opposite end of the house where the two lay sisters who cooked for us slept. "Hark the Herald Angels Sing." "Angels We Have Heard on High." The very carols I'd dared on the muted organ all those weeks. Sung now legitimately. Christmas was upon us.

Sleepers wake! Other sounds began to accompany the singers — water in the pipes, slippers on hardwood floors as sisters moved out of their cells, emptied water in the sink room, donned their habits, headed out into the upstairs hallway.

Here stood Sister Thomas with the satisfied look of a mother about to watch her child open a present. (Only now does the analogy strike me.) No more moss. No more cold. She motioned us through the dark hallway to . . . the front stairs! From the day of our arrival when our novice mistress first descended them to greet our parents, it had been made clear that these were *her* stairs. No novice or postulant walked on those hallowed boards except to clean them. For two months, in fact, that had been my charge. In the early days of my postulancy, morning after morning I'd knelt on each step, carefully wiping away invisible dust, hating every minute of it.

And now we were motioned toward them, to descend.

The banister had been wound about with shining tinsel. Through the window at the top of the stairs (I stopped to look out, it was Christmas Eve) I saw snow falling heavily. And at the bottom, there, surrounded by singing novices watching us, smiling, a Christmas tree! A huge tree, floor to ceiling, bedecked with garlands and lights and balls and small figures (not only liturgical symbols, either) and tinsel icicles. Red and green and yellow lights winking in the darkness, their dance reflected in the patio doors at the far side of the room whose panes we'd polished that very week. Small bright lights, colourful static against the snow-falling dark.

The novices were singing. Mother Theodore stood there with them, gesturing us five to join in. Her ageless face, was she fifty, sixty?, usually stern though not unkind, looked relaxed now, softened by the Christmas lights shining on her. She watched us as if to say, "See? Christmas isn't so bad here. It's special." Even before this we had noted in her hints of humanity. She was what we called in those days a woman of prayer.

After a few moments, she gestured us to silence, indicating that we should follow into chapel.

The sanctuary glowed, bathed in light. Red poinsettias everywhere — on the steps leading to the altar, beneath the side altars, and gold vases holding other red flowers on the altar itself. What were they? Gold and red everywhere. Tall golden candlesticks. The only other lights in chapel came from two tall tapers standing beside the gold lectern in the middle of the nave. From here, choristers would intone the invitatory.

I took my place, opened my liber, waited. Chapel was still chilly but it would warm up. My stomach was on edge. Getting up for midnight vigil always brought on nausea. Sister Dolores and Sister Thomas walked to the centre of the nave, bowed, faced the altar.

Never had I heard anything like it! Not even on the cold darkening afternoons when their voices cut the blue light of a December sky. Shadowy chapel, brilliant sanctuary, nuns in their white veils standing in choir on either side of the nave, two choristers in the centre by the lighted tapers — calling into the dark, toward the lighted sanctuary, those same divisions of history I'd heard before.

I watched them. I wasn't to watch them, but I did. I couldn't see their faces, just the black habits, the long soft white novice veils. I closed my eyes to listen to words I'd practically memorized in the weeks before and could now easily translate. I followed as they counted from Adam, from the flood, from Noah, from Abraham, from David — from all the points in Time Before that marked the inevitability of His coming . . . until that great beginning moment, the moment of new time, which, as they chanted, we knelt to acknowledge.

". . . in the sixth age of the world, Jesus Christ, eternal God, and son of the eternal Father, desirous to sanctify the world by His most merciful coming, having been conceived of the Holy Ghost, and nine months having elapsed since His conception, is born in Bethlehem of Judea, having become Man of the Virgin Mary."

Their voices dropped. They bowed, turned, walked back to their places in choir. Who cared if their arrangement of history was a fiction (what arrangement isn't?), an ingenious device to help memory. We knew about literary forms, multiple authorship, synoptic boondoggles, the perils of translation. We knew things could be only *so* literal. Still . . . the beauty, the urgency of it.

Our own voices followed — less dramatic, a sustained singing of the Hours that told us Christmas was almost there. "Take comfort, my people, says your God. Speak tenderly to Jerusalem, and proclaim to her that her service is at an end, her guilt is expiated . . ." Now Isaiah could be believed.

The words flew by me. St. Leo telling us: "It would be unlawful to be sad today, for today is Life's birthday; the birthday of that Life which, for us mortal creatures, takes away the sting of death and brings us the bright promise of an eternal hereafter. No one is excluded from sharing in this joy . . ." Part of my mind took it all in, but underneath everything it seemed to me nothing could match that soaring invitatory, the pure high voice of longing nourished by faith, human desire singing its own fulfilment.

ANN COPELAND

Near the end of Matins I must slip out of my stall and head to the organ at the back of chapel, warm it up, prepare the registration, be ready. Just before I left my place, from the corner of my eye, I saw the family who farmed for us bundle into the balcony. Five children, snow on their hats and coats, and their vigorous father who came to the back door every morning with the huge milk pails and collected the empties. Who cared for the pigs we fed once a day. Who watched the cows we did not milk. Who slaughtered the chickens yearly with our help. It comforted me, in some unfathomable way, that Mr. Riordan and his wife and girls had joined us, were part of it, waiting with us. That October he'd taken us postulants to the corn field at the very moment when asceticism and housecleaning weighed especially heavy. The envelope of self-denial burst open as we piled into the back of his truck and headed off, singing, toward the golden ripe cornfield. Up and down the rows we moved, harvesting, our blue and white aprons hidden in the waving sea of ripeness. The hillside was bursting with life and we were part of it.

When I sat at the organ now, I felt them behind me in the small balcony. Reverend Mother was beside me in her stall. On the seat beside her lay the plaster-of-Paris baby. I saw now that she would have to put it in the crèche. That had never occurred to me. It was so concrete, so literal.

I moved softly into the carols. "Hark the Herald Angels Sing," "O Little Town of Bethlehem." I played strings, flutes, shorter pipes, one principal. We were still waiting. Finally, on the stroke of midnight, as I'd been instructed, I opened registration to a plenum and played "Silent Night." Reverend Mother rose from her place, took the battered looking babe, carried it down the centre of the nave to the crèche. I couldn't watch, though I'd already caught sight of one thing when the lights went up on the side altars. Moss. There it was, lining the crèche. Our scraping and scrabbling had found moss on which to rest the baby. I noted this almost casually, busy as I was finding the right keys. Already that afternoon excursion and my contest with resistant earth seemed as remote as the world I'd left six months before. A remnant of dirt remained beneath my nails, but my fingers were busy making music. The sisters sang quietly, three full verses. Reverend Mother returned, eyes down, to her place.

Into the sanctuary padded the small Capuchin who served us. Tonight he wouldn't need the basin of steaming water Mother Theodore usually prepared for his bare feet. He wore heavy white socks inside his sandals.

"*Dixit Dominus ad me . . .*"

Mass began, the organ quietly underlining voices that rose now to heights and depths not heard in the stuffy library on Advent afternoons. I could forget the literalness of the plaster baby. It seemed so pitiful in the midst of this sacrament of history we were creating, enacting, so pitiful to carry a plaster baby to the crib and put it before kneeling Mary and Joseph. But what would I have had? An empty crèche? The child mysteriously appearing there when no one was around to see where it came from? Perhaps.

Mass proceeded. The *Gloria* shone, bells and voices shimmering praise. The sisters had never sounded better. I felt my power. My feet moved as I wanted them to, found the right pedals, my wrists did not tighten, the organ merged with their voices in a satisfying Christmas harmony. Incense. Bells. No sermon. Our Capuchin spoke little English. Communion. Palestrina.

Then, quickly it seemed, it was over. The lights in chapel were dimmed as the sisters knelt to make their thanksgiving. Sister Henry moved about the sanctuary, dousing candles, fixing the altar. I stayed at the organ, waiting. After a few moments, Reverend Mother rang the bell she kept on her stall, a small silver dome like the nuns in elementary school had on their desks.

Eyes down, hands in their full sleeves, the sisters left their stalls, met by the lectern, bowed to the altar, and proceeded out, two by two, past the organ. I was into "Jesu, Joy of Man's Desiring," playing carefully, hoping I'd get through it. Reverend Mother left last. No one else in chapel except Sister Henry out in the sacristy. I'd keep playing to the very end, let the sounds fill the chapel. I opened the swell box. Behind me the Riordans were still sitting in their pew. I played for them. If I delayed now, I'd get to bed ten minutes later than the others. The sink room would be empty. I could go through my ablutions undisturbed.

The end. At last. I closed the organ, clicked off the switch, slid from the bench.

I went through the library, in darkness now, oak chairs in their perfect rows, piano keyboard covered. Through the foyer — usually dark, lighted now by the winking Christmas tree. I headed past the stairs, her stairs, still festooned with tinsel. And into — the refectory. *Lighted! Full of novices and postulants!* Candles on tables, a beautiful full wreath suspended on the wall behind Mother Theodore's table where usually the white alabaster crucifix of the suffering Christ gleamed. Food. I took my place.

"*Benedicamus Domino,*" said Our Mother quietly. "Merry Christmas."

Never had anything like this occurred. Talking — at midnight in the refectory, a place of great silence. And presents on the table! In front of my place were two small packages carefully wrapped. And candles, lighted, spaced along the table. Perfect miniature chocolate logs, candles in them, decorated with holly and red berries. By each place a whole unwrapped candy bar.

Such were the gifts: a toothbrush, a box of notepaper. A candy bar. And the greatest gift of all — joy where I'd expected none. Human warmth I recognized, partly of the old kind, partly new. Novices and postulants, weary from weeks of prayer and preparation, celebrating together.

Tomorrow would come intrusion, the other world, parents arriving with their gifts, their anxious concern. But for this moment, for just this one hour, the wholeness felt different.

The Time That Was

ROBERT B. RICHARDS

Lights with circuit-breakers wait on shelves.
Our puss is neutered and she has no claws;
Ask us why, we'll tell you it's because
We don't want cat or kids to harm themselves.

A purring clock accumulates its twelves;
Come the time, there'll be no pregnant pause
Before angelic chimes cascade; no laws
Say Christmas is for either Christ or elves.

But, oh, there was a time this time was ripe
And real, and rife with, yes, both love and joy;
Santa tamped tobacco in his pipe
And Jesus was no ordinary boy
But mad with love for sods like you and me
And dangerous candles on a living tree.

The Montreal Aunts

MAUREEN HULL

Lizbeth and I climbed spruce trees. We only did this in winter when our snowsuits, hats and mittens protected us. We squeezed past dense branches and needles that wanted to poke our eyes out, but it *had* to be a bushy tree or we'd fall between the branches on the way down and break our necks. We climbed as high as possible, then sat on a big branch, feet pointing out and down. Laid back and shoved off. It was a fall — broken by branch after branch as we sped groundward. As we dropped from each one, it would spring back up and shower us with snow and spruce cones. It was a glorious ride down — and a game we never described to our parents, or played within view of the house. We had a kind of a feeling about it.

So I was up as high as I could climb, with a prickly green and white view of the world, and just about to launch myself, when I saw Dad coming across the field. He was heading for the woods, straight towards us.

"Don't come up, Lizbeth," I hissed. "Dad's coming, and he's got the axe." I let go and whooshed down without my usual kamikaze yell, so I he wouldn't notice me. When I hit the snow drift at the bottom, Lizbeth had already run off. Dad in the woods with an axe meant it was time to cut the tree, and Christmas could start. I staggered after her, beating clumps of snow and spruce cones from my hat.

In our house, the tree went up on Christmas Eve day, after lunch. Once Dad had built the stand and set the tree up in the bay window in the living room, it was Mum's to decorate. I helped, putting my favourite decorations in a cluster at the front, where I could see them all at once. Lizbeth couldn't decorate, she dropped the glass balls and broke them, and she threw tinsel instead of hanging it.

"Get out of here and let me finish in peace," Mum would say. She'd turn the radio on to Christmas Carols, and hum and not care how many mince tarts we ate off the racks cooling on the kitchen table. She'd undo Lizbeth's tinsel and move my favourite ornaments around. When she was finished, it was always more beautiful than the year before.

After supper and a bath, Lizbeth and I would lie on the floor in our nightgowns, cross our eyes, and stare up at the magnificent sparkling blur while Dad read from St. Luke, 2: 1-19.

"And it came to pass in those days, that there went out a decree from Caesar Augustus, that all the world should be taxed."

The minute I heard those words my heart ballooned out in every direction. By the time he got to, "And she brought forth her first-born son, and wrapped him in swaddling clothes, and laid him in a manger; because there was no room for them in the inn," I was sniffing back tears. It is the best story.

It was hard to settle down and fall asleep, but neither Lizbeth nor I ever wanted to stay awake to see Santa. If he caught you up late, you were naughty, not nice, and you would get a lump of coal. We went to bed at the usual hour, squeezed our eyes shut and tried desperately to pass out. Besides, we were Baptists, and we knew that Christmas was supposed to be all about Baby Jesus. We were to be good for Him, not for a present from Santa. And greed was a sin, so we were only allowed to ask for one present, although I had friends at school who wrote letters asking for twenty different things, quite sure they'd get at least half of what they asked for.

"Santa's not a millionaire," my father said, "He has all the other children in the world to think of, not just you."

When I brought up the matter of my friends' bounty, he told me that Santa really only brings one present for each child, the rest are bought by the parents who then pretend that Santa has brought it all. Well, that settled that. We didn't have That Kind of Money.

We chose our Santa present after weeks of deliberation. We thumbed the pages of the toy section of Eaton's catalogue ragged until time was up, and a final decision had to be made, and the letter to the North Pole printed and mailed. On Christmas morning it was the one present we were allowed to open before breakfast. The rest had to wait until my parents were good and ready to get up and we had been fed a bowl of porridge to steady us.

Our parents gave us new slippers, boxes of sixty-four Crayola crayons, collections of Illustrated Bible Stories. At the back of the tree, in bright foil wrapping and store-bought bows, were the presents from the Aunts.

Our family was decidedly skimpy in the blood-relative department. Most of my schoolmates had crowds of cousins, kitchenfulls of aunts, Legionfulls of uncles, three or four grandparents and at least one great-grandparent mumbling the rosary and spitting in a back bedroom. We had no uncles, no grandparents. My mother and her two younger sisters had been orphaned when their parents drowned in the St. Lawrence River on a canoe outing. They were taken in by an elderly cousin twice-removed who ran a boarding house in Montreal. She made them scrub and cook for their keep and sent them out to work at Eaton's as soon as they turned sixteen.

Dad's parents were dead, too, his father of pneumonia when Dad was seventeen. We had moved into his mother's house in Glace Bay to look after her when I was a baby. When Nana had finished reading the bible for the eleventh time (one for each of the apostles, except for that traitor, Judas Iscariot), she took herself off to heaven and left us her house.

Dad had two sisters, too. The Ottawa Aunts. They were much older than he was, they both worked for the government, and they were both war widows. One had a son, Cousin-Richard-the-Divinity-Student, who was grown up and was going to go to Africa to convert the heathen. Dad said he didn't need to go all the way to Africa, there was plenty of work to be done at home, and why didn't he start a Mission in Montreal? Mum would fold her mouth and leave the room. I knew he meant the Montreal Aunts. By accidentally listening at keyholes and such, I knew that the Montreal Aunts smoked, drank gin, went dancing, and wore red lipstick, which they used to kiss the boyfriends they weren't in any great hurry to marry.

The Ottawa Aunts sent us copies of the New Testament, bound in white leather with gold-leaf printing, and cream coloured writing paper with matching envelopes. They sent us white cotton blouses with lace, like strings of snowflakes holding hands, sewn to the collar, and blue diaries that locked with a golden key. They sent us Fair Isle tams and matching scarves and gloves. Mum said they had Good Taste.

The Montreal Aunts, unconstrained by a Baptist upbringing or a steadying marriage or Good Taste, sent us whatever amused them. Back when they were sending cartons of chocolate bars, or dolls that walked, talked, and peed on the living room floor, it had become a tradition that we were allowed to wear whatever we liked from our Christmas pile to the church service we went to before we sat down to Christmas dinner. This meant cotton blouses or Fair Isle tams for us, leather gloves or a silk scarf for Mum, a new Arrow shirt for Dad. But when I turned five, the Montreal Aunts decided we weren't babies any more and sent Lizbeth and me a jug of pink bubble-bath and a quart of highly scented cologne apiece. Lily of the Valley for me, Lilac for Lizbeth. Of course we wanted to wear *that* to church. Mum showed us how to subtly dab behind our ears and at our wrists, but we wanted more of the wonderful stuff, so when she wasn't looking, we poured on a generous amount. Dad made us sit at the very end of the pew, as far from him as possible, because, he said, we made his eyes water.

Next year — lace underwear and a dozen silver bangles each, and oh, what a fine clash and clatter they made every time we turned the page of the hymnal, or scratched an itch, or stood up, or sat down again. The following year — purple velvet clutch purses and gobs of gaudy costume jewellery — women's jewellery. Painted plastic and glass and gold beads as big as marbles, three rows of them hooked together. Matching clip-on earrings made of clusters of the same beads. Dad was speechless, Mum rolled her eyes. Lizbeth and I thought we looked just grand.

The year I was eight and Lizbeth was six, the Aunts Went Too Far. They sent us nylon stockings and red plastic high heeled shoes with rhinestone butterflies on the toes, butterflies as big as my fist. The shoes fit perfectly. Dad was horrified to think they made such things in children's sizes, but Mum assured him that you could find *anything* in Montreal. Lizbeth took over the front hall, practising so she could wear her new shoes to church, one hand held against the wall for balance. I was swooning with delight, dancing around the dining room table in my nightgown and heels and hardly falling at all. Since I could walk I'd been sneaking into my parents' closet to stand in Mum's Sunday shoes: navy blue leather, solid square heels lifting me up. When we played dress-up, I stuffed a wooden block into the heel of each sock and minced about until my feet were crippled with the pain and I had to take the blocks out and rub my feet better.

Lizbeth and I hurried to get dressed for church. We struggled into layers of warm, practical things: Stanfield undervests and bloomers; garter belts hooked to the nylon stockings we substituted for the thick brown ribbed stockings we usually wore; cotton petticoats and starched white blouses; pleated navy-blue jumpers and wool cardigans (blue for me, pink for Lizbeth). And red high-heeled shoes with rhinestone butterflies. I wouldn't have traded them for all the velvet Christmas dresses, all the lace flounces and clusters of artificial pink roses pinned to satin bows . . . every year I didn't envy my friends their Christmas dresses. Envy was a sin. It wasn't allowed. So I didn't. And Baby Jesus had finally rewarded me, with the help of the Montreal Aunts.

". . . looking like streetwalkers!" he was saying, his voice very loud.

". . . just little girls," she was arguing.

They were fighting in the kitchen downstairs.

Lizbeth crouched down by her bed and put her thumb in her mouth. I felt sick to my stomach, felt the peppermint surge of candy canes wanting out.

". . . sequinned g-strings next!" he was yelling.

". . . my sisters you're insulting," she was yelling back.

I clomped downstairs and into the kitchen to try to make them stop.

"You're scaring Lizbeth." I threw my arms around my mother's middle and burst into tears. "Baby Jesus says you have to love everybody, even if they live in Montreal!"

"Oh, Christ," said my father, sitting down.

My mother started to laugh.

Lizbeth and I were carried off to church with toffees in our pockets and our gorgeous new shoes on our feet. The Senior Choir sang "O, Holy Night" and made a lump in my throat. Reverend Miles read the story of the Wise Men and their gifts. Our whole family held hands while he prayed Christmas thanks, and in the quiet minute after, when you were supposed to add your own private PS, I thanked Baby Jesus for Lizbeth and my parents, for six Excellents and two Very Goods on my report card, for the new baby we would have by Easter (another girl would be fine) and, most fervently, I thanked Him for the Montreal Aunts.

One More Wise Man

DAVID HELWIG

The only warning I got was a telegram from Montreal. It said "ARRIVING TOMORROW LOVE JACOB." Just that after five years.

The last time I'd seen him was in England, in a London tube station, Tottenham Court Road I think it was. We were taking trains going in different directions, and as we separated, Jacob grinned back at me. He was wearing a heavy overcoat that made him look like a bear, and his teeth were very white in the middle of his dark beard.

"I'll see you tonight," he said.

The next day I got a telegram from Rome. It said "COME TO ITALY LOVE JACOB." Then two years of silence while I poked away at England and finally packed my life in a bag and came back to Toronto. Then three more years, happy enough, I suppose, with a job that was not too demanding and not too rewarding, a few friendships, and most recently, an arrangement of sorts with Laura, something that could have ended in marriage but hadn't.

Laura had been a widow for a year and a half now, and I had known her for about a year. We had spent gradually more time together as the months went on. I let things happen but never seemed to act, to be in control. Her dead husband was a presence that I could not exorcize. I had never known him, Laura never mentioned him. And I did not ask. So his presence continued to haunt us. The only honest one, I sometimes thought, was Laura's nine-year-old daughter, Cathy, who disliked me because I was not her father, and she would allow no replacement. Laura and I went on, politely, foolishly, as friends. I didn't tell her that I loved her, didn't ask her to marry me. I don't know quite what I was waiting for, but I was still waiting.

Now Jacob was about to arrive in my quiet world. Over the last three years I had received two letters from him, one saying that he was separating from his wife and another two days later asking whether he'd ever written to say he was married. It was three days before Christmas when I got his telegram, and I assumed he was planning to stay with me over the holiday. The next morning I decided I would get some extra food and liquor in, to be ready to celebrate his return.

Jacob, my old friend, how to tell about him, where to start? I think I met him when we were both ten years old. It seems to me that he was a fat, grinning ten-year-old boy with a thick dark beard, standing on a street-corner, in the snow maybe, and laughing. It was always hard for me to keep the facts straight in my mind where Jacob was concerned.

His father, who had left Austria for political reasons, directed the United Church choir in which Jacob and I sang, I in a remarkably high soprano and Jacob in a rough but powerful contralto. His mother was a round smiling woman who baked buns and bread and cookies and cakes and pies and pastries and loved to see us eat them. She kept Jacob almost as round as she was herself by filling him with her food.

And Jacob, my friend for years. He had a brown sweater with a hawk on it. He had an old short wave radio. The biggest collection of Captain Marvel comic books in town. A single copy of a sunbathing magazine full of naked women. When we got to the age for real girls, he would tell me everything, and I would tell him nothing.

Holding Jacob's telegram in my hand, I looked out the window of my apartment and saw a Christmas wreath in a lighted window across the road. I remembered how we had loved Christmas. When we sang carols in church, Jacob insisted on singing the melody instead of the dull contralto harmonies that the hymn book offered him. And I, not to be outdone, would invent soaring descants. We would look across

DAVID HELWIG

the choir loft at each other and only keep from laughing because we loved the singing, especially the wild joyful carols, "Joy to the World" or "O Come All Ye Faithful."

As I stood there, I decided I'd better phone Laura. I was expected to spend Christmas Eve and Christmas Day with them, and I thought I should tell her (did I mean warn her?) about Jacob's coming.

I phoned, and as I knew she would, she said to bring him with me, perhaps a bit apprehensive or not really happy about it, but determined to do the right thing. I like to talk to Laura on the phone, she has a nice voice, but this time I let the conversation die quickly because I didn't want to say too much about Jacob or try to make her imagine him. I have lots of funny stories about him, but he becomes unreal in the stories, and there's some kind of disloyalty in telling them. Anyway she'd meet him soon enough. Let her judge for herself. I had a suspicion she wouldn't like him. He certainly wasn't like any of her friends. I put on a record and sat staring out the window, wondering what Jacob had been doing for the last five years, what I was going to do for the next twenty-five.

In the morning I found myself a bit puzzled about when he might arrive, and whether I should make any attempt to meet him. He might be coming by train or plane, even by car for all I knew. There was nothing to do but tape a note on the door saying I'd be back at five-thirty and set off to work.

It was a busy morning and at noon I forgot to buy extra groceries, but I left early and arrived home just before five-thirty with my arms full of food and liquor. As I walked up to the door of my apartment, I could hear music from inside, "Gottes Zeit ist die allerbeste Zeit" sung by a choir and a loud extra baritone. My arms were full, and I wasn't sure I could get my key without putting everything down so I knocked on my own door and waited.

The door opened, and Jacob's familiar bearded face smiled at me. He had the same bright, scrubbed look that I remembered and the same tattered clothes.

"Jerry," he said, "it's great, goddamit, it's great."

I could see he wanted to shake my hand or throw his arm around my shoulders, but he couldn't really get at me for the bags. I went into the kitchen to put them down.

"How did you get in?" I said. "I didn't think the caretaker would ever open up for you."

"That's a funny thing," he said. "I was standing there at the door looking at your note and figuring how much trouble I'd have getting anyone to let me in or even finding out where you work when I noticed the lock was made by a company in Germany that I used to work for. That particular design has a weakness. If you know about it you can take it apart from outside. I put it back together after I got in."

"Same old Jacob," I said.

Then suddenly I didn't know what to say anymore. It was five years and I was different. I didn't know where to start.

"It's great," Jacob said again.

"Do you want a drink?" I said.

"Yeah," he said, "I want a drink."

We drank and talked a bit and then drank some more and then ate, and within a couple of hours, it had all come back so that we didn't have to think of things to talk about. He was surprised that I'd never got married. I was surprised that he had. I wanted to tell him something about Laura, but I held off for a long time. When I did mention her, he wanted me to describe her, and I tried, said she was small but not really small, had brown hair with a bit of grey coming now, and then gave up and told him to wait and see. He let it go at that, and we talked about other things, his family, my family, five years of time, and as we got drunker and more relaxed, sat in the dark listening to music and talking less. Sometime after midnight, Jacob suddenly stood up and turned to me.

"This Laura," he said, "she's a widow, not young and innocent, so you must go to bed together, eh? I mean there's nothing wrong with you is there?"

"Dammit, Jacob," I said, "why don't you mind your own business? Of course we go to bed together sometimes, and of course there's nothing wrong with me. Is there anything wrong with you?"

DAVID HELWIG

"Not a damn thing," he said. "But what I want to know is why you don't marry her?"

"I don't know why. Maybe we don't want to get married." I was shouting a little.

"Don't get touchy," he said.

"I'm not," I said. "I'm just going to bed."

I had an extra bedroom that I used for a study, and the bed there was made up, so I only had to turn on the light and point to it before I wandered back to my own room and fell into bed. The last thing I remember was hearing Jacob talking to himself.

I didn't wake till almost eight o'clock. I got organized in a hurry and left Jacob a note saying I'd be home about four. There was a party at the office, but I planned to leave early.

When I got home that afternoon, it was later than I'd expected, and I only had time to wash up before we drove to Laura's for dinner. During the short drive over, Jacob asked more questions about her, and I tried to answer them. He didn't seem to be listening to what I was saying.

When we got to the house, it was Cathy who answered the door, very polite and mature, giving away nothing. I wondered, as I often did when I saw her, whether she ever cried over silly things. Laura came in, wearing an apron, and apologized for not meeting us at the door. Because I'd been trying to describe her to Jacob the night before, I kept noticing things I could have mentioned: she has brown eyes and a funny mouth, she looks good in an apron though I don't know why, she's good at covering how she feels. I introduced her to Jacob and tried not to notice how they reacted to each other. I kept telling myself that it didn't matter. Two days from now Jacob would disappear and not come back for years. Still I caught myself listening to them. They didn't have much to talk about, but they seemed to want to be friends. I gave Laura the bottle of wine I had brought, and we all had a drink before she went back to the kitchen.

After we'd spent a few minutes sitting around, Jacob had the bright idea of asking Cathy to show him the house. At first she didn't want to, but before long she started to enjoy it. As we followed her about, Jacob carried the wine bottle with him and drank from it every couple of minutes. The part that Cathy enjoyed most was showing us the cellar. She had to ask her mother if she could go down, and I guess because it was an unusual thing her excitement started to show. She even relaxed enough to tell us how old the house was and that there was an old cistern under the kitchen. Jacob wanted to see that too, and the pair of them got quite involved over it. I could see that Cathy was starting to like Jacob, and I felt a bit jealous. After they were through with the cistern, Jacob wanted to see the furnace and the fuel tank.

"For God's sake, Jacob," I said, "you don't want to see the furnace."

"Of course I do," Jacob said with a big smile. "When I see a house I want to see everything. Don't you think that's right, Cathy?"

"I guess so," she said, but I'm not sure she really agreed.

Jacob had a good poke around the furnace, and we went back upstairs. Cathy had already eaten, and Laura got her off to bed before she served the dinner. It was a fine meal, and Jacob did it credit. He made me think of his mother's huge meals as he crouched behind his plate chewing happily, warm and content, like a stove that took in food for its fuel and gave out some rare spiritual heat. Every now and then he would wink at me, and I was puzzled but assumed that he was just expressing his delight in Laura and the food.

It was with the coffee that I started to feel cold, and by the time we had done the dishes, I was shivering and so was Laura. She went to turn up the thermostat, but when she did, nothing happened.

"Must be something wrong with the furnace," Jacob said. He seemed pleased. "I'm beautiful on furnaces," he said and headed downstairs.

"Does he know what he's doing?" Laura whispered to me.

I shrugged. There was some soft noise from the cellar, then a loud noise and the sound of Jacob running upstairs.

"Bit of a problem," he said. "I punched a hole in the fuel line somehow. I don't think there's anything to set it off, but maybe we better get out anyway. We can drive over to Jerry's place after we phone the firemen and the furnace people."

"Jacob," I said, "did you really?"

He nodded his head.

"Laura better get Cathy."

Laura looked as though she didn't know whether to be mad or scared, but she went to get Cathy. When she was gone, Jacob turned to me with a big smile.

"Beautiful, eh?" he whispered.

"You didn't do that on purpose?"

He nodded.

"I figured, what's nicer than to have all your friends at your place for Christmas? You and Laura and Cathy are all too well organized."

"You're out of your goddam head."

He grinned. I could hear Laura coming. Cathy had wrapped herself in a blanket and was walking along still half asleep. I went to the kitchen phone and found the number of the Fire Department. They wanted to know how the fuel line got broken. Then I got the number of the heating company and phoned them. They asked if I'd phoned the firemen and then wanted to know how the fuel line got broken.

Cathy hadn't said anything, but she looked a bit frantic, so Laura took her out to the car. Jacob offered to stay till the firemen and heating people came. We left him there and drove to my apartment. Almost every house we passed on the way had some kind of coloured lights up. Even without snow everything looked nice, but I didn't think I'd mention that to Laura.

We got Cathy up to my apartment, and I suggested that Laura make her some hot chocolate before she went to bed.

"Are we going to sleep here?" Cathy said.

Laura nodded.

"Just for tonight," she said.

When Laura went to the kitchen, Cathy sat in silence. I could see she was trying not to cry.

"Don't worry," I said. "We'll leave a note. Santa Claus will find you."

"I don't believe in Santa Claus," she said.

Laura came in with the hot chocolate.

"Cathy and you can have my big bed," I said. "Jacob can have the little bedroom, and I'll sleep on the couch."

We didn't say anything while Cathy drank her chocolate, and even when Laura had taken her off to the other room and put her in bed, we were silent, everything made strange by the child sleeping near us in a bed that was not her own. Still, I was happy in a way that we were there, ready to admit Jacob's wisdom, or maybe only one part of it, for I could see that Laura was worried and afraid that her house might be in flames. She kept fiddling with the back of her hair. I'd never seen her do that before.

"Do you want me to phone back to your place," I said, "and see if everything's all right?"

"Would you mind? I'm pretty nervous."

I dialled her number. For a long time nobody answered, but finally Jacob came. He said everything was under control, that they had all the oil out of the basement, but that the fuel pipe wouldn't be fixed for a few hours at least.

I hung up and gave Laura the message.

"I'm sorry about this," I said. "Jacob always makes a little bit of chaos wherever he goes."

"In two weeks I'll laugh about it," Laura said. "Afterwards I'll think how refreshing it was, but right now I'm not sure I'm up to it." She reached out and took my hand.

I kissed her on the top of the head and went to put on a record.

"We'll have to go and get Cathy's presents," she said.

"Wait till Jacob gets back, then we'll go. We'll leave him to babysit."

"Do you think we'd dare?"

"I suppose not."

I sat down beside Laura on the couch. For an hour and a half we sat and waited for Jacob, and as we waited, we talked. It was strange, different from any other time. I even asked about her husband. Once or twice I called Laura's house looking for Jacob, but there was no answer. It was after eleven when the phone rang. It was Jacob.

"Where are you?" I said.

"At a police station."

"What in hell are you doing there?"

"They thought I was trying to steal a dog."

"What dog?"

"At the pound. I thought I'd get a dog for Cathy for Christmas."

"She doesn't want a dog."

"She'd love one. A great kid like that should have a dog, but when I went to the pound it was closed. I could hear dogs inside, and I figured if I could get one I could pay after the holidays. But when I climbed over the fence I got stuck and they saw me, and now they won't let me explain."

"All right," I said. "I'll come." I found out where he was and hung up.

When I tried to explain to Laura, I started to giggle, and then she started, and I never got the whole story out. I wanted to keep Laura with me, so I got a teenager from down the hall to stay with Cathy, and we drove to the police station.

The cops weren't too difficult about it. They hadn't charged him with anything, and one of them was a man I'd met a couple of times, a friend of a friend, so eventually we got Jacob out after I'd given my word that I'd keep him out of trouble. They thought he was just drunk.

As we drove home, everything started to seem unreal to me. I guess I was probably tired. I pulled into the parking lot and we all got out.

"Oh, Jerry," Laura said, "I just remembered the presents."

"Back to the car," I said.

"It isn't far, is it?" Jacob said. "We can walk. It will wake me up. You should always go out walking Christmas Eve."

I looked at Laura.

"It's a nice night," she said.

"Let's go," I said, and we started out. It was cold, but we walked quickly and kept warm that way as we passed through the streets and parking lots that lay between my apartment and her house. Within a few minutes we were there.

We walked up the steps to the dark house and stood at the door while Laura looked for her key.

"Don't you have a key?" Jacob said to me.

"No."

Laura fumbled a little harder in her bag.

"Why not?" Jacob said.

"Here it is," she said. She got the door open. The house still smelled of oil, and it seemed as cold inside as out. Jacob beat his arms as he walked up and down the hall making a roaring noise. Laura stood at the door of the living room.

"I guess we'll just take the presents," she said.

"No," Jacob said, "we have to take the tree. We can't have Christmas without a tree."

"How can we take it?" I said.

Jacob looked at me. He was really surprised.

"Of course we can take it," he said. "We'll take off the decorations while Laura gets the presents packed."

I was too tired to argue. We began to take the decorations off. Jacob whistled happily, but I kept thinking that my eyes were going to close on me. Once or twice I stopped to watch Laura as she packed up the presents. It didn't take her long, and when she had finished, she sat down in a chair and closed her eyes. Sitting there, she looked small and old, vulnerable and desirable.

We had the tree stripped in a few minutes but had trouble getting the decorations packed away. I dropped a silver ball and broke it, then dropped another one.

"Out with you," Jacob said. "You take the tree and Laura take the presents and get on your way. I'll finish packing these and be right behind you."

"Okay," I said. I tried to pick up the tree and dropped it. Tried again and got a face full of needles. Jacob manoeuvred me and the evergreen and got us in some kind of order. He pushed me out the door and helped Laura get the parcels settled in her arms.

"I'll be right along," he said.

Laura and I walked down the street and started across the parking lot. We didn't speak, just walked. The high buildings stood guard over our mad pilgrimage through the crackling cold, and above us a thousand stars gave their silent fire to the night. My face hurt from the scratching of spruce needles against my skin. Loaded down, we walked slowly, and there was no sound but the sound of our feet on the cold ground. Then, from behind us somewhere in that huge silence, came Jacob's voice, loud and raucous, but still a courageous noise in the face of winter, singing "O Come, All Ye Faithful." We stopped and listened.

"Laura," I said, "I don't agree with Cathy. I believe in Santa Claus. I can hear him singing to me."

She, my poor tired friend, tried to smile at me, or as much of me as she could see through the branches of that big spruce.

"Laura," I said, "I want to marry you."

In the distance I could hear Jacob singing. Then I joined in.

Waiting for Gabriel

KELLY COOPER

It seems like we've tried everything, Ron and I. We've done it every other day for a month. We've used a thermometer and done it only when my temperature was up a degree. We've even done it in the back of a borrowed car, because that seems to work for teenagers. Nearly three years. Nothing. Now it's Christmas again, and all the talk is of trees and Santa, and clerks are getting injured in department stores trying to intervene in fights over stuffed toys and it's family this and family that.

We don't have a tree. It seems a shame to cut them down. But when I was a child, the tree was important. It marked time. It was brought into the house ten days before Christmas Day. A promise. Time for the gifts to start coming. My brothers and I were allowed to circle one toy in the Christmas catalogue. One wish. And we knew never to pick the most expensive thing, even if it were what we truly wanted. One year, I hoped for new skates, but I didn't circle them.

Just because you don't seem to want a thing, doesn't mean you don't want it. That's what people have trouble understanding. It's like being fourteen and wanting to ask that boy to dance, wanting it so badly that tears come to your eyes, but not asking. I read a lot when I was that age. Harlequin romances. In one of them, I found the perfect word for what I was then and still am now. Reserved. The heroine was reserved. Not cold. Just waiting. And I'm no different with children.

Some people come right out of themselves when there's a baby in the room. They walk over, pick up the baby and talk to it just as if it were the most natural thing in the world. Not me.

Just because there's no tree in our living room doesn't mean we don't celebrate Christmas. I believe in God, hard as it's been sometimes. The first year we were married, Ron gave me a Nativity set carved out of real wood. It's olive tree wood from the Middle East, smoother than skin, and marked with dark rings that look like ripples in water. There's a stable, with two cows that look a bit like dogs and two sheep that look a bit like the cows, only smaller. I set it up yesterday. The people are hard to tell apart if you don't know the story. The wise men are the ones with gifts in their hands. The shepherd has a crook. Joseph carries nothing, and neither does Mary, but he's taller. The baby is the only figure that will fit in the scooped out block of wood that is the manger. There are no details in the faces, no eyes or noses even, so it's hard to tell what they are thinking, but I wonder, especially about Mary, when I set them in their places. What did she think when the angel Gabriel came and told her she had been chosen?

Ha, ha, tell me another one?

No problem, just give me a minute to do something with my hair? Why me?

The last few years, when Mary comes up in church services I've attended, ministers go on about how afraid she must have been, and how hard it was for her, being pregnant before she was even married to Joseph, and having to give birth in a strange place without her mother there. Maybe. Ministers say all kinds of things. All I can think of is how sure she must have felt. There was no doubt. She was going to have a son. God said so. Who can feel sorry for Mary? The only thing I feel sure of is that, so far, I have not been chosen.

Ron and I spend every Christmas Eve in the car, driving to my parents'. They live just outside Fredericton, and it takes twelve hours to make the trip. Ron said we didn't have to go this year, but we do, especially this year, because there will be talk if we don't. My brother's wife just had a baby. Tomorrow, I'll see their little girl for the first time.

The store stays open until noon on Christmas Eve. I'm the assistant manager in Produce. Ron is in Meats. He cuts and wraps. It's been a madhouse for the last two weeks. One of the magazines at the checkout featured some sort of artichoke egg dish and everyone wants artichokes for Christmas brunch and we ran out long ago because who'd have guessed artichokes? Meats was down to their last turkeys. Parents are not at their best shopping for groceries with children. It's hard to watch them wish their babies elsewhere.

I'd like to be back at our house, just Ron and I, rubbing each other's feet and eating cherry chocolates. Sometimes I look at Ron and think, even if this is all there is, if this is my share, then I'm lucky. Ron says he knew right away that I wasn't a cold person, because at the staff party where we first met, I was willing to listen to one of the clerks tell me all about how badly she felt when she had her cat declawed. Such guilt, she'd said, with tears in her eyes, but the couch in the living room was new and expensive, so what else could have been done? Ron came along with a tray of cocktail meatballs he was passing around as a sort of market test. They went over quite well, and Meats has sold them ever since. Ron sat down when he saw how upset the woman was. Eventually, she left to get another drink, but he stayed. Eight years ago and married for seven.

Road conditions are good. We've got some nice music playing and it's warm in the car. A little while ago, we stopped for a quick coffee and Ron took off his jacket. Now he drives in just a T-shirt. Lovely. The man has arms. Not all big and bulgy. Not hairy. Ron's arms are long and smooth, muscle visible each time he moves. Working in Meats requires a fair amount of heavy lifting. There's a motel at the next exit. We've stayed there before. Is it especially wrong to lie on Christmas Eve? I hope not, because I'm going to tell Ron I'm tired. But what I'm really thinking of is not sleep, far from it. He looks so good. Besides, I have a theory. A baby is more likely to happen on a journey.

If you're just past thirty when you marry, like we were, people start asking right away about children. Like it's their business. I used to say plenty of time for that, and then you should have heard them.

Wait too long and you won't have the energy to raise them.

Who will look after you when you're old?

People without children grow odd.

They said all those things, and more, when they thought we weren't trying. They don't say them now, of course, but that doesn't erase the memory of the words. And they still believe what they believe.

People without children grow odd.

The baby is called Melissa, a ruffles and lace sort of name that I'm surprised my brother agreed to. When Ron and I arrive, the whole family is assembled in the living room around the tree, waiting. I've piled my arms high with gifts, making a place to hide if need be, but it's not too bad. I pretend to look at the baby, but really focus on the embroidered edge of her cap.

Presents are passed around. The pile for the baby is large. Talk is about colic and crying and sleeping. Stories are told of when my brother was Melissa's age. Ron sits right beside me, and every now and then his hand comes up to stroke my back. It is not easy. A less reserved woman would have to excuse herself and leave the room. I stay.

Carla is a pretty girl. The baby is only a few months old, but she holds it on her lap easily with one hand, using the other to pass gifts. My brother can't stop smiling. The telephone rings and he goes to the other room to answer it. It's for Carla, her parents calling to say Merry Christmas from their winter home in Florida. Carla gets up. All eyes in the room but mine are on the baby. Hands lift, eager to hold her. My arms are stiff and motionless.

Carla walks past my father. Past my mother. Maybe she's going to take the baby with her. She stops in front of me and says, "Ginny, would you mind?"

The baby is in my lap. A warm lumpy bundle in a blanket. Is everyone staring? No. There's the sound of paper tearing, then laughter. Someone has given my brother a pair of earplugs. Ron's arm is around my shoulders and the baby isn't crying, and more importantly, I'm not crying. I look at her and push the blanket aside so we can see each other better. Her eyelashes are long and straight, like my brother's.

All those people in the room, all those reaching hands, and Carla chose me.

Let her be my angel Gabriel, Lord.

Let it be a sign.

Green Knight

ANNE SIMPSON

"Tell us a story, Granddaddy," said Sam, pressing his spoon into his ice cream. "You always do at Christmas."

"Granddaddy doesn't want to tell a story right now," said Christy, Sam's mother.

It was true. John sat at the head of the table feeling weary. He had asked the family to come to Halifax this year so that he wouldn't have to fly to Toronto or New York. It had been a selfish thing, really. And they had come. Christy, Leonard and Sam had come, and Michael and his girlfriend Indi had flown in for three days, which was all they could spare, they told him, before they went on to Greece.

"I can't think of any stories," said John. He'd made the cranberry jelly and the pecan pie. He'd stuffed the turkey. It wasn't as though he'd done it all by himself, because Christy had worked tirelessly. Leonard had peeled the potatoes and whipped them. But it had been strange not to have Emma watching over everything, one hip against the stove as she stirred the gravy.

Sam began moving his spoon around the ice cream, turning it into mush. He slouched in his chair. Soon he might slide under the table and crawl around like a dog, even though he was eight and beyond that sort of thing. Then Christy would get irritated and take him off to bed.

"There's one I know," John said, eating the last bite of pecan pie. "About a knight."

"A knight in shining armour," said Indi.

"Well, no." He wasn't sure how he felt about Indi. She'd been named after a racetrack. Her parents lived in Los Angeles. She wore bright red nail polish and tight leather skirts. "This one was headless."

"He was?" said Sam, putting the spoon against his chin so it left a little mark of vanilla ice cream.

"Not at the beginning," John went on, leaning back in his chair. "You see, the Green Knight went to the court of Camelot at Christmas. Perhaps a little after Christmas, I think. Yes, New Year's. And Camelot was a good place to be: it was comfortable and peaceful. And so everyone there was relaxed and happy, but nobody had to do very much of anything. They'd forgotten something important about being knights. That's how it begins. Anyway, the Green Knight went to the court and there he told the most valiant knight — "

"What's valiant?" asked Sam.

"Brave and good. The best knight of the Round Table."

"Oh." Sam stood his spoon and knife on their handles on the tablecloth and walked them around his plate.

"He told them that the most valiant knight would have to take up his challenge. And so Gawain was chosen. He was asked to behead the stranger, the Green Knight."

"Why?" Sam inquired, halting the spoon and knife in their progress.

"Because the Green Knight asked him to. He said it was all a game. A Christmas game. So Gawain cut off his head, and the Green Knight picked it up in his hand, picked it up by the green hair, in fact, and challenged Gawain to meet him in a year's time at the Green Chapel. Then off he rode into the night on his green horse."

Sam chopped the spoon with the knife. He put the spoon down on the plate. "Is that it?"

"There's more. I'll tell you tomorrow."

"No, tell me now."

"No Sam," Christy told him, getting up. "It's bedtime for you."

There was no question that Indi was a very pretty girl, thought John. She was sitting by the fire with her legs turned gracefully to one side, one ankle hooked over the other. She had very long, shiny hair, almost like a Japanese woman's hair, it was so dark and fine. Her eyes were lustrous and her brows arched in a questioning way, so that whenever she looked at Michael it seemed she was waiting for an answer. Michael had gone out to fix coffee, so it was only John, Leonard and Indi staring into the flames. They had temporarily exhausted the conversation about on-line browsers, which Leonard had started. It had gone nowhere, because John didn't know much about that sort of thing. The internet was a mystery to him.

Now Indi uncrossed her legs and leaned forward. "They say that if a person had bought into Stars&Stripes Online last September, the stock would have gone up over seven hundred per cent by now."

"Well, that's true." Leonard looked at her with new interest, and Indi shook her mane of hair back over her shoulders. "It's the same with so many of the IT stocks in the States."

"I watched a program on it the other night," she confessed, smiling. Her smile was extremely charming. She had even, white teeth and lips that were perfectly tinted with dark coral gloss. "I really don't know anything about it."

Christy came into the room and flung herself down beside Leonard on the sofa. She was getting a little thick around the middle. But she still had the same rosy cheeks, the same auburn hair that she'd had as a girl. Leonard put his hand on her thigh. He patted her, John noticed.

"I'm done in." She turned to John. "But Sam loved that story. He didn't want me to read him anything. He only wanted his granddad to come and tuck him in."

John rose, trying not to wince at the pain in his lower back. He smiled. "There's nothing I'd like more."

It was dark in Sam's room, but a wedge of light from the hall shone on his pillow, his face, part of his bed. John sat down and smoothed his hand over his grandson's soft brown hair. Sam wriggled his body closer to his grandfather's.

"Did you have a nice Christmas, Sam?"

"Yes," he said simply. He picked at the duvet, extracting a feather. "I miss Grandma, though. Do you?"

"Yes," said John.

"The thing I miss most," Sam went on, "is her smell. She smelled of fudge. I asked Mom to make fudge, but it wasn't the same. It wasn't Grandma's smell."

"Fudge," repeated John dumbly.

"She smelled good."

A little snow was falling on Boxing Day morning, whirling festively in the air. There was already quite a lot of snow on the ground and now more was coming down. It might play havoc with the flights at the airport the next day, when Michael and Indi would fly to Athens. But no one was thinking of that: Leonard took Sam tobogganing and at the last moment Indi decided she'd join them. So they tramped through the backyard and ravine to the golf course. John went out an hour later to chop wood in the backyard. He liked to do it with an axe, though it would have been faster with a chain saw.

He'd chopped a neat pile of wood before Michael came out, snugly dressed in a black parka, sunglasses, and good leather gloves. He might be dressed for the weather, but he looked as though he came straight from New York.

"Need help, Dad?"

John didn't particularly want help: he liked chopping wood by himself. But he handed the axe to Michael, who took off his sunglasses and put them in his pocket.

"I'm not as good at this as you," he said, glancing at his father.

"You're all right."

The snow came down more thickly, falling on Michael's parka and making tiny white blotches on it. It was wet, and the piece of wood he rested on the block slipped when he tried to chop it.

"We don't need much more wood," said John. "You don't have to do anymore if you don't want to."

"I'll just do a few."

He chopped neatly through a log, set the pieces down and put another on the block.

"She's something, don't you think?" he said, as he brought the axe down exactly in the right place. "Indi."

"Yes, she is," said John. There happened to be a few thin slivers of wood attached to his old ski jacket. He took them off one by one. "She's got a mind of her own, doesn't she?"

"Yes." Michael got the axe stuck in a piece of wood. He began trying to work it free. "She's independent."

John watched Michael futilely wrenching at the axe in the wood. He longed to help him, but didn't. "She likes her job, then?"

"She doesn't work. She's got an inheritance."

John looked towards the ravine. The snow was a frieze of dancing figures in front of his eyes. Through them, vaguely, he could see Leonard and Indi coming up the bank. He saw them stop for a moment, just at the top of the ravine, and Indi started laughing. She bent over, laughing. Leonard was pulling the yellow plastic toboggan, but Sam wasn't on it. They had both stopped in their tracks and were laughing, though Leonard wasn't laughing as hard as Indi. Now she put her hand on Leonard's sleeve — a fake leopard skin glove — to keep herself steady.

"They're back," John said.

Michael had taken the axe by its handle, lifted the recalcitrant piece of wood and set it on the ground. "Dad, I can't get it out."

But his father wasn't listening. He was walking towards Leonard and Indi, his eyes fixed on Indi's spotted glove. She moved it from Leonard's sleeve and stopped laughing. The snow was a pretty screen between them as John approached; it kept fluttering down on his eyelashes. "Where's Sam?" he asked.

"Isn't he here?" said Leonard, in alarm. "He said he'd had enough and he'd go back through the ravine by himself."

"No, he's not here." John strode over the brink of the ravine and plunged down into it. He didn't follow Leonard and Indi's tracks. Instead, he went another way that took him to the little creek faster. But the snow was deep and he floundered through it. He could hear Leonard coming after him, but Leonard would go straight along the path he'd come from. John took a different path. There was a place Sam had shown him in the summer and he went there, treading carefully on the log as he crossed the creek. But Sam wasn't at the fort he'd made in the summer, at the roots of the great oak tree.

"Sam," he called. "Sam."

John paused for a moment and then followed the creek down its course, his boots sinking in the deep, wet snow by the creek. Children liked water. They liked playing with the little shelves of ice at its edges. But Sam wasn't anywhere along the creek. The ravine ended abruptly at the road that went around it. The park where they'd been tobogganing was just beyond it. Would Sam have gone across the road by himself, back to the park? It didn't seem the sort of thing he'd do, but John stood looking at it through the sugar maples, the thin birches, the falling snow. The painted yellow line on the road seemed broken by the trees, but it was vivid all the same.

He went towards it. For some unaccountable reason he thought of the story of Gawain and the Green Knight, wondering why he'd told it. It wasn't really a Christmas story. There was a note in John's leather-bound version — handed down from his father — informing the reader that it had to do with vegetation rites. The green man supposedly embodied the earth. There was more that John couldn't remember. But it was clearly a pagan story. It had to do with folklore. It had to do with myth. It made him angry. Here he stepped into a mushy bit of snow and sank into water, into a little pool that was really part of the creek. He yanked out his foot, but the water had already seeped into his boot.

"Sam," he called.

There was no answer. Two crows brayed, flapping up through the trees by the road.

John climbed a little slope and lifted first one leg, then the other, over the guard rail. He started along the road where it sloped up between the ravine on one side and the park on the other. If the child were dead, he wanted to be the first to find him.

Sam was not dead. He was in the ravine, but not in a place anyone had thought of yet. In the summer he had discovered a sort of teepee made entirely of branches laid together. A stick house, he'd thought at the time. He remembered it when his father and Indi were taking him home from the park. Tobogganing had been all right, but a bit slow, because of the snow. It was heavy and wet. Sam was a little disappointed and kept dragging his feet when they started home. After they crossed the road, he'd hesitated, thinking of the stick house. Should he go and see if it was still there? Should he tell them? In the end, he'd decided not to, because Indi had sat down on the toboggan after they crossed the road and his father was laughing, saying he couldn't pull her. Sam slipped away, up a little slope above the road. The snow was so deep he had to drag his boots out of the snow one at a time. He was hot in his snowsuit.

The teepee was still there. It was not as perfect as it had been in the summer, but it was still more or less intact. He crept inside, careful not to dislodge anything. Then he lay down, his boots sticking out the entrance. He could see the trees through the openings between the sticks. And the white sky was cut into precise bits by the dark arms of the trees. The snow came down between the sticks and touched his cheeks, his nose, his lips. He licked the snowflake that fell on his lips. It felt good just to lie still.

After a while he got up and started patting snow carefully on the sticks, thinking that he would turn it into an igloo. It seemed only fitting that the stick house be a teepee in summer and an igloo in winter.

"Igloo," he said, and paused. "I'm making an igloo," he said louder.

He felt strange all of a sudden, struck by the fact that he was alone. He was making an igloo, but he was making it alone. Perhaps he wouldn't make an igloo after all.

"Dad," he called. "Daaaad."

But his father was nowhere to be found. It was John who heard him, striding quickly up the road.

"Sam?" John hurdled over the guard-rail and ran as fast as he could in the direction of that flute-like voice. The snow hindered him though, and he could not run as he'd done when he was younger. "Where," he puffed, "are you?"

"Here."

Sam was all right, John thought. They would go back together to the house and everything would be all right. Now he came to the top of the slope and found Sam bundled in his red snowsuit. His hat with the blue stars and the pom-pom was a little askew. His face was white. John hugged him close, still panting a little.

"Sam," he said.

They lay in the teepee, though it was a tight squeeze. John could fit in his head, shoulders and torso, but his legs were outside. Sam's boots were outside.

"Tell me the rest of that story," said Sam.

"Well," said John, thinking that they should go back soon because the others would still be worried. "Where was it we left off?"

"That good knight had to go find the green one, I think."

"Well, that good knight went everywhere. He went everywhere he could think of, but he couldn't find the Green Knight. It was getting late, too, because he had to find him before the year was up. He went through all kinds of trials and ordeals, and then, finally, he came to the Green Chapel. He was afraid."

"Why?"

"Well, because Gawain had promised that he would take the same blow that he had given the Green Knight the year before."

"You mean the green one was going to cut his head off?"

"Yes."

"But you said it was all a game."

"Well, it was partly a game."

Sam's face was puzzled. "So did he cut his head off?"

"The Green Knight made him put his head down. Then he lifted up his axe and brought it down, nearly taking off Gawain's head."

"But he didn't, did he?"

"No, he didn't. But he gave his neck a little nick."

"Why did he do that?" asked Sam, a little frown knitting itself between his brows.

John watched the snowflakes whirl up and whirl down. He was content here. He could stay for hours.

"Why? To remind him." He shifted himself carefully out of the teepee and stood up outside.

"I don't understand," Sam said, sliding out.

John couldn't think of what to say. Sam would want an answer, but he didn't really have one. He couldn't remember more than that. He glanced over to the crescent of road he could see through the trees.

"To remind him of what?" Sam persisted.

"That he would not always be alive," said John. "That he was mortal." He looked away from the road. From here the ravine looked different. He looked down the little slope at the inky line of creek, where it meandered under ice and came out in the mushy pool by the road. The pool he had stepped in earlier. "That's all."

Apples

SUE SINCLAIR

When she went back at Christmas time, her father had a bowl of apples
on the table. She hadn't been home for several years and now the fruit
seemed a sign of her father's life without her — without her mother
too, of course. Martha had been gone so long she almost forgot.

It seemed a reassuringly good life. There were six apples, Golden
Delicious, all of them ripe and yellow. You could no longer imagine
them on the tree, the branches would never hold them now, and this
had left behind a trace of sadness. The bowl made you sad too; it made
you think of the moon. Matte white. Even its shadow had that kind of
pallor and that kind of privacy — like the privacy of pain or illness. Or
perhaps more like the privacy of convalescence, an interiority that is
a move toward wholeness and, if not quite contentment, is very close
to it.

They talked until midnight, which was late for both of them. Memories
and family jokes. "Do you remember when you gave me a quarter to
find your lens cap?" When they were on a weekend trip — they had
done this often when she was young — and he was taking photographs,
he would inevitably lay his lens cap down somewhere. The absent-
minded professor. It was her job to find it, and when she did he would
fish a quarter out of his pocket for her. They were very precious, those
quarters.

When they were both too tired to talk anymore they went upstairs.
She slept in the bed she had slept in as a child. It was too short for her,

so she curled up. The sheets were fresh and smelled the same as they had when her mother had washed them. He must be using the same detergent. She imagined her father with his first batch of dirty clothes, searching for the soapbox under the bathroom sink. He would find it and look inside, under the tab that her mother had opened by pushing in the perforated edge, although he wouldn't know how to do this yet. He would read the instructions, precisely, holding the box up in front of him. Then he would follow them slowly, step by step. Soon, though, he would have become more efficient. And the thought of this efficiency touched her more than his fumbling. It made him seem distant. She could already imagine how, when she was gone, he would strip the bed neatly, like whisking a cloth out from under a set table. But she wouldn't think about it now. She slept. She kept her socks on because the heat wasn't turned up; the wooden board at the end of the bed was cold.

"Did you sleep well?" her father asked in the morning. He had his reading glasses on and was marking a stack of student papers. She was happy to see him working.

"Yes," she said. She was well rested. She felt as though she had slept several nights instead of one, scores of nights. She would have kissed him but they had never been that kind of family. Instead she went to the kitchen for a cup of coffee.

Her father, she noticed, had started drinking decaf. She brought the coffee upstairs with her and sipped it while she filled the little sink in her bathroom. Then she bathed herself. She used a bar of green soap her father had left out for her; it smelled of apples.

She had woken up with strange wistfulness upon her. Her body was light, almost too light. And the air was cold. Now she felt she was bathing in that almost imperceptible sadness. Splashes of water. When she had woken up the pillow had been cold except for the spot where her head had lain. But it was so fresh she lifted her head and laid it down again there, then there. Bathing in the cold room gave her the same pleasure.

When she went back downstairs again, she discovered that the room was bright. She hadn't been able to tell the night before and hadn't noticed earlier. Now there was a sharpness, an edge to each object, even to the shadows, that made it all unreal. The bowl with its six apples seemed so entirely remote that she had to touch it — it was like the moon again, hanging in the daytime sky. She half expected it to recede when she put her hand out. She picked up an apple and bit into it. It made her feel better. She carried her father's breakfast dishes into the kitchen then sat down to finish the apple. Several juncos were clustered around the bird feeder outside. She was humming to herself by the time she threw the core away.

That afternoon they went for a drive to the cove they used to visit sometimes on their weekend trips. Snow was falling. Christmasy, her father said. The shore was deserted. There weren't any horses in the field where they used to graze, but she could smell the manure mixed into the salt air. Maybe it was too cold for horses. Her father had brought his camera and now took several pictures. The ice on the cliffs, the patterns of frost on the rocks. "Your mother never saw it snow here," he said. As though that were the reason for the pictures. As though he could send them to her.

They walked to the edge of the water. "Will I take one of you?" she asked. "I suppose so," he said and gave her the camera strap, placing it over her head. It was an intimate gesture, almost an embrace. He buttoned up the top of his coat, drew himself up, and stood looking straight into the lens, and she knew what he was thinking. It was at moments like these that she could see his thoughts as clearly as if they were written on him. He could see her mother somewhere behind the lens — if that wasn't it, it was something close — he was imagining her flipping through the photographs, pausing at this one. Martha was looking at exactly what her mother would see. The waves crashed in behind him. She clicked the shutter and looked up. The sky was low and grey, like a passing bird. "It is beautiful here when it snows, isn't it?"

A week went by. Christmas was only days away. She started expecting to see him in the morning, sitting in his chair, wearing his reading glasses, doing his marking. Or listening to jazz in the evening. The thick blurry lenses made him more familiar than he was without them. They were like Allen Ginsberg's glasses, the same ones her father had worn when she was a child. So they brought him closer. But they also made him seem further away — sometimes she seemed only to be remembering him. It was as though, wearing those glasses, he couldn't exist in the present. The glasses belonged to another time, and so did he when he put them on. She remembered him as he was a week ago, standing in front of the camera on the beach.

They went shopping, they cooked dinner. It snowed. She continued to wake up feeling sad. And although she had never thought of yellow as a sad colour, the apples always looked sorrowful in the morning. The way there would be six or seven of them, and how they lay — yellow, all of them — in the curve of the bowl. As though they were thinking something quietly to themselves. Only once she had her bath did the feeling go away, or she forgot about it. She forgot everything once she had bathed; the day began.

On Christmas Eve the phone rang. Martha answered and was startled to hear her husband's voice on the other end. It was as though this were the first time she had talked to him, like a premonition, someone she knew instinctively she was bound to love. Her heart raced when she hung up the phone. "I can't wait to see him again," she told her father, and it was true. But she felt it would be several years before she even met him.

"You'll be back there before you know it," her father said. He filled the kettle and placed it carefully on the stove. And she realized this was what he would do when she was gone. That this was what was required of him, each day needing the same attention. Living had become more deliberate than it had been. He was greyer than she remembered. He kept his hair shorter. And the bowl of apples. It was what her mother would have done.

The Feast of Flesh

DAVID HELWIG

Christmas night out on the highway,
few cars, everyone home somewhere,
a night of bright stars, a half moon
lying on its back. Beside me
your voice cries out. Ahead of us
the two animals, big, unreal
in the bright channel of the lights,
racing across the road and into
the frozen trackless acres, two
coyotes trailed by the low thick
brush of tail. Chances are they're
a mated pair loping across
the night fields to harry foxes,
rabbits, rats. Recent arrivals
these bush wolves, migrants coming
over the ice under the cold
pastel of winter skies, a pack
running through moonlight to the black
line of unknown shore, all drawn
as surely as the compass is
to the magnetic pole. Have come
to join the ghosts of Christmas night,
its season of astonishing arrivals.

Dene Christmas

SUSAN HALEY

"7 DIE OF GUNSHOT WOUNDS, 23 PRESUMED BURNT IN FIRE."

Robert lay on the upper bunk in the shack, reading *Time* magazine out loud to Haga.

"MANIACAL SECT LEADER'S THREAT OF COMMUNAL SUICIDE PROMPTS FBI ACTION. Oh, boy!" He turned a page.

Haga was cooking; he had been cooking all morning. First he had carefully scraped the hair off a caribou head, and now he was boiling it in a large pot on the stove.

It was Christmas Day.

"Look at this picture, Haga. 'Federal investigators hold hooded suspect at gunpoint beside site of mass grave.' Another serial killer, I guess."

Haga came over to look.

"How can those whitemen stand it?" he remarked. "I'd be scared to live down south. With those murderers everywhere — you can't hardly walk to the store or go out of your house to a card game without getting murdered."

"There won't be any trees left down there pretty soon," Robert said. "The rivers are all polluted."

"Boy, what a place to live! No wonder so many of them have to come up North."

"Yeah, and now the Americans are trying to get hold of our water." Robert had just been reading an in-depth perspective on this subject.

"Our water?" Haga was alarmed. "How are they going to get it? It's up here. Not down there."

"They'll dig trenches, probably," said Robert. "You know, like the Panama Canal."

"To take away the Big River?"

"Maybe they'll build a tunnel." Robert was not just teasing Haga. He had been trying to figure out how they would do it himself.

"You know how the water goes into the Ramparts above Sans Sault? It kind of all just pours down in there?" Haga looked up at him, his mouth open. "It'd be like that. Only the water would disappear into a big hole."

"But what would happen to the people who live in Aklavik?" Haga protested.

"Well, I guess it would get dry there, like the Sahara Desert. I wonder whether you could have camels in this country? That would be kind of interesting."

Haga said, "This is bad, Robert. You know that prophecy of our people. When the river dries up — the world will end."

"Well, cheer up," said Robert. "The world could come to an end tomorrow if the Americans wanted it that way. So I guess we're kind of used to that idea."

Haga was horrified. "I don't want the world to end," he said.

"Well, it will anyway." Robert put his magazine face down on his chest and looked up at the bare boards of the roof above him.

"It will?" Haga was no longer just horrified.

"In a couple of million years," said Robert. "That's all I meant, partner. A couple of million years."

Haga turned back to the preparation of his soup. The fire crackled. The water in the pot bubbled. It was cosy in the little shack. Robert turned a page and began looking at pictures from the war in Africa. They were terrible pictures, grisly, haunting. Then he stopped looking at them and stared again at the ceiling, reminded of something that had happened last night, something that he felt good about for a change.

SUSAN HALEY

The Red Baron had finally relented on Christmas Eve and sent in a couple of planes full of turkeys, oranges, toys, wrapping paper, votive candles, snuff, cigarettes, chewing tobacco, formula, baby diapers and, what was most important of all, mail. This was how Robert had got his *Time* magazines, a bonanza, four of them at once.

He had been passing by the hamlet office after dark on his way home to the shack, intending to burn a little lamp oil that evening, when he had noticed that the lights were on in there for a meeting, even though it was Christmas Eve. And a warm, well-lit government office was a wonderful place to read. Robert ran up the steps and went in, intending to read his way through the hamlet meeting.

Local Government was there: the two officials, Mike and Shelagh. Shelagh was explaining something to Herod McCrae, the only other person present, and he was responding patiently.

"We understood from the Red Baron that the strip wasn't being ploughed."

"Yeah, but that was because he never brought in the parts we needed to fix the grader."

"He said he couldn't bring anything in because the strip wasn't being ploughed," she said.

"We needed those parts first," said Herod. "And he never brought them in."

"Well, he was just telling us how he couldn't land the plane on the strip. Because it wasn't ploughed."

"We could stop going around and around right there, I guess," Herod commented. "We got the parts. Old Elvis Woodcutter went into the Forks and got them with his Ski-Doo."

"Well, it's why we had to postpone your Capital Plan meeting till tonight, that's all I'm saying."

"Yeah, Christmas Eve." Herod sighed. Then he brightened, seeing Robert, who had already settled down in one of the armchairs, his feet up on a coffee table. "Hi, Robert. Here for the meeting?"

"Nope," said Robert, opening the first of his magazines, the one dated November 3.

The door opened and Billy McCrae entered and took off his parka. He was a member of the Council.

"Good, now Billy's here." Herod was in a hurry to get started. "So maybe we could start talking about that capital plan you guys brought down here for the hamlet."

The two government people were silent. It was not a quorum, only two members of Council, one of them the mayor.

Robert was reading to himself: "POLITICAL CHAOS IN THE CARIBBEAN. In the small hours of the morning, people take cover and huddle on the dirt floors of the primitive shacks thatched with banana leaves and flattened kerosene tins that are their homes as the sound of gunshots reverberates through the slums. . . ." Gun-toting voodoo men. That would be one to read to Haga. He began to flip through the magazine to see if there was anything else like that. Acid rain. Pollution. Iraq. Saddam was using poison gas again. The bad state of the economy.

The door now opened and Tommy Douglas entered.

"Oh, good. Here's Tommy," said Herod. "I'm going to start this meeting. Just to get it off the ground. Take the minutes of the last meeting as read? All in favour?"

"Aye," replied the other two.

"So we'll start with open floor. We're going to go through the Capital Plan tonight with Mike and Shelagh from Local Government, but first, we've got a member of the general public present. Robert, got anything you want to say?"

Still flipping, Robert had found the pictures from Africa and come to a dead halt. He looked up.

"This is pretty horrible, Herod," he said. "Look at this! Just little kids!"

He got up and went over to spread the magazine pictures out in front of Herod.

"Their legs and arms are just like little tree branches," Herod said, appalled.

"'Children, the most terrible casualties of the "forgotten war," are left dying on the road by their dead or dying parents in the search for supplies of relief food provided by the UN. Some of these children are later dragged into hospitals in the city, suffering from shrapnel wounds or burns, only to be left to die untreated on rat- and lice-infested rag beds in the hallways. There is no medicine for burns, no penicillin, no nursing staff, and there are almost no doctors,'" read Robert out loud.

"Geez." Herod continued to stare at the pictures, swallowing hard.

"God, this is awful," said Robert, reading rapidly to himself. "You know what the awful thing about this is?" he demanded of the others. "It says here that the big problem is that there's no money to send them anywhere near the aid they need. The UN is just about broke, and besides, it's bogged down in this big deal in — what's the name of that other place? Bosnia."

"Oh, yeah," said the others vaguely. But they were clustered around Robert's magazines, staring hard at the pictures, which were brightly coloured like a centrefold: children, their bloody wounds covered with flies, babies with sunken, haunted eyes, wrapped in white rags with the blood soaking through, the ghastly images of war and starvation.

"Uh, Herod, the meeting . . ." suggested Shelagh from the sidelines.

"Oh, yeah, well, let's get this show on the road again." Herod came to himself, tearing his eyes away from the pictures. "Anything else from you, Robert?"

Robert took his magazine away with him to the corner where he had been reading.

"I'll just read you this piece here. 'The situation once again exhibits how we don't want to stop armed conflict in Africa. For if there were world peace we might have to share our wealth with the poor people of the earth.'"

"You know, that really makes me mad," said Herod angrily, staring at Robert with his large, hard-boiled eyes. "People not being willing to share. Especially when it comes to food. There's those poor little orphans and we aren't even willing to give them a little piece of meat?"

"Yeah, it makes me mad, too," agreed Robert. "We always shared our stuff. I never heard of Dene people not sharing food."

"Herod. This meeting? Could we . . .?" Shelagh was getting anxious.

"Oh, yeah. Well, I guess that's all the open floor we've got time for." Herod came to again. "So now maybe Mike can get up here and tell us about the hamlet Capital Plan for next year."

Mike got up and passed around a set of Xeroxed handouts showing the breakdown of the Capital Plan over the next five years. He gave one to Robert as well.

"As you see it breaks down into sixteen categories. Roads, Airport, New Staff House, and so on."

Herod nodded. "We need a new grader."

"We got the message," said Mike. "Look on page two there."

There was a long pause as the three members of Council present studied the pages of the plan rather helplessly. Robert was also looking it over. He had been so starved for reading material lately that he read everything that came his way, even a dry and, in his opinion, largely irrelevant document like this one.

"I've got an idea," he remarked.

"Okay, shoot, Robert," said Herod.

"The grader's fixed, right?"

"Yeah. Till next time."

"Getting a new grader's going to cost us $100,000 minimum. And it's in the plan for this year. That's what it says here."

Robert flourished the plan, open to page two.

"So what about if you guys take that money and put it into relief for those kids?"

"Then we wouldn't get a grader." Herod was slow to follow.

"Come on," said Robert. "You can still fix the old one."

He dropped the plan on the floor and jumped up, bringing his magazine back over to the table. Then they were all looking at the ghastly centrefold pictures again, and there was a long silence.

Mike decided that it was time to intervene. "Well, I'm sorry about this. But you really can't use Government funds earmarked for —"

"$100,000 isn't going to go very far to help those people," Herod interrupted him. He ignored Mike, looking at Robert.

SUSAN HALEY

"Well, look in this budget here and see if you can cut some more things. How about the swimming pool?"

"But we want the swimming pool to keep our kids from swimming in the river," objected Billy.

"Hey, the kids have always swum in the river," replied Robert. "Go down there, take off their clothes and make a little fire. You remember, Billy. That way they can pretend they're real Dene and don't have to live in houses."

"Okay. That's a point. Anything else?" said Herod.

Tommy Douglas now spoke for the first time. His opinion always carried a lot of weight with Herod because he wasn't just a younger relative. He said, "I don't see that it's real sharing if you just give away the stuff you don't want. Like when somebody cuts up a moose and gives you the hoofs and a piece of the insides. Why don't you put the whole shebang into relief?"

Both the government people present were by now thoroughly alarmed. Herod cast an ironic glance at them. They were trying frantically to intervene, their hands up.

"It's ten o'clock," he said. "And we've got a rule here that says we don't go on with meetings after ten. So does somebody want to make a motion right now? You, Tommy? All in favour?"

Everyone was in favour. Robert voted as well.

"Okay. I guess we'll just work out what we're going to do without the Capital Plan budget at our next regular meeting." Herod was already pulling on his enormous tent-like parka as the others also got up to go.

"Boy, I want to go home! It's Christmas Eve, you guys!"

The door slammed several times and everyone was gone, leaving the government to pick up its papers and regroup. Even Robert was gone; he didn't want to stick around and argue with them about this one. Of course, as he fully realized now, there had not been a quorum at that meeting, and even if there had, someone in Yellowknife would have found a tricky way to overrule the motion. But it made him feel good that it had been made. And this was why he had not got much reading done the previous night.

"Boy, Haga, that soup sure smells good." It smelled so good that he jumped down and went to look in the pot.

"There's nothing like soup made with a caribou head," said Haga, lifting the lid for him. "Fish soup is good, but you get kind of tired of it in the winter."

They both took a deep sniff of the steam. Then Haga gave the bubbling broth a good stir.

"Nobody wants soup like this any more, Haga. Not even Dene people. They're all eating pizza."

"And those vegetables," said Haga.

Robert always enjoyed having this conversation with Haga.

"Well, I like an onion in the stew," he remarked.

"But what about lettuce?" demanded Haga.

Robert nodded. "And that broccoli."

"And fruit." This was a real hobbyhorse of Haga's. "What is it, anyway? Some kind of candy?"

"Candy?" Robert was only mildly surprised to hear that he thought this. "No, it grows on trees. You know, the way blueberries grow on bushes?"

"Yeah, but it's all kinds of funny colours, like orange and yellow," said Haga.

"Well, blue is kind of a funny colour, too, when you come to think of it," commented Robert.

"Well, this here's a real Dene Christmas dinner. Just meat," said Haga. He again lifted the lid of the simmering pot and inspected the contents with pride.

Robert began collecting up soup bowls and spoons, setting the table. They had only a few things of this kind, knives, the sugar spoon, an odd glass they had found in the woods. One of the soup bowls was in fact a metal pie plate, while the other was a chipped blue enamel coffee mug. Haga dished out the soup with a flourish, using the mug as a ladle. Then they both settled down at the table, eating with their knives and drinking the broth.

Christmas was on Robert's mind now.

"Are you going to visit anybody?" he asked Haga. Visiting was what most people did on Christmas Day.

"Well, I was going to go to my sister's," said Haga. "But she's got so respectable she doesn't want to see me any more." Haga's sister was married to the school janitor. Like almost everyone on town, Robert hardly ever thought of the two of them as related.

"She said I'd just go to sleep on the floor like I usually do. She said she was going to wake me up and kick me out if I did that."

"Your own sister." The conservative in Robert was shocked.

"Well, it's not like the old days, that's what I say," Haga complained. "Back in the old days a brother was a brother, no matter how much he snored."

Robert thought now of his own family. It was a mess. He had gone to see his mother the previous afternoon, but she had hardly had anything to say to him. She was in a bad mood because Danny had had a Christmas party without inviting her. She was angry at Michael, now openly drinking and playing cards again, who was sleeping off the night before on her sofa. And she was still annoyed with Robert, both because she was almost always annoyed with him anyway, and also because he had been at Danny's party.

They ate in silence. Finally Haga sat back with a sigh of repletion. "Was that good!"

Robert got up to get the tea. Still silent, he poured a bit of the hot liquid into Haga's soup bowl — the mug — swished it around and threw it out the door. Then he put a steaming cup of tea in front of Haga and poured out one for himself into the glass they had found in the woods. Haga took a spoonful of sugar out of the bag. Robert watched him take another spoonful. Apparently feeling Robert's eyes upon him, he quickly took two more, making four in all. He liked a sweet cup of tea.

"Well, it's Christmas, isn't it?" he said defiantly.

The door suddenly flew open, letting in an arctic blast, and three male visitors entered. Robert's cousins, heroic drinkers and cardplayers all of them. Suddenly there was a lot of noise. Someone was singing a country-and-western song about low-down friends.

"What are you guys doing?"

"Something illegal, I hope."

"Got some cigarettes, Robert?"

"Wipe your feet, you guys," commanded Haga. "You're getting snow all over the floor."

"We came all the way out here to see what you're up to, Haga. There's nothing going on in town."

"Nothing but eating and church."

"Have you guys got a pack of cards anywhere?"

One of the visitors had sat down on Haga's bed, dropping the long ashes from his cigarette over the blanket. Then he took the remains of the butt and ground it out on Haga's pillow.

"Hey, what's your problem, Haga?"

Haga was getting quite upset with these guys, Robert noticed.

"A beer would taste pretty good right now."

"Why didn't you bring one with you, then?" Haga had taken possession of his bed again and was dusting it off assiduously. Meanwhile, someone else had climbed to the top bunk and lain down.

"Geez, Harold's going to sleep up there! Don't go to sleep, Harold!" But it was already too late. Harold Woodcutter was a championship snorer, almost in Haga's league.

"For God's sake, wake him up!" Haga was alarmed and astounded by the noises proceeding from the bunk above. But their visitors were already getting restless.

"Why are you guys just sitting here like this? You got no wives to bug you like the rest of us do."

"Yeah. You could be drinking and smoking and playing cards all day if you felt like it."

"But this is Christmas," said Robert. "We were having Christmas."

"Well, you're not having much of a good time, if you ask me."

"We were eating dinner," Haga told him.

"Caribou head soup. Dene food. Like it was in the old days," said Robert.

They found themselves grinning at each other. In the ordinary course of things they would both have been out roaming the streets in search of entertainment, too. But now, in their special position as outcasts and exiles, they were living a life of sobriety and upright virtuous behaviour. It was a strange outcome, a kind of paradox. And it was entirely too dull for the taste of their visitors, family men, all of them.

"Okay. I'm going home."

"Nothing going on here anyway."

"Hey, you guys, take Harold with you," pleaded Haga. But they were already gone, slamming the door behind them. Haga was still nursing his injured pillow, feeling the burned place tenderly with his fingers. He had never had a pillow till Robert borrowed one for him from his mother, but apparently he liked it now. The man in the bunk up above rolled over on his back and began to snore in a rich, full-throated fashion, like a caterpillar tractor engine turning over at full throttle.

"Why'd they have to leave Harold behind?" moaned Haga.

"Well, at least they took off," said Robert. "Probably looking for a card game." He felt a slight twinge as he said this. But it was in the longing for cards, not in any wish to join his cousins out on the road in their fruitless search for something to do on Christmas afternoon.

Harold was still snoring loudly, and the volume and also the absolute regularity of it astonished Robert, who was more used to the heart-stopping arrhythmia of Haga. Of course, Harold was a big, strong man in his prime, and he had probably eaten a dinner of turkey, cranberry sauce, hot buttered buns, mashed potatoes, jellied salad, macaroni salad, and two slices of pie sometime within the past two hours.

"Geez," whined Haga.

"I thought you said that back in the old days a brother was a brother no matter how much he snored." Robert gave an ironic shrug. It was almost as though Haga was getting respectable: he cooked soup for Christmas dinner, he put four spoons of sugar in his tea, he had sugar around to put in his tea, the pillow he was nursing . . .

But no, Robert thought, taking another look. Haga wasn't going to get respectable. There was no need to worry about it.

Waiting for Santa

MARK TUNNEY

It's one of those memories that you are unsure of, not because it didn't take place, but because it happened so long ago and because you were too shocked and ashamed to share it with anyone else. But as much as the rational adult mind may question that it really happened, it remains very real to the boy inside.

I think it was when I was in grade one or grade two.

We were called out into the hall — four or five at a time — to answer some questions. I didn't know then who the people asking the questions were, but in retrospect they must have been psychologists from the school board. I think they asked a range of questions about our families, our attitudes toward school and our beliefs.

I'm not really sure, because I only remember one question: Do you believe in Santa Claus?

I was standing at the back of the line, listening as each of my classmates was interrogated. I couldn't believe their answers. Everyone in front of me said, "No, I don't believe in Santa Claus." I didn't believe them then, and I don't believe now that they actually felt that, but it was as if these weasel-eyed bureaucrats with their sharp, thin smiles had planted a seed of doubt that rippled through the line.

The line kept getting shorter.

By the time it was finally my turn, the next batch of classmates was already pressing up behind me. I don't remember any of the other questions, because all I was thinking about was Santa Claus and how, all of a sudden, it seemed that I was the only one in the world to believe in him. Finally, they asked the question: Do you believe?

Conscious of the line-up behind me, the pressure of fitting in and already indoctrinated into an education culture that rewards what is correct if not necessarily right, I whispered, "No."

They asked me again, and I said it louder.

I remember feeling so confused and ashamed as I walked back to my small desk. I had betrayed Santa Claus, and I had no idea how to make it up to him.

It's funny how you can lose your ability to see Santa Claus, to feel him in the months leading up to Christmas, to hear him on the roof Christmas Eve. Sure, we see him everywhere around this time of year: in malls, on television, as a merchandising tool for every conceivable product. But we see right through him, walk right past him, in a way a child never could.

We talk about the spirit of Santa, the spirit of giving, the real meaning of Christmas, peace on earth. But these too can become words, hollow cants we beat on without ever creating the resonance and magic that once stirred us. Although we continue to celebrate Christmas, eventually Santa stops visiting us.

We accept this as one of the burdens of adulthood. It is not that we don't believe our words, or even that we don't try to live them, it's just that we are stuck in line, and magic doesn't work in line-ups; credit cards do. When I'm waiting there, sometimes I think back to the child in the line and feel the sense of betrayal creeping over me as I inch towards the desk.

We bring our gifts over such a long journey, over so many years, only to realize when we finally arrive that our destination is a simple one. Nothing but a child.

It had been many, many years since I had seen Santa. And although I have children, I still had not heard him on the roof; although I had seen Rudolph's teeth marks on carrots left out near the fireplace, I had a hard time imagining him in my living room. I will even admit to cursing Santa for bringing the Barbie Van — a flimsy, mind-numbing collection of plastic that should never be assembled after partaking of eggnog and which takes hours more to put together than it can possibly survive in the ghetto of a playroom.

Yet there I was on a plane with my family, flying home on Christmas Eve. The flight was a gift — for my mother felt that this would be my father's final Christmas. She proved to be right.

The pilot's voice came over the p.a. system with breaking news.

"We have a sighting. Santa's sleigh has been located on our radar screens approximately forty degrees to the north. If you look out the windows on your right, you may be able to spot Rudolph's nose."

And sure enough, there was a flashing red light, streaking across the sky. My oldest daughter, then nearly four, had no problems making out the entire sleigh and excitedly tried to describe it to me. The sky was very black, but as I gazed into her eyes, I think I may have seen its reflection — for the first time in a long time.

Earlier this month, my family was at a Christmas party for children at the hospital. Santa arrived, and the kids gathered around, waiting for a chance to sit on his lap and receive a gift.

My youngest daughter noted that one four-year-old girl seemed to get an especially large gift from Santa.

"She must have been *really* good this year!"

That little girl — whom I remember so vividly because my son had harassed her with kisses at a Christmas party when they were both only two — would not quite make it for Santa's visit this Christmas Eve.

"Yes, Eve," I said. "Santa Claus knows."

MARK TUNNEY

Home for Christmas

HARRY BRUCE

When my father was a boy, his sisters were schoolmarms at assorted villages and shores in Nova Scotia, and Christmas was the only time in winter that he saw them together. He once wrote, "I knew about a gentleman named Santa Claus. I may have sent him an occasional postcard. But if I did it was only to be polite, a kind of insurance just in case. He never took rank in importance with Bess and Anna and Carrie and Zoe." Each came home with a suitcase full of parcels, which she promptly locked away so little Charlie couldn't get at them till the Big Day. The expectation of what would be in those packages, of hearing the laughter of his sisters fill the house, of knowing that for a few precious days the bedrooms would once again hold the girls who belonged in them — these made the days before their arrival a time of almost intolerable excitement for him.

On December 10, 1919, he used *The Shoreham Searchlight* to remind Zoe to "DO YOUR XMAS SHOPPING EARLY" and to give her a shopping assignment: "This *Searchlight* is all blots but I can't help it. Find enclo. $1.00 part payment on presents for Mama, Harold [MacIntosh, his chum from the farm next door, and now my eighty-three-year-old neighbour], etc. I will send more when I get my fur money. Just now, half-broke. Kid."

One or two of the girls might show up at The Place aboard the mail-driver's sleigh on the weekend before Christmas, but Will Bruce always made at least one trip to Boylston, five miles away, to pick up a daughter who'd arrived by steamship from Mulgrave. He'd use the family sleigh, hauled by the skittish family mare, Doll, and he'd cover his lap with the family buffalo-robe. The boat had to steam up Chedabucto Bay to reach Boylston, and from The Place you could see her moving inland. Once, Sarah Bruce and little Charlie stood in the snow outside the back porch and waved a red tablecloth at the vessel, just in case Bess could see it from four miles out on the bay. Surely she'd be looking in their direction.

All his life, my father carried memories of those Christmases, of raisins, oranges, roast goose, red-and-green tissue-paper bells, real bells that tolled over moonlit fields of snow, sleighbells at the gate, frost on the windows, the far blink of a lighthouse, the hot kitchen where birch and maple crackled in the Waterloo range, and The Room. That was the dining room, and in there the light of a second fire flickered in an open Franklin stove, and a tinselled fir brushed the ceiling. It was in The Room that Charlie stripped the wrapping from a red tin pig that ran when he wound it up, from a flashlight, a box of paints, and, above all, the Daisy air rifle he'd been dreaming about ever since he'd seen it in a summer catalogue. His stocking — boys wore long ones then, gartered above the knee, hung in the kitchen some years — and in The Room other years, but it was always "sure to bulge on Christmas morning, like something with mumps."

As Charlie grew older, he got more books as Christmas presents from his parents and the girls, but the book he most clearly remembered was a volume of poetry sent by someone in the States, not to him but to his mother. It was by George William Russell (1867-1935), the Irish intellectual who signed his works AE. Charlie was ten or twelve, and decades later he wrote, "I can still recall that tingling of the spine, discovering from the printed voice of that wonderful Irishman what men could do with words.

The peacock twilight rays aloft
Its plumes and blooms of shadowy fire.

If Christmas brought to The Place a book that fanned the flame of his ambition to write poetry, it also shone in his head in a way that cast later Christmases in shadow. He put up a good act during the Christmases of my boyhood in Toronto. He never let me and my brothers know that he found the jolly Yuletide season depressing. He hated its commercialism, the greed it aroused in us, the bills it dumped on his shoulders and the way it disrupted work routines that normally made the world turn as it should. It also plunged him into memories of Christmases at The Place, Christmases he would never know again because he was no longer a boy, and Will was dead, and Sarah and the girls were scattered across the continent, and the old homestead had been rented to a fellow named Brown. My father died in Toronto in 1971, escaping his sixty-fifth Christmas by six days.

After Will Bruce died in 1934, Sarah lived for a while in the States with the families of Carrie and Zoe, but she ended up in Edmonton with her oldest daughter, Bess, a spinster. When Bess's long career as a schoolteacher was done, mother and daughter came back Down Home to live out their last years, and The Place was once again The Place of the Bruces. That was in 1953, but the summer visits had begun long before that. In July 1946, for instance, while Harry Brown and his wife Georgie were still renting The Place, a horde of folks with Bruce blood descended on them: Sarah and Bess from Edmonton; Zoe and her son and daughter, from California; Carrie and her daughter, from Detroit; and me, an eleven-year-old from Toronto. I got the small room over the kitchen that had once been my father's, but I can't imagine where everyone else slept. Bruce invasions occurred most summers, and I've a hunch no one along the shore looked forward to September as eagerly as the Browns did.

From 1953, Sarah and Bess lived in The Place year-round till Sarah died at ninety-nine in 1966, the year Canada, too, was ninety-nine. They'd shared a dozen quiet Christmases at The Place, but Bess soon began to close the home in November and to spend the winter at Anna's house in nearby Boylston. Anna and her husband, Robert MacKeen, had moved to Saskatchewan in 1928, and almost four decades later, just before his death, they, too, had resettled Down Home. So the spinster Bess and the widow Anna endured the winters together in Boylston, but each spring Bess went back along the road to The Place, and both sisters began to anticipate visits from Zoe in California and Carrie in Detroit. Even by the homecoming standards of ex-Maritimers, the returning record of these two frail, witty women is astounding. Zoe is ninety now and Carrie ninety-three, but in the past twenty years they have failed to get home in the summer only a couple of times. They were here last summer. They'll be here next summer.

When Bess died — at ninety-four, in June 1986 — our daughter Annabel sat with Carrie beside the open coffin at the funeral home in Guysborough. Men and women whose forebears Bruces knew in the nineteenth century flowed into the room to pay their respects, and Carrie, who was so deaf she could not have heard a bomb explode, simply watched the kindness in their faces and then murmured to her grandniece, "Mine own people." Much later, while rooting among crumbling, water-stained, and bug-ravaged books at The Place, I found *Mine Own People* by Rudyard Kipling. On the front flyleaf, written in black ink in the neat, flowing hand of a conscientious schoolmarm, was "Miss Carrie Bruce. Xmas 1914." She was twenty-one when she unwrapped that book by the shining tree in The Room, and my father was eight. He was too old for the mechanical pig and too young for the air rifle. Maybe that was the Christmas when he got the flashlight.

Penny and I still had an apartment in Halifax in December 1986, but our oldest son and his brood were coming back from Toronto for Christmas, and we decided that The Place was the place to be. Not for twenty years had the house been open in the winter, and cycles of freezing and thawing had buckled wallboards, left rooms reeking of mould and dampness and spawned armies of sowbugs. But the beds were good, and we had enough of them. The oil furnace in the basement still worked. Where the old Waterloo had once stood in the kitchen, we had installed a new Resolute, a cute, pricey, and efficient air-tight stove. The previous summer, I had bought three cords of sixteen-inch birch and maple, and somehow I had managed to split it all without breaking a foot or losing a toe. If the power failed, we'd still be cosy. We had kerosene lanterns, too. We were ready for whatever winter might throw at us during the most historic Christmas our own little family had ever celebrated.

On December 18, Penny and I drove the hundred and eighty miles from Halifax to The Place, cut a little spruce, set it outside the front door and festooned it with lights. The house smelled like the inside of its own ancient Leonard refrigerator, but the oil furnace and a snapping fire in the trusty Resolute drove out the clamminess. We drank rum, wrapped gifts and listened again to a record we've dragged out of one cupboard or another every Christmas for a quarter century: *Songs of Peace and Goodwill from the Welsh Mines* by the Rhos Male Voice Choir. The singing miners sounded more glorious than ever, and never before in our lives had we managed to wrap the bulk of the presents a full week before Christmas. We wanted everything to go right.

This would be the first Christmas that a real crowd of Bruces had spent at The Place in more than sixty years. Melinda and Jessica were coming from Toronto; they were four and two respectively, children of Alec and Vivien Cunningham Bruce. The last little kid to awaken in this house on Christmas Day in the morning had been their great-grandfather, darling Charlie, the Prince of The Place, who had turned four in 1910.

To round up our gang, I had to travel farther than Will did to pick up his daughters in Boylston. Decades have passed since the last ferry steamed up Chedabucto Bay with rail passengers from Mulgrave. Indeed, months may go by before we see *any* ship on the bay, though the Queensport lighthouse still offers its rhythmic glimmer. To meet my daughter Annabel and my son Max, both students at the University of King's College, Halifax, I drove twenty miles to a windswept stretch of the Trans-Canada Highway near the village of Monastery. I arrived just as a blue-and-silver Acadian Lines bus, jammed with homeward-bound Cape Breton Islanders, came arrowing east, pulled over to the shoulder and released just two passengers, Annabel and Max. Annabel waved good-bye to the driver, and she and Max, grinning like beautiful fools, walked toward me with their gift-filled paper bags with handles, and the bus roared back onto the traffic lanes, and the Tracadie River made its way through brown eelgrass to the marching waves of St. Georges Bay, and how come, at moments like this, I have always forgotten to bring my camera?

My son Alec's job was with the *Globe and Mail* in the heart of Toronto, where the atmosphere sometimes stank, and the moment he stepped outside Halifax Airport he said, "The air! I can't get over it. It's so *clean*." His wife, Vivien, and their two daughters had arrived before him, and I had picked them up at her parents' house in town. Her father had made a superb teddy bear, and her mother had bought another one, a supermarket special. I happened to have bought an identical super-market special, and now we had three bears for two girls. With me and Alec up front, and Vivien, Melinda, Jessica and the wrapped bears in the rear seat, and gift-stuffed luggage farther aft, the little Toyota was tested, but the three-hour drive to Port Shoreham went as smoothly as sailing on a broad reach in a soft breeze.

Snow had dusted the fields, the sun was out, and as we swung between the familiar dark hills, hundreds of millions of years old, that flanked James River, the setting sun behind us filled the flurries ahead with pink light, a light to make atheists believe in angels. We arrived home as darkness fell on the shortest day of the year, and when Alec got out of the car he said, "Boy, if I could get a decent job down here, I'd be back in a flash." In the spring of 1971 a Halifax businessman had told me, "We don't ask to be rich. We aren't greedy. We just want the economy to be healthy enough so our children won't have to keep on goin' down the road, that's all."

Now we were all Down Home together. The term has many meanings. If a Maritimer says "Down Home" while sitting in a Toronto tavern, he could be talking about all the Maritimes, or Prince Edward Island, or a valley, cove, county, village, or the house where he grew up. "Down-homer," in its gently derogatory sense, is also relative. "The first time I ever heard the term down-homer was a bit more than thirty years ago," my father wrote in *Mayfair* in 1955. "It was used by Bill Fraser, a brakeman in Antigonish, to describe a freight-handler from Mulgrave. Now, Mulgrave is only forty-five railway miles down the line from Antigonish; and I suppose that whenever Bill swung down off a gondola a few miles farther west and talked about the way things were done in his home town, he too was a down-homer to the more cultivated citizens of New Glasgow and Truro."

But the most intimate use of "Down Home" I've ever heard came from the lips of Floyd Grady when he dropped over to give me a Yuletide bottle of navy rum. His childhood home was adjacent to The Place on the east, and his mother, Kay, still lived there. Floyd was off to Prince Edward Island to visit relatives. Jerking his head over his right shoulder, he explained that he would not be Down Home on Christmas Day. To him, Down Home was a few hundred feet away. Every house along the shore was a specific Down Home for a specific family. At the Down Home of Carl and Carol MacIntosh, our neighbours to the west, the house was brim-full. Grant, the oldest son, a bricklayer in Oshawa, Ontario, had driven his pickup truck nonstop for more than eleven hundred miles to get to his Down Home for Christmas. Stewart, the second MacIntosh child, had recently been crew aboard a 230-foot vessel that sailed across the Atlantic to the United Kingdom. London had not impressed him much. It was too tough. Nobody cared for you there. As his father said, "It's just been a city too long." It would never be a Down Home.

Down Home was the kind of neighbourhood where, when you went out to your highway letter-box on December 23, you found a bottle of homemade spiced grape jelly, and for your granddaughters, two candy canes, each with a little horse's head, made of red and green felt. They were from Jean Grady, widow of Floyd's uncle Oscar. She had never met Jessica and Melinda, but she knew they were at The Place. Down Home was also the kind of neighbourhood where, on December 24, the girls next door walked their pony around to your front door just to give two much tinier girls a Yuletide thrill. The visitors were Jennifer, Jane and Sarah MacIntosh, and the pony was Fiona, a reddish-brown beastie with a straw-coloured mane, a barrel belly and a fat scarlet ribbon tied in a bow at her throat. Melinda had come from Queen Street in downtown Toronto, and when she saw Fiona strolling down our driveway, she squealed, "Yikes, get me outta here. There's a *camel* coming!" Within five minutes, however, both she and Jessica were aboard Fiona's beamy back, as giant snowflakes fell.

Down Home was the kind of neighbourhood where, when your distant cousin Clayton Hart dropped in — he was the fellow who built our cottage — he brought a box of the world's best chocolate fudge, made by his wife, Rose. When Carl and Carol MacIntosh came over, trailing a couple of daughters, Carol handed us pillow-sized loaves of brown raisin bread, fresh out of the oven. When Grant showed up, he gave us oysters in the shell. When Stewart arrived, he produced English toffee. Grant and Stewart sat around till midnight on December 23, downing Mooseheads, talking, yarn-spinning and dreaming out loud. We dubbed them the Two Wise Men. Grant thought he'd pull out on Boxing Day, heading south in his pickup truck for New Jersey. He had a friend down there, and the friend might fix him up with a job in Florida.

From before Christmas till a blizzard on New Year's Eve, the weather was God's gift to the Bruces. Most days, Christmas was green. After Carl MacIntosh delivered three cords of sixteen-inch firewood, Alec split some of it with a six-pound maul every day for a week, and he never once wore anything heavier than a shirt and sweater. (He split the whole pile, Vivien stacked it, and Penny and I were still burning it during the lonelier Christmas of 1987.) On Boxing Day, Alec and

I dug out baseball gloves we hadn't used in years and played catch for an hour with a shiny, time-blackened hardball.

The weather sometimes staged shows, our own vast meteorological pantomimes. One morning, after midnight winds had roiled the floor of the sea and violent water had torn at the sandstone of Ragged Head, a pink stain split the cold blue of the bay, and even though the storm had long since passed and the air was still, big combers kept crashing ashore. Bahamians call this phenomenon a dry rage. While the dry rage continued — and we could hear it way up here at The Place — huge, soft snowflakes swirled around the house, and we felt we were inside a glass paperweight that chimed a carol. Through the fat flakes, we could see splashes of blue sky, and late in the afternoon the snow stopped falling, the waves quit crashing, and a swath of purple cloud sat on the stone hills across the bay. The rest of the sky was pure blue, and low sunlight slanted all across our sweet field of grass — yellow, russet and blotched by snow.

Clayton Hart built a little box sleigh with steel runners, painted it fire-engine red and brought it over, and we dragged the little girls around on it whenever the snow was thick enough. One day, Annabel discovered a miraculously hard crust on top of the snow, and she climbed aboard Clayton's creation, and, whooping and screaming, she shot down our slope for a hundred yards. Dragging the sleigh by its yellow cord, she trudged up toward the house. Behind her, a curve of hairy evergreens on Bruce's Island stood out against the sheet of the bay, and something in the way she laughed made me think the impossible was happening: we were all getting younger.

When she and Alec were small they were such pals they could read one another's minds, and they played for hours at a stretch in worlds they invented together. But long before Alec married Vivien — he was barely twenty — the pull of different schools, ambitions, and sets of friends and enemies had destroyed that fine old closeness. In recent years, Annabel and Alec had scarcely even seen one another. During Christmas at The Place, however, she gave him Paul Simon's record "Graceland" (he brought the same record from Toronto for me and

Penny), and in the evening they sat by the hot stove, wearing their parents' sweaters and they listened to the driving rhythm of the music, drank beer, made jokes and dredged up memories. They went for walks, too. They found their old skates in the shop where I store firewood, and defying all warnings about weak ice, skated on the long pond where James Christopher Bruce had launched his first trading schooner while David Livingstone was exploring Zambezi.

In 1970, when Alec was nine and Annabel seven, I had written about their skating together in a column for *Maclean's*. In the piece, I lay in bed in Ottawa on a Sunday morning. I was suffering from the kind of hangover that Dorothy Parker once said "ought to be in the Smithsonian Institute under glass." Thoughts tormented me, too, thoughts like pecking ravens. Environmental doomsayers had predicted that, thanks to population growth and industrial activity, there soon wouldn't be enough oxygen in the air for people to breathe. We were bound to run out of oxygen in only twenty or thirty years, and I just lay there, torturing my mind in my already-tortured head with hideous fantasies about what would happen to our children in the 1990s. The column ended with my edging my way downstairs for a cup of black coffee just as Alec and Annabel came bursting in the kitchen door: "They've still got their skates on, their faces are red, a gust of knifing Arctic air tears around the kitchen, we all start laughing and hollering and, sweet dying Jesus, they are beautiful children."

Now, sixteen years later at The Place, they burst into another kitchen, after another skate, and their cheeks were once again red, and a gust of Atlantic air tore around the room, and Annabel said, "God, we felt just like little kids out there." Later, each one got me aside to tell me how much the other loved The Place and its fields, woods, streams and bay. The Place was even growing on Max. The other two had childhood memories of our houses in Toronto, on Toronto Island, in Newcastle, Ontario, Ottawa, and Prospect, Nova Scotia, but since Max's infancy his only hometown had been Halifax. He loved the city, and even as a high-school student, he often lurked all night in the radio station at Dalhousie University. He detested the long drive to Port Shoreham.

Being there bored him. It meant doing without video games, video music, movies, television, clubs, restaurants, street traffic, junk food, friends and, aside from his parents, anyone even to look at, much less talk with. But with all of us together again, he liked The Place. With my old Pentax hanging from a shoulder, he took long walks by himself and took the best photographs anyone has ever taken of his ancestral home.

When Anna came over for Christmas dinner and to meet her great-grandnieces, four generations of Bruces sat down at two tables to gorge on roast turkey, cranberry sauce, gravy, mashed potatoes, carrots, cauliflower, plum pudding with hard sauce and butterscotch pie with whipped cream. Jessica, Melinda and Anna were the only teetotallers. The rest of us downed white wine. In the entire history of The Place it's doubtful if wine had ever graced a Christmas feast, but out of deference to Anna's principles and respect for the gentle ghosts of earlier teetotallers within these walls, we offered no raucous toasts to the fact that wine on the table was another "first." Later we opened the doors of the Resolute and installed a screen, and Anna sat in her father's rocking chair beside the flames. He'd been dead for fifty-two years, and she talked of times long gone.

She'd been told as a child that before the pioneers built schools here, male teachers had tutored children while boarding in the youngsters' houses. The only classes were for singing lessons, and a favourite song began, "Here we go to Miramichi, to get a load of sugar and tea." Maybe it was the chair, but something reminded Anna of the evening Bess vanished. She remembered that after Will's grocery store near Boston had failed, he and Sarah and the girls were living not here but at the home of Sarah's mother — the property now owned by sleigh-maker Hart — a little way inland on the McPherson Lake Road. With another little girl, Bess, who was eleven or twelve, went out to fetch cows. During the search, they met Will, who asked if they knew their way home. Bess said yes, but she was wrong. A search party scoured the woods till midnight, began again at dawn and found the girls at midmorning. They'd spent the night under a tree, no doubt praying. "I can still see the men coming down over the hill with them," Anna said.

Before I drove her back to Boylston, she opened her purse and started to hand fifty-dollar bills to me and Penny, and twenty-dollar bills to Alec, Vivien, Annabel, and Max. We all protested. "Oh no, Anna, you mustn't do that. You really shouldn't."

"I certainly should," she said. "I'm the great-*great*-aunt of these little girls, not just the great-aunt. This is one Christmas in a hundred years."

And so it was.

"To a kid of four or five or six," my father wrote, "time is the Pool of Now." When you looked back later, the pool was still there, but it had become the Pool of Then, in which "people and events and places, laughter and tears and the words of songs — they drift and swirl and circle, far off and yet immeasurably close." The Christmas of 1986 has slipped into my own personal Pool of Then.

I remember Melinda and her aunt Annabel charging across our snowy field to greet one another and Melinda "treating" her uncle Max with the toy doctor's kit she found under the tree. The best patient she'd ever have, he lay moaning on the chesterfield for much of Christmas afternoon. I remember Jessica, at two, dancing to "Grace-land" in all the glory of her nakedness and Annabel showing both her nieces how to make sugar cookies that looked like fish and teddy bears. I remember the friendly racket at midafternoon on Christmas Day when half a dozen MacIntoshes came into our kitchen. The room sounded like the corridors of Maple Leaf Gardens between periods of a hockey game in, say, 1946. That was the year I first saw The Place, and I gave swimming lessons to a sunny nine-year-old named Carl MacIntosh. Carl was a sunny forty-nine-year-old now, and he outweighed me by fifty pounds, and we sat by the stove, tossed back a rum or two and swapped jokes.

A few days later, Alec and I explored our property lines, and he considered sites for the house he would build when the time was right for him to return for good. Neither of us knew whether that time would ever come. As Annabel pulled on her snowboots before going back to Halifax, she said, "God, I hate to leave this place. I wish I could take it with me, on a key chain or something." She would graduate in journalism in the spring and head for Upper Canada. Alec and his family were about to fly back to Toronto, and Max would soon go to Montreal to study film production. As for Penny and me, we had lived in seventeen different apartments and houses since our marriage in 1955, and we knew we would never move again. But having found our home, we had lost our children.

Down Home, of course, there's nothing new in that.

Folding Bones

BERNICE MORGAN

"Not all year around?" "Think of the winters!" "Think of the isolation!" colleagues said when I told them I was going to live in Newfoundland. For all that, I could detect a certain relish, almost admiration, in their voices — as if my abandoning Ottawa and the civil service mitigated somewhat their own preoccupations with mortgages and retirement funds.

In fact, I am the most cautious of women. No act in my life — apart from the conception of my son — has been done impulsively. I gave up my job knowing I can always get contract work in Ottawa, and my house there is leased, not sold. I remind myself of these things each morning as I gaze down on the mound of snow under which my car is buried. From my bedroom window the shape looks more like an upturned boat than a car. But car it is, and with muscle power can be uncovered. Two hours digging, a two hour drive in to Gander and a three hour flight. Seven hours and my son and I could be back in Ottawa. Davisport is not the Gobi desert or a polar ice cap.

Reassured by this knowledge, I go downstairs. I get David Saul's breakfast, make sure he is well protected for his short walk to school, cap, mitts and boots pulled on, coat buttoned. My son loves it here, thrives on the freedom. There are only four children in his kindergarten class, but his summertime friendship with Todd Pardy next door has continued.

Summer after summer I have been content here. Winter after winter in Ottawa, the thought of this place kept me sane, the thought of driving down this coast, taking the turnoff to Davisport, driving until there was nothing before me but blue — endless blue stretching all the way to Ireland. I would sit in my hermetically sealed office and picture myself stepping out of the car with David Saul in my arms and all around us the smell of roses, the smell of sea, Selina waiting in her shady garden.

I loved it all then, without caution, without discrimination, as if feelings for my baby had overflowed to include Davisport and everything in it, the plastic motels and ugly takeouts as much as the white churches and weathered wharves, the gouged-out gravel pits as well as the deep bays, the long sweeping beaches and fragrant marshes. And the people, of course — what passion I had to protect Selina and her friends, to protect everyone in Davisport from the unkind appraisal of outsiders.

I don't feel that way anymore. My impulse now is to protect outsiders from Davisport, to take up for Nurse Johanssen, to tell Mr. Richards he must stop carrying that briefcase, stop wearing that tweedy cap the men make fun of. It's myself I'm really worried about, of course, myself and David Saul. I see now that one can be a stranger here forever. It doesn't take much to be considered odd in Davisport and I'm already eccentric — likely to get more so as time goes by. I remember my step-father Saul, his lonely last years, wonder if I can live in a place where I will be considered strange and a stranger for the rest of my life.

On Friday there is another snow storm. "Savage weather," Selina says, looking out at the whirling whiteness, not mentioning that Ruby hasn't been by for days, not since our argument about the nosy bank clerk who turned out to be her niece.

I suggest we keep David Saul home from school, and we do. He and Selina make five batches of cookies, "One hundred and sixty three — for the mummers!" my son announces. He is in a fever of anticipation, wound tighter each day by Selina. With her own grandchildren gone she has only David Saul to make promises to: promises of a Christmas stocking, Christmas concerts, Christmas fireworks, now Christmas mummers.

On Saturday the sun is out. I open the library but no one comes, not even Angus Vincent to replenish his weekly supply of science fiction. I content myself with dusting and indexing four boxes of books Selina found in the room she cleared out for David Saul. The books are old, worn volumes of poetry: Tennyson, Yeats, Shelley, English schoolboy adventures, a beautiful but tattered set of children's books called the Collins Crusader Series.

I would like to repair the books, to peel away their broken spines, cut new covers, wrap them in leather as my stepfather used to do. I remember Saul lighting the gas ring under a pot of honey coloured glue. It would be a winter's night, us alone, me doing my homework and him reading, my mother visiting her friend next door. It would be quiet, just the sputter of gas and, in the snow-silenced streets, the occasional clank of a loose chain hitting the undercarriage of a car. I would know by the smell when the glue was soft, when it was time for Saul to take the felt-wrapped package from the bottom drawer of his desk.

I remember Saul's hands unrolling the cloth, lining up his tools on the desk, the long curving needles, the ball-peen hammer, square-tipped knives and, my favourite, the eight inch strip of worn ivory that Saul called a folding bone. He would let me hold the cream coloured bone, a small piece of some wild animal, silk smooth between my hands.

Slowly, careful as a doctor uncovering wounds, my stepfather would peel away the worn binding, expose crystallized glue that looked like brown sugar. Old covers falling away from the body of the book would be used as a pattern for new covers. After cutting a set of cover boards, Saul would pluck the round brush, fat with glue, from the pot. Without getting a speck on his hands he would spread hot glue over the new leather binding.

Then I would pass him the folding bone, which had grown warm in my hands, watch as he folded soft leather deftly around the edges of the spine, over the cover boards, nudging neat corners into place with the little awl he cupped in the palm of his hand. He would turn then to the pages, stacked in what he called signatures. Using the curved needle he sewed these together, restitching the spine before attaching a set of beautifully marbleized end papers. The last thing he'd do before setting the book in his bookpress was to apply white paste to the backs of the end papers. Then, with a magical snap of his hand, he would wrap new covers around the book.

Saul often sang when he was bookbinding. It was the only time he ever sang, a low chant in a language that was not English. Other times he recited poetry: Blake, ". . . and sands upon the Red Sea shone, where Israel's tents do shine so bright," and Yeats, ". . . and therefore I have sailed the seas and come to the holy city of Byzantium." Sometimes he asked me to read poems out loud to him. Our tastes matched, or maybe his tastes became mine. "Where the Great Wall 'round China goes, And on one side the desert blows," I would read, or "Morning's all aglitter and noon's a purple glow . . ."

A wonderful thing for a child on a winter's night to stand in that warm core of safety, to smell glue and leather, to be surrounded by a whirl of words. Fingering old books in an empty library, I think of those nights with Saul, remember them as the essence of happiness and childhood innocence. I wonder if I could recreate such times for my son. I still have the folding bone.

I am thinking this, wondering if I might be able to order bookbinding supplies from St. John's, when David Saul comes into the library. He scuffs in, complaining that his mitts are wet, that he has no one to play with. When I ask where Todd is he becomes cross, reminds me of the concert Todd is in. "I know the songs as well as Todd, but the teacher says I'm too small this year — they're all practising, and there's no one outdoors," he whines.

I tell him about Saul, about the bookbinding, but he is not interested. I find *A Child's Garden of Verses*, pull him onto my lap and read, "Where the great wall 'round China goes, And on one side the desert blows . . ." I am caught by the words but he is not; he squirms away, "Someone might come in," he says. "They'll think I'm a sooky baby!"

There is nothing for it but to lock the library and go home. Outside, where the evening really is all aglitter — with silver thaw and sunset — David Saul becomes cheerful. He sings the Star Song for me. His voice is thin and off key. Still, I think, they could have let him sing. We smile at each other, he lets me kiss his red cheek, tells me that Selina has promised a little tree for his bedroom, a tree with lights. He lets me hold his hand until we come opposite Todd's house.

This week David Saul is coming straight home from school. "It's lonely," he says, lolling in front of the television, challenging us to coax him out of the sulks. We try. Selina makes toffee, finds an old Crokinole set her sons used forty years ago, teaches him to shoot wooden rings towards the centre. I read to him, tempt him outdoors, show him how to make snow angels, how to draw in the snow with food colouring. But we are dull, we cannot hold him, cannot distract him from the hall where older children are kings and shepherds, where Todd is practising the Star Song, where Mr. Richards has promised he will take everyone out for pizza before the concert.

Today, the day of the concert, David Saul did not come home from school. By three-thirty I had been back and forth to the lane six times. There was no sign of him on the road or in the field where he and Todd sometimes slide. The Pardy house was empty. At four I phoned the school but there was no answer.

"They'll all be over at the hall gettin ready for tonight. And I allow that's where our young lord is, bound and determined to be on that concert," Selina says. She is chuckling, recalling some long-ago prank of her own as she pulls on her coat. "You stay put in case he turns up — I'll phone from the hall."

The hall is right across from the school. The first floor, once a storage shed for salt cod, was converted some years ago into a recreation centre for teenagers. Since there are no longer many teenagers in Davisport, the centre is now used as a community auditorium. It was almost five before Selina phoned. "David Saul's not here. Young Todd says he saw him putting his cap and jacket on when the rest of them left school." There is no humour in her voice now.

I grip the phone and listen. Around me, Selina's cream and green kitchen looks just as safe and shiny as it did before the phone rang. I am struck by the impossible sameness of household objects, the permanence of walls, chairs and tables — the impermanence of flesh. I must have made some sound because Selina snapped, "Stop that!"

"He's around somewhere. Don't let yourself get all worked up," she says after a minute, then: "He'll be all right — he's just off somewhere sookin' cause he's not on the concert."

"I'll come down. I'll circle around to the highway and loop back to the school." I am already dragging on my coat, am searching through pockets for my car keys.

Selina reminds me of the snow-covered car. She tells me I must stay where I am, "You stay by the phone so's the people searching can check back," she says.

"Searching?" the word has a cold, news report feeling.

"Yes, searching," Selina says. She explains that Dunc and Ruby have gone out in their four-wheel drive, that the principal and several other men are out on snowmobiles, coasting around snow covered woods paths. Mr. Robinson and some high school boys have been dropped off over at the old boy scout camp back of the pond — they've taken snowshoes.

All this has been done without me knowing, done even before she called me. I feel grateful, yet resentful, "I can't stay here — I'll go mad," I said.

"No, bide there. Get yourself a cup of tea, scrub the floor, that's what I used to do," Selina orders, and I recall some of the stories she's told me, times when she might have scrubbed floors to keep sane.

"Look," she says, trying to sound cheerful, "we'll hear from the little imp soon. Everyone's out looking. Ruby even called the RCMP road cruiser, they got flares and spotlights. I'll keep by the phone here in the hall and you stay by that one — the minute one of us knows something we'll phone the other. Now, make yourself a cup of tea, girl. Mark my words, he'll be found before dark!"

But it is already dark. Has been dark for some time. I make myself a cup of tea, then pull a kitchen chair over to the phone, as if the seconds it would take me to cross the room might make a difference. I sit in the dark, holding the tea, waiting, telling myself that children stray away all the time, telling myself they turn up — always. Not always.

The tea is cold. I cannot stand another minute in this silent kitchen, cannot stand this waiting for someone to come and tell me what has happened to my son. I stand and rush outside, leave the door wide open. The freezing cold stings my face. Did I put an extra sweater on David Saul this morning? I cannot remember. I walk down the lane; there is a full moon, the snowbank covering my car shimmers like the back of a blue whale. On the far side of the harbour I can see lights: cars or snowmobiles. Over here nothing, not a sound, not a light, only the moon and the snow.

Realizing suddenly I will not hear the phone from where I am, I run back to the house, return to the kitchen, to the shattered teacup and spilled tea. I sweep up the broken china. Then I get a bucket of water and begin to scrub the floor.

I am still scrubbing the floor, scrubbing unnecessarily, when the phone in Selina's kitchen rings. I scrabble towards it, tripping, almost upsetting the bucket.

As soon as I hear Selina's voice, I know the worst thing has not happened. "Found! He's been found — Found, Found, Found!" she screeches, repeating the word until I order her to shut up. I ask if my son is all right.

"He's fine, fine, just a bit cold. He was hiding all the time, in the back of the teacher's van, under an old jacket. Right there in the van all the time they were driving around looking for him! The little nuisance!" she says with admiration. "Apparently he heard Mr. Richards promise the youngsters he'd take them for pizza before the concert, not the best idea if you ask me. Still, David Saul wanted to go, too." Selina babbles on, describing where each searcher had gone, what each one said when they came in. It is ten minutes before I can interrupt, ask her to put David Saul on the phone.

"Oh, he's not here, girl! Gone off happy as a lark with the rest of them. Three or four parents, Ruby and Dunc, most of the teachers and all them youngsters, traipsin' all the way up to Greenspond for pizza. They've decided to set the concert back an hour." She paused. "I told Ruby we'd meet her over at the Lodge." The triumph in Selina's voice makes me wonder for a minute if she could have arranged all this in order to get us together, to devise a celebration we are all part of.

It is almost nine when we get to the hall. The room is filled to capacity. For this night the pub must be deserted, television sets abandoned. Ruby has managed to save only two seats so I take David Saul on my lap. A dozen or so young people, most of whom I've never seen before, stand near the back — sons and daughters come home from St. John's, from Lab City and Goose Bay, from Toronto, from Fort McMurray. Home for Christmas. Ruby reaches behind Selina to tap my shoulder, points our her three good-looking boys around whom a bevy of girls have clustered.

As the hall becomes hotter, more overcrowded, a briny smell seeps up from the planked floor, the spirits of salt cod once stacked by the thousands in this room. The smell is euphoric — it reminds me of my stepfather's binding glue. I glance at Selina, hoping to convey the happiness I feel sitting here with my son safely in my arms. But she is focused on the opening curtains, on Jesus, Mary and Joseph who occupy centre stage. They sit rather uncomfortably, this holy family, arranged atop a blue plastic fish crate onto which evergreen boughs have been stapled. This year there are not enough student voices, so the church choir has been brought in, adults arranged in a semicircle behind the children. To one side Nurse Johanssen stands by the piano, peering down into the audience, waiting sternly for the pointing and whispering to stop.

Nurse Johanssen is a large woman, not fat but tall, with breasts that have become a single unity. At the clinic she wears white blouses and firm gabardine skirts, but tonight she is flamboyant in red velvet, long and flared and embroidered with green and gold. When the audience is quiet, she moves regally to the piano, sits and begins to play "Silent Night."

Scene follows scene; meek sheep and dancing stars, shuffling angels, self-conscious shepherds and kings mime their parts. Older students, standing to one side, read appropriate sections of the Christmas story. In between, choir members are efficiently herded on and off stage by Nurse Johanssen who seems to be in charge of all.

I watch in a daze of tiredness, leaning into the pungent dark, my lips brushing David Saul's hair. His hair is still wispy soft, angels' hair, but with a musty smell — probably from the jacket he'd covered himself with in the van. The worst thing about not believing in God is not that you cannot ask him for help, but that you cannot thank him for happiness.

Near the end, when every performer is on stage for the grand finale, Nurse Johanssen comes to the front again. Holding her hand above her eyes she peers down into the audience.

"Looks like a Christmas rooster, her Ladyship do," Selina whispers.

It is true. Ruby and I start to giggle. Then we realize that Nurse Johanssen is looking at us, see that she is beckoning to David Saul, inviting him to come forward, to join in the last carol. "Bless her heart!" Selina says, repentant now, though I know that tomorrow she will again refer to the nurse as a CFA. She takes my son's hand and, all smiles, leads him to the front, lifts him onto the stage.

Nurse Johanssen sits down at the piano and, with great relish, ripples out a few notes. She points a commanding finger towards the fifty or so people on stage. "Star of the East, Thou hope of the soul, Guiding us on while dark billows roll . . ." they sing, the music rolling out, filling the small room.

It is the Star Song David Saul talked so much about. He is standing next to Todd, fair and square in front, singing with all his might. He is flushed with happiness, any moment he might burst into tears or throw up, as he often does when excited.

I will lose him. I know I will lose him. But not now, not yet. For the moment he is mine, for the moment he stands before me safe — safe and loudly happy. "Gladly we follow in thy holy light, Pilgrims of Earth so wide," he sings.

The words remind me of my stepfather, of Saul the wanderer — of my mother, too — of myself — perhaps of everyone — pilgrims moving across a vast spinning planet. Pilgrims of earth so wide.

Enclosed by the smell of salt cod, sitting in an over-warm room on the edge of nowhere, I watch my son's face. I let myself sink into happiness — wrap myself in it, as I might wrap myself in a good dream, knowing it is a dream, giving myself up to its fragile safety.

Cousin Gifts

BRIAN BARTLETT

The names of three dozen cousins shook
together in a hat. Our mothers always
chose the gifts, always wrapped them
neatly, with clean creases. Cousin gifts
were never revolved near lamps. Buried
under more promising packages, shoved aside,
they were the orphans under the tree.

One autumn your name wasn't put
in the hat, and you knew you were aging,
adrift in your teens.

Two decades later at Christmas, family news
gathers like darkness on shedding boughs:
Doris unemployed after ten years selling
train tickets, Wheeler's bank account emptied
by his fleeing wife, a fatherless child
born to Sylvie in high school, Donald
tongue-tied, on tranquilizers . . .

My cousins have scattered to Corner Brook,
Mississauga, Burnaby, New Guinea.
Some are happy, says my mother,

but those who aren't
I try hardest to recall — voices
drifting across a picnic table, breaking
a lake's calm in two; then only
their hands turning over and
over, eyes facing kitchen tiles.

My cousins . . .
I do not know what gifts to give them.

Christmas in the Country

SYR RUUS

She was not looking forward to this visit.

It would be nice to see her grandchildren certainly, and Jane, her daughter, her only child, was all the family she had left. They had been on good terms until Michael came along. Then everything changed. Jane became resentful and evasive. When Meredith asked about anything personal, she would answer, but never look her directly in the eye.

Meredith sighs loudly and presses her lips together, leaning back against the faded plush seat.

First her daughter. Then her husband. Gone. He had stayed until Jane was married off, then felt free to live his own life. She could hardly mourn him, for he was already living with another woman when he died. But she mourned for Jane, still alive and claiming to be happy, though Meredith doubted it. Michael had long hair and no steady job. Jane taught school to support him and the kids. Even when they were babies, she had to be the breadwinner in the family. It wasn't right. She could have done better. But she would never admit it, especially to her own mother. Jane didn't accept criticism well. She could never face up to a mistake.

Meredith sighs again and looks absently out the window at the soggy, grey city. Not like Christmas was supposed to be. Across the parking lot she sees a skinny girl in tight jeans and pink parka, the fake fur matted and yellow around the hood, dragging a small boy behind her. His short pudgy legs in baggy corduroy trousers move twice as fast as hers to keep up as she tugs him toward the waiting bus.

"You goin' to Western Shore?" she asks the driver.

"No," he says. "This here's the Express. We don't stop in them little towns."

The two stand silent in the icy drizzle looking up through the open door.

"The house is right beside the highway," she said finally, "with a white picket fence around it? You can't miss it. Will you just stop so's we can get off thar?"

The driver considers a moment, looking at the girl and then at the kid.

"Yeah," he says slowly. "I guess we can do that. But you gotta pay full fare anyhow. And you gotta tell me when to stop."

She has no suitcase or anything, just a green vinyl shoulder bag and the kid. They pick the seat right in front of Meredith, and at the first traffic light, the kid starts in:

"Are we thar yet, Ma?" he whines, standing up on the seat and pressing his face against the window.

"No, not for a while yet," says the mother, keeping her voice low, though it seems obvious to Meredith that she is a type more used to shouting.

"Look at that, Ma," the kid hollers, pointing. "What's that thar, Ma?"

"Shush. You gotta be quiet on the bus," she says.

"What fur, Ma?" he asks.

She has no answer to that one.

She seems to be no more than eleven herself, until you look closely. Then the dead ends of her dyed hair and the sallow skin over her cheekbones give her away.

"When we gonna get thar, Ma?" he whines again after a space of two or three minutes.

It nearly drives Meredith crazy, the whining. Why did they have to pick a seat right in front of her? The bus was still half empty when she got on, its motor idling softly, the driver busy outside filling the luggage compartment with packages. Meredith had taken a taxi to the station early, so as not to be late. She didn't know how she'd manage by herself with the two heavy suitcases, one of them full of presents. She wasn't the type to travel in buses. There was no reason they couldn't have driven to the city to pick her up, no reason at all, she thinks resentfully, but she has learned over the years not to speak her mind. It would only lead to an argument, the same old accusations making the rounds and spoil Christmas for them all. As it was, she always felt uncomfortable at Jane's with Michael there. Unwelcome. The mother-in-law. Jenny and Mike Jr. would latch on to her right away of course, eager to see what she had brought them. They'd have to wait until Christmas morning, but she might be allowed to give them at least one of their gifts early.

As she thinks of her grandchildren, her face softens. An expression close to a smile plays around her lips. She is caught unawares by the boy, standing backwards on the seat, staring at her out of sombre dark eyes. Quickly she fixes her face to its accustomed severity, opens her purse and pretends to be searching for something until the boy tires of looking and settles into his seat. Not for long. When the bus stops at the next light, he scrambles to his feet again.

"Are we thar now, Ma?" he yells. "Is this the country, Ma?"

"No," she says. "Hush. We got a long ways to go yet."

But the kid won't hush.

"What's Nanny's house like, then?" he asks, tugging at her sleeve.

"Nice," she tells him. "I ain't never been there myself, but it's sure to be nice. Houses is nice in the country."

That seems to satisfy him.

Soon the traffic thins out. The bus pulls onto the highway and picks up speed. Over the steady drone of the motor she hears the clack of windshield wipers and muffled voices from the young crowd in back. The little boy must be asleep. But now that everything is quiet and the boy no longer a nuisance, Meredith wants him awake and talking. Is there really someone waiting? she wonders. Is there truly a Nanny in Western Shore in a house surrounded by a white picket fence? She looks out the window at a grey landscape punctuated by scraggly evergreens clutching at thin rocky soil. Not many houses to relieve the monotony of the view. None with a white fence. Clumps of withered yellow grass the only patches of colour.

Across the aisle sits a youngish woman, prissy and spinsterish, black sensible shoes set neatly side by side on the muddy floor. Every once in a while she underlines something in a small volume, then gazes off into space. Meredith tries to get a glimpse of the title. Probably a religious tract of some kind, judging by the woman's demeanour. Perhaps she's a nun. Since they have stopped wearing the habit it's hard to tell.

In front of her sits a plump girl, unattractive, with greasy brown hair and a bad complexion, reading also. A tabloid. Meredith can make out a red headline predicting dire events in the New Year. The girl's attention seems to wander to the delicate pink rose wrapped in cellophane which she has placed on the empty seat beside her. Several times she picks it up to sniff it. Who could it be for? Meredith wonders.

The bus is almost full, most of the passengers being college students returning home for the holidays. They sit together in the back, their duffel bags carelessly flung on the racks above. Meredith hears their faint laughter and imagines talk of parties, those past and those yet to come. She feels like crying. Somehow, somewhere, life has passed her by. Every Christmas she feels it. She had tried to convince herself that her life was full. She kept herself busy. She had her bridge club, her volunteer work. But maybe, after all, it was quite empty.

All these other passengers had somewhere to go, something they looked forward to. What did she have? A daughter who no longer loved her. A son-in-law she despised. Grandchildren she really didn't know, who were only interested in the gifts she brought. Are we thar yet, Ma? the little boy's voice asks again in her mind, though the questioner himself is now sound asleep, drool oozing out of the side of his slack and peaceful mouth. Meredith wants to doze off herself in the stuffy warmth of the bus, yet a strange compulsion keeps her wide awake, looking out the window for a house with a white picket fence. The bus driver seems to have assumed the same responsibility judging by the number of times his concerned blue eyes glance back into the rear-view mirror.

Suddenly the bus slows and then stops altogether on the shoulder of the highway. The passengers become attentive as the driver turns around.

"You never did tell me to stop," he says accusingly. "We're a ways past Western Shore now."

"I didn't see no picket fence," she whines into the silence. "What am I supposed to do?"

He thinks hard before he answers.

"We're not that far past yet," he says. "Maybe you oughta get off here. Before we go any further. There's a service station up the hill. You could call someone. Maybe they would come and pick you up."

They all gape at her as she moves down the aisle, pulling on the little boy, still rosy and muddled from sleep. The bus door opens with a hiss.

"Is this the country, Ma?" the kid is shouting as they disappear down the steps into the cold.

Barely visible in the grey mist, a tiny pink figure drags a smaller one up the barren icy slope as they pull away. It is silent on the bus. Even the students in the back are watching her ascent. Everyone is hoping the same thing — that somewhere someone will welcome them home.

SYR RUUS

Hilda Porter's Christmas

HERB CURTIS

Hilda Porter's face had more lines on it than an Illinois road map. Dark around the eyes, frail, growing weaker and more forgetful every day, she spent more and more of her time beside the stove.

One day just before Christmas she fell, and Shad had to help her into the chair. She made light of it, chuckled, but Shad knew there was something terribly wrong with her. She had forgotten to flush the toilet on a few occasions, and Shad had seen the blood.

"I think we should get you to a doctor," he said.

Hilda knew that Shad was right, but she also knew that if she went to a doctor, she'd be hospitalized and kept, perhaps for weeks. She did not want to spend Christmas in the hospital.

"I'll be all right, dear," she said. "Maybe, if things don't improve, I'll go after Christmas. Will you be going home for Christmas, darling boy?"

"Don't know . . . s'pose I should."

"Well, do what you have to, dear. Don't let me stand in your way."

"Maybe I'll just go home for a little while, see the folks and come back again."

"Christmas don't mean anything to me, dear. I haven't celebrated Christmas for years. It's just for kids, young people. Is it tomorrow or the next day?"

"Day after tomorrow. Thought I'd get a tree."

"For here? I . . . my goodness, we don't need a tree. "

"Just a little one. We can put it in the parlour."

"But your parents will have a tree. That's good enough. I don't need a tree."

Shad could have been a philosopher, a psychoanalyst or an ecologist when he said, "Everyone needs a tree."

He grabbed the axe and headed out.

"But we haven't any decorations," said Hilda.

There was no more arguing — Shad was already heading for the road.

The snow was too deep to go into the woods any distance without snowshoes, so Shad walked along the road searching the ditch for something suitable. He didn't go far until he came to a little fir, sparse, but with a certain uniformity, slightly better than a Charlie Brown tree, but not a caricature. He cut it and carried it home.

He took it in through the front door and stood it in the parlour. Then he went to the kitchen to find Hilda standing by the table — she was making gingerbread.

Shad watched the thin little white-haired person for a moment before he spoke. She wore a white apron, blue dress and pink knitted slippers. She was humming a melody with a shaky voice. For some reason she reminded Shad of a little girl playing house, making mud pies.

"Makin' gingerbread men?" he asked.

He sat on a chair by the table to watch, to talk.

Hilda began to sing the words to what she was humming —

> Put me in your pocket,
> So I'll be close to you . . .
> No more will I be lonesome
> And no more will I be blue.

"You never hear them old songs anymore," she said.

"That a Christmas song?" asked Shadrack.

"No, just a song. I was thinking some gingerbread men would work for the tree. We don't have any decorations. Got thrown out, I guess.

We used to make strings of popcorn and cranberries. I don't think we have either. I was thinking you might go to the store."

"Yeah, sure. Maybe I can find something to make a star out of."

"Have I given you any money lately?" asked Hilda.

"No, but that's all right."

"You need money. Christmas coming up and all. Goodness me, I'm getting stupider every day. Go into my purse there by the door and take fifty dollars."

"Fifty dollars!"

"I've been saving it for you; I just never got around to giving it to you. And here it is almost Christmas! Go get it, and go shopping. Bring back some popcorn and cranberries!"

"But fifty dollars?"

"You earned it. Go get it."

Shad went to the purse, took fifty dollars came back, sat.

"Tell me more about the Tasmanians," he said. "You haven't talked about them for a long time."

"The Tasmanians? I told you about the Tasmanians?"

"Yeah. The last thing you told me about was a lad called King Billy."

"King Billy. The last male Tasmanian."

"Only women left?"

"And not many of them. It wasn't long before there was only one — Trucanini . . ." Hilda sighed, growing tired with the work. She had finished cutting out the gingerbread men and placing them on a cookie sheet. She carried the cookie sheet to the stove and slipped them into the oven. Then she sat in her rocking chair.

"By this time, these lads, anthropologists, I think they were called, were studying her."

"Studying her?"

"She was the last of her kind, you see, and they were realizing it for the first time. All of a sudden she was very important to anthropologists, men who study man. She was the only living specimen of what was probably the most primitive people on Earth. Not only were they studying her, but they had done something that was very taboo to her way of thinking — they dug up King Billy and dissected his body. They had been dissecting the bodies of the Tasmanian aborigines for quite some time, but Trucanini hadn't known it. When she found out, she was terrified. "Don't let them cut me up," she cried. "Bury me behind the mountains!"

"So, did they?"

"Yes."

"And that's it?"

"No. They took her to the woods in the cheapest coffin they could find, on an oxcart. They buried her. The premier and some other big shots were there. It was supposed to be very secret. They did it in the night."

"Well, they did that much for her, anyway," commented Shad.

"Well, yes, but they dug her up. Imagine! They dug her up and wired her bones in a sitting position, put them in a museum."

Christmas Eve, Bob and Elva Nash went to Blackville to do some shopping, then dropped in to Hilda Porter's. Hilda sat in her chair by the stove; Bob, Elva and Shad sat by the table.

Hilda had very little to say. She knew they had come to get Shad, to take him home for Christmas.

"Are you feeling pretty good, Hilda?" Elva asked this so loudly she could have been heard upstairs. Hilda was looking very tired and old; Elva assumed she was deaf.

"Oh, pretty well," said Hilda.

"Ya can't kill them old Porters," said Bob. Bob was nearly shouting as well.

Shad saw the amused look appear on Hilda's face. She has a way of smiling without smiling, he thought.

"I'm the last, you know," said Hilda. "Would you folks like a cup of tea?"

"No. No tea, no!" said Bob. "I said, ya can't kill them old Porters! You could live to be a hundred yet! Women always live old!"

Elva chuckled, then grew serious. "You gonna try to get to church?" she asked.

"I don't think so," said Hilda.

"You should try to go to church, dear!" said Elva. "I hope you pray, dear!"

"I might try to go tomorrow if I can find a way . . . if it doesn't snow," said Hilda.

"Your father lived old!" said Bob.

"Yes, yes, he was nearly ninety when he died," said Hilda.

"You got a good many years ahead of you yet, then!" said Bob.

Hilda knew by the way Bob and Elva were shouting that they thought she was deaf. She also knew that they thought she was dying. It amused her. She decided to play along.

"Eh?" she asked.

"I say, you'll live to be a hundred!" shouted Bob.

"I hope you've been saying your prayers," said Elva to Shad.

Shad looked away.

"I got your present," said Elva. "Couldn't afford very much. You like them laminated jackets, dear?"

"Yeah," said Shad.

"You should get your stuff ready and come home with us," said Elva. "We'll be going to church tonight."

"If you call John Kaston's church a church," grumbled Bob.

"John Kaston's havin' a sermon tonight?" asked Shad.

"He wasn't gonna, but he come around this mornin' and said he was. You'll have to come home with us, dear, and go to church like a good boy."

Shad could only sigh. He didn't want to leave Hilda Porter. He did not want for Hilda to spend Christmas alone.

"You taught me in school!" shouted Bob to Hilda. "Must be thirty-five years ago! I guess that makes you . . . I'd say you were pretty near eighty!"

"Shad got us a tree," said Hilda, changing the subject.

"I saw it as I came in!" yelled Bob. "I think he must have got it in an alder swamp."

Hilda looked at Shad and smiled.

"I say, I think he must've got it in an alder swamp!" repeated Bob.

"I think it's a beautiful tree," said Hilda.

"Your mother didn't live that old, did she?" asked Bob.

"She was sixty-five . . ."

"Old enough! Old enough! A person can't expect to live much older than sixty-five!" said Bob. "My mother died when she was in her sixties. How old are you, Hilda?"

"I'm older than that. You folks sure you won't have a cup of tea?"

"No! No, can't stay," said Bob.

"We just came to get Shad, dear! We don't want to bother you with tea!" said Elva.

Shad grinned at Hilda, winked.

"I can't go home with you," he said to Elva.

"Oh, you'll *have* to come home, dear! It's Christmas. John's havin' a sermon."

"Well, old Hilda here is pretty near dead. Gittin' awful old. I think I'd better stay with her tonight. I'll try to get home tomorrow."

"You not feelin' too well, are ya, Hilda?" asked Elva.

"No, no, I'm pretty near dead, dear," whined Hilda. "I'm not long for *this* world."

"Maybe Shad should stay the night with you!" said Bob. "He kin come home tomorrow!"

"Oh, no," sighed Hilda. "He'd better go home . . . when's Christmas?"

"Today's Christmas Eve! Tomorrow's Christmas! Shad's gonna stay the night with ya!"

Hilda looked at Shad, searched his eyes for the truth. "Don't you want to go home?" she asked softly.

Shad smiled, nodded a quick, barely distinguishable negative.

"That okay, Mom?" asked Shad.

"Well, I . . . I suppose . . . you . . . well, I do have your present in the truck . . ."

"I have yours here, too. I'll come home tomorrow."

"Well, all right, dear. You still wear a medium jacket, eh?"

"Yeah," said Shad.

At eight o'clock Shad told Hilda that he was going over to see Bamby, but that he wouldn't be gone for long.

"Will I wait up for you?" asked Hilda.

"Yeah, I'll just be gone for a little while."

As he walked across the bridge, he whistled "Jingle Bells." It was a frosty, clear night; Shad figured it must be twenty below zero.

He found the village quiet, uneventful; there would be church services to attend later, but otherwise everyone stayed in on Christmas Eve. He passed the post office, a church, the mill, crossed the Bartholomew River bridge, entered Swingtown.

He walked up to Bamby's door, knocked. Bamby's mother greeted him and showed him through the kitchen where Bamby's father sat blurry-eyed drunk.

"She's in there," said Bamby's mother, gesturing to the living room.

Bamby was watching TV, her eyes shifting periodically from the screen to the presents beneath the tree. She was wondering if Santa, her father, had somehow managed to get her all she had asked for.

She was wearing a pink blouse, unbuttoned at the neck; Shad could see her cleavage, the straining bra. She had one foot in her hands, rubbed her fingers between her toes. She was positioned in her chair in such a way that the black polyester of her slacks threatened to come apart at the seams as it stretched around her nearly obese thighs. She had a piece of ribbon candy protruding from her mouth.

When she saw Shad, she reluctantly removed the candy and placed it on the coffee table in front of her.

"What're ya watchin'?" asked Shad.

"Church service."

"Nothin' else on?"

"No, only got one station, can't get CHSJ. Ya hear that, Dad?" she yelled. "We can't get CHSJ!"

"Brought you a present," said Shad.

"Put it under the tree," Bamby yawned.

"Don't you wanna open it?"

"No! It's only Christmas Eve!"

Shad shrugged.

"Did you get your hair dryer?" he asked.

"How should I know? I think it's in the one with the green paper."

Shad put the box of chocolates, Bamby's present, under the tree.

"What's Santa bringin' you?" asked Bamby.

"Laminated jacket, I think."

"MOM! I'M HUNGRY!" yelled Bamby to her mother, who was in the kitchen.

"For God's sake!" yelled her mother. "You just ate!"

Bamby sighed. "What'd ya bring me?" she asked.

"Can't say. It's only Christmas Eve."

Bamby stood, sighed once again and went to the tree, picked up the chocolates, shook the box. "I know what it is," she said.

She picked up and handed Shad a little present wrapped in red paper, ribboned. "Here's yours," she said.

"Thanks," said Shad.

"You'll never guess what it is," said Bamby.

Shad shrugged.

"C'mon!" said Bamby.

"C'mon, what?"

"Guess!"

"I don't know what it is."

"Well, guess!"

"It's a pair o' socks."

"No."

"A tie?"

"Hardly!"

"I don't know."

"See? I told ya you couldn't guess."

"Well, anyway, I gotta be goin'," said Shad.

"I love you, you know," said Bamby.

"Do ya?"

"You know I do."

"That's good."

Bamby took Shad in her arms, held him to her massive breasts, kissed him.

"You love me?" she asked.

"You're a cream o' tartar. You're my little heifer."

"What's that supposed to mean?"

"Jerseys have the prettiest eyes in the world."

"Silly."

They kissed again.

"Well, I'll see you tomorrow," said Shad.

"Promise?"

"Yeah, if I can. I have to go home sometime tomorrow."

"I hope you like what I got ya."

"I will."

When Shadrack returned home at nine-thirty, he found Hilda Porter sitting in the living room. All the lights were out except for a couple of candles. He could hear the radio in the kitchen, Bing Crosby singing "White Christmas." There was a pot of tea and a fancy plate of fruitcake on the coffee table in front of her. She looked very old, fragile, cozy.

"I'm glad ya waited up," said Shad.

"You said you wouldn't be long," said Hilda.

Shad sat, poured himself a cup of very weak-looking tea. He did not like fruitcake much but took a piece anyway; after all — it was Christmas.

"We should be drinkin' wine," he said.

He sipped his tea. It was not tea but brandy. He realized there was a whole teapot full of brandy. He couldn't help grinning from ear to ear.

"Bamby says hello," he said. "She gimme a present."

"You like Bamby a lot, don't you?" said Hilda.

"She's all right," shrugged Shad.

"So, what did she get you?"

"Don't know. She won't let me open it till Christmas, till tomorrow mornin'."

"Of course," smiled Hilda.

Hilda wore a blue satin dress; her cheeks were rouged to a bubble-gum pink.

"She's kinda nuts," said Shad. "But I like nutty people. She eats a lot."

"See what's under the tree?" asked Hilda.

Shad looked under the tree. There was a small package there wrapped in blue paper, red ribbon, a bow.

"You can open it tonight, if you'd like," said Hilda. "I'm planning on sleeping in tomorrow, and later you'll be off. I thought we'd celebrate Christmas tonight."

"I have a present for you, too," said Shad. "I'll open mine, if you'll open yours. I'll even open Bamby's."

Shad drank from his cup, sat it down, stood. "That's good tea," he said and ran to his room for Hilda's present.

While he was gone, Hilda replenished his cup. Shad was only gone for a moment, came back with a present the size of a shoe box.

"Here you go," he said. "Open 'er up!"

"You first," said Hilda.

"Well, okay." Shad removed the little gift from under the tree, went to Hilda and sat on the arm of her chair. "What is it?" he asked.

Hilda had an overwhelming urge to reach up and scratch Shad's back. She stifled it, said, "Open it and see."

Shad untied the ribbon and fingered open the pretty paper, trying not to rip it. He opened a little velvet box and feasted his eyes on the contents — a very ornate pocket watch.

"A gold watch," he breathed. "A beautiful gold watch."

"It was my grandfather's," said Hilda. "It's very old. My father gave it to me years ago. That's a real diamond. It comes from South Africa."

"A real diamond! It must be worth a fortune! Hilda, I . . ."

"I want you to have it, Shadrack," said Hilda, touching his arm. "You're my darling boy."

"But it's worth a fortune."

"It's only worth something to me if you keep it and look after it. When you get old, give it to your son or grandson. Give it to him and tell him the story I told you."

"Yes, but . . ."

"Say no more."

"Thanks, Hilda." Shad kissed the old woman on the bubblegum-pink cheek. "It's the nicest thing anyone ever gave me."

"Oh, Shad, don't start. You'll have me in tears."

"Ain't no time for cryin', little lady! Here. Open yours."

Shad passed her the present he had bought her.

Hilda sniffed and began to unwrap her gift.

"Now, I wonder what this could be?" she mused. "Did you wrap this yourself?"

"Well, I wasn't much good at it. I had the lady at the store do it."

"I thought so. No man could wrap a gift this well."

"I hope you'll like it," said Shad.

"It's . . . it's a make-up kit! Shad, look! Rouge! Lipstick! Perfume! Eyeshadow!"

"Like it?"

"Yes, but . . ."

"I thought we might take a drive to Tasmania next summer, steal Trucanini's body from that museum. Thought you'd need a disguise."

"Ha, ha, ha, ha, ha! Shad, you're crazy! But . . . I love you . . . and thanks very much."

"I must see what's in this thing," said Shad, picking up his gift from Bamby.

He unwrapped it, stared at its contents, first with disbelief, then with a broad grin.

"You ever hear tell of a girl givin' a man a pair o' shorts for Christmas before?" he asked.

"Now, Shad, don't make fun of her gift. What's in it, really?"

"I'm serious," said Shad, grinning. He held up a pair of red men's briefs.

Hilda was amazed. "Well, I never!" she said, chuckled, laughed.

"I guess you'd have to call her practical, anyway," laughed Shad.

Hilda took a deep breath in an attempt to stifle her laughter. She didn't think that it was right to laugh at someone's gift, but she couldn't help herself.

"I should lend that woman to Dryfly for a while," laughed Shad. "I imagine he could do with a new pair of shorts!"

"Now, Shad! Ha, ha, ha, ha! It's the thought that counts! Ha, ha, ha, ha!"

"I think we should have some more tea," said Shad.

Hilda was laughing so hard at her last remark that the tears were running down her cheeks. She held out her cup. Shad poured.

The Three Marys

LYNN COADY

Up in the hospital's teen lounge were bruise-eyed thirteen-year-olds who sat with IV skeletons behind them, cutting holes into folded pieces of white paper for gluing the shapes together to make bells, candles and holly. Once these were finished, the craft lady would string a piece of gold thread through the top, because they were to be sold at the Christmas Craft Fair — all proceeds going to the Hospital for Sick Children — as tree ornaments.

Bridget was there, too. She and the rest of them from Four South — the Psych Ward — were being forced up daily to create their own individual masterpieces. Byron complained about it. He said it was hideous and "Dickensian" to force these children, who uniformly wanted to lie down and die, into the lounge to listen to Burl Ives and toil on a felt-and-glitter production line. Nurse Gabby told him that a lot of the children found doing crafts to be therapeutic.

"What about those of us who don't find it therapeutic, but a sadistic torment?"

"Some people don't know something will be therapeutic until they try it," Gabby soothed, shooing the herd of them into the elevator.

If Bridget got any pleasure from seeing Byron hacking a swastika out of green felt to the tune of "Holly Jolly Christmas," it was only when she looked at him alone, and not at the others sitting in a row with them at the long table. The sight of them made her think that he was right. Dying children shouldn't be expected to make Christmas ornaments out of felt. People would buy them at the craft sale and put them on their trees: Look! An actual dying child made this manger. We understand it was cystic fibrosis. And here's our leukemia candy cane. And we got this wreath from the Indian reservation.

There was no denying that some of them probably did enjoy the diversion, or were at least being diverted by it. One translucent fourteen-year-old — whom Bridget, with her new-found expertise, would have diagnosed as anorexic, but later learned it was full-blown AIDS — had a particular flair for the decorations. She could even twist the felt in elaborate ways to give the finished product a three-dimensional effect, and the craft lady would always hold her latest creations up for everyone else to be inspired by and talk about the new dialysis machine or surgical laser it would help the hospital to buy. The girl would sneeze, picking up another wad of felt and eating glue off her fingers.

Bridget was another of the craft lady's stars. Sick of the felt and glitter, she had been looking through some of the lady's craft books and come across what looked like a fairly easy method of making lovely, ornate snowflakes simply by curling strips of white paper and gluing them together. She soon found out that it wasn't easy to do at all. It was extremely intricate work, and it took Bridget four days of her teen-lounge time to complete the first one, which by all accounts was a masterpiece. The craft lady exhorted her to come up with at least five more before the sale, so Bridget began taking her work downstairs to the ward with her. The snowflakes required tremendous concentration. Bridget worked on them every spare moment, which in her present mode of existence meant practically all the time. Gabby and Doctor Solomon could not have been more supportive of this new interest, Bridget's first and only interest since being admitted.

It seemed to make Solomon all the more certain that her decision to send Bridget back home for the holidays was the right one. For the first time since informing Bridget of her discharge, on report of the snowflakes, Solomon came round the ward to view Bridget's handiwork.

"These are just lovely."

"Ya want one?"

"I'd love to have one. And maybe you could donate a couple for the ward's tree."

"Take your pick."

"Thank you, Bridget. You've got a wonderful eye. I'm sure you'll do very well in pottery."

"Pottery," said Bridget, looking up.

"Have you enrolled at the college yet?"

"No. I guess I better do that, eh?"

"I would think so. It must be getting rather late."

"Yeah, I'll do it."

"Are you looking forward to going home?"

"Oh, I dunno."

"I'm sure your family will be glad to have you back. Your Uncle Albert especially."

"Albert doesn't even live with us."

"Oh!" The doctor moved her electrolysed eyebrows slightly. "I was given to understand that he did. He was so insistent you be sent home."

It was because Albert liked for people to be where they goddamn well belonged. He had been harassing the entire ward ever since Bridget's arrival. Gabby told her this. Gabby had related that sometimes he would call up on the pretext of wanting to speak to Bridget and instead take the opportunity to blast whichever nurse had picked up the phone.

"Hello, Four South."

"Is Bridget Murphy there, please?" Polite, older-male-relative voice.

"Yes, if you'll hold a . . ."

"Well, Jesus liftin', when are you fag psychiatric sons of whores gonna let her out of that hell hole?"

"Would you like to speak to Bridget, sir?"

"I'd like to speak to her all right. I'd like to speak to her sitting in her own goddamn kitchen is where I'd like to speak with her, but I can't do that until you bastards decide to turn her loose — as if she's some kind of Jesus menace to society or something."

And the nurses, being psychiatric nurses, wouldn't be as quick to respond in the same way that someone else in the same situation might — namely by hanging up on the raving old fart. They were psychiatric nurses who had been trained for every eventuality, and this sort of thing they were eternally ready for. The family was a volatile thing. The family — usually the organism responsible for the child's internment in Four South in the first place — could not normally be expected to comprehend why one of its number would need to be there. Bridget gathered that phone calls like Albert's were more or less par for the course in Gabby's line of work. Leaning back into the chair and lighting a cigarette, whichever nurse was on shift would robotically switch into a mode of soothing rationality once the first note of hostility reached her ears.

"It's not that she's a menace to society, sir, that's not the case at all. It's just that she needs a bit of sheltering right now."

"Shelter she can get from her family!"

"No, obviously not, or she wouldn't be here."

"What the eff is that supposed to mean?"

"I only mean that your daughter has come through a hard time, and often, following events as overwhelming as a pregnancy and adoption, a young woman will need a period of . . . hibernation, if you will . . ."

"She's not my goddamned daughter."

"Oh. To whom am I —"

"This is her uncle, by god! Albert Patrick Murphy!"

"Well, Mr. Murphy, we do appreciate your concern —"

"Yah, well, you may as well appreciate me hole for all the good it does."

Bridget often thought her uncle must be unique. He was the only man she knew who saved his temper for strangers rather than his family and friends, and not the other way around. When she'd lived with him and Bernadette in the late summertime, Albert would curse at the TV news and its single mothers ("welfare sluts"), simultaneously leaning

LYNN COADY

over to pour Bridget more tea and berate the little bastard who was her undoing.

"You're a good girl," he would tell her over and over again. "You're a good girl and a goddamn smart girl and no little puke from Home Hardware is going to mess up a future as bright as yours, good girl." Bridget tried for a couple of minutes to envision it, a future as bright as hers.

Her father was a craftsman. Once, he had worked for the government, had practically run the town at one point, but residents soon became appalled at the kind of upheaval he was constantly trying to achieve. He had wanted to build a senior citizens' home, for one thing. He had wanted "Causeway Days" — the spring festival — to attract more tourists, to entail more than a five-float parade down the main street, two of which were furnished by the mill, three of which were no more than locals in toilet-paper-decorated pickups with signs on the front reading stuff like "Jimmy Archie's Lumber," or "Come to Dan Hughie's Garage. Two for 99 on O Henrys."

Bridget's father had also wanted some kind of musical event other than the traditional bagpipe contest that had led him to refer to the festival as "Catkilling Days" during an interview at the local radio station. Many residents had been offended. They were proud of the bagpiping contest. It was one of the many things that made the community unique. They found Mr. Murphy to be overbearing and unduly aggressive. One day her father came home late from a meeting and announced, "Piss on 'em. They can play the bagpipes until their foolish lungs implode. I hope they all go deaf as me arse." And he went downstairs to work on his craft.

Woodworking was his craft. He called it that, but it was really more like art. Nobody dared suggest this to him. Once a TV station out of Halifax had called him up to be on some program about Maritime folk art. "I'm not some kind of dope-smoking hairy-faced fruit," was what he'd said. "Unlike you and yours." Television was television to her father — Halifax no different from Los Angeles. "Ar-teests," he'd spit, whenever the subject came to mind, making flitting gestures with his short, yellow fingers. "Arse-tits is more like it."

So her father was a craftsman of wood. He drove off into the hills every Sunday to pick choice pieces. He especially liked the trees that had some kind of disease that made the trunks bulge monstrously out in places, as if gourds had become lodged in there somehow. Her father would take the diseased trunks home and carve all sorts of faces into the bulges. If there were a lot of bulges, the effect was very much like that of a totem pole — caricatures of bulbous-nosed hobos and sailors replacing those of owls and wolves and ravens. Big-nosed, heavy-lidded men's faces were one of her father's specialties.

At other times, he would come home with what appeared to be an average piece of wood, spend a few hours sanding and varnishing it, and then present it to the family — a smooth, polished piece of wood.

"Whaddya think of that?"

"It's really nice!"

"Do you see what it is?"

"Um. A fish?"

"It's a wolf's head. See, there's its snout. By god, nature does the work, I just bring it to the fore."

Mr. Murphy also delighted in any chunk of wood that bore a passing resemblance to parts of the human anatomy. He stole a pair of Bridget's mother's shoes once to put on a branch that had been uncannily like a bum and a pair of legs — right down to having little protrusions where the feet would be. This was where he hung the shoes. Bridget's mother got mad because they were good shoes, but he wouldn't let her replace them with a pair of old slippers or anything. He referred to the artifact, for some reason, as Mrs. MacGillicutty, and pretty soon, after he had returned gleeful from the woods one day with what he said was a husband for Mrs. MacGillicutty, Bridget's mother wouldn't go down to his shop any more.

The shop did a fairly good business because he made cabinets as

LYNN COADY

well, and because he overpriced his art work outrageously, for the tourists. He had also acquired a reputation for being a character, and local people were always stopping by to see what he'd do. They found his insults endearing, but if they ever loitered too long, he'd bark. "If you're not buying, you're leaving," in such a way as to make the people fear that they had offended him somehow. In such a way as to prompt them to buy, perhaps, one of his twenty-five-dollar golf balls. With those, he peeled away half of the ball's pitted skin and then carved more goofy faces into the hard rubber beneath. Everyone thought this was ingenious.

What a lot of people really came for, though, were Bridget's father's decoys. His decoys were simply beautiful, more perfect than any actual duck. They were entirely smooth and flawless — he did not bother with feathers or any other realistic detail that might disturb the decoy's linearity. The result was a perfect, liquid platonic ideal. Perfect duckness. He stained — never painted — and then varnished them. The wood was what mattered, the acknowledgment and refinement of the wood, as opposed to any attempt to deny it, that was what made the carvings very nearly sublime. People came from far and wide to purchase one of Bridget's father's ducks. They were all exactly the same.

When Bridget got home from the hospital, there were two pieces of news right off. One was that the trial of the girlfriend-murdering Archie Shearer had finally gotten under way, and the other was that her father had taken to bringing Rollie down to the basement with him, and now Rollie was an artist, a craftsman, too.

Rollie's school had been shut down. Rollie used to go to a special school every day where he would make bread with other adults like himself. The bread was very good, and Bridget's mother bought loaves of it every week. It spoiled the family for the store-bought kind, and on weekends, if they ever ran out, Gerard would sometimes go on rampages, rummaging through the deep freeze in the hope of finding a forgotten loaf, hollering, "Where's the retardo bread?"

Rollie loved going to school, and if Bridget's parents ever wanted to punish him for not going to bed when they told him to, or taking a piss out of doors, or pulling his shorts up over his belt and ripping them, then they wouldn't let him go. It was a very effective punishment, and they were relieved to finally have discovered some kind of leverage to use against him. It was widely acknowledged within the family that Grampa and Margaret P. had spoiled Rollie most of his life — cutting his meat and pouring his tea and putting his mittens on for him — and so when it came time for Rollie to live under Bridget's father's rule, Rollie knew how to be quite stubborn. Bridget's father didn't know any way to make him do anything except for cursing at him and giving him the occasional shove up the stairs. It was still a little difficult with Margaret P. around. Sometimes Rollie would stumble into her room in tears, and Margaret P. would bang on the wall with her bedpan, wanting to know what had been done to him.

"Jesus Murphy, Ma, I was just trying to get him to take off his own goddamn shoes!"

"He's never had to take off his own shoes, for the love of God!"

Bridget's father saw that changes had to be made, so he sent Rollie to the "special school" as soon as it opened up. And Rollie surprised everyone by loving it. He had even managed to acquire something like a girlfriend, a woman named Emma, overweight and smiling. Every night before going to bed, Rollie would ask Bridget's father, "Who's going to wake him up see Emma?" — and her father would revel in his new-found power.

"Well, now, I don't know if anyone should wake you up for school tomorrow, not coming in for supper when Joan calls you."

"He'll come in for supper."

"You will, eh? You're not going to do that again, walking around in circles going No no no no like a Jesus lunatic?"

"No, he's not."

"You're going to come in next time, then, are you?"

"No he's not, no he's not," Rollie would say rapidly, putting his hands over his ears.

"Well, are you going to come in next time or aren't you?"

"He's going to come in next time."

"All right then. Go on up to bed."

"Who's going to wake him up for school, Raw-hurt?"

"Robert will wake him up for school."

But now — due to lack of resources — Rollie's school was shut down. It was a trying time for everyone. Bridget's father didn't know what was to be done with Rollie during the day. He sat in his chair with the television on and would complain. "When's Rollie going to school see Emma?" every time Bridget's mother or father went by. This, along with his constant inquiries over the last few months about where Bridget had gone, was combining to drive the two of them up the wall. So one day Bridget's father announced, "Shit on this. You come downstairs with me, sir. We'll get you going on something."

This was how Rollie became an artist. Not just an artist, but, according to Bridget's father, a religious artist, the best kind of artist to be. Her father had stuck a piece of wood into Rollie's hand and let him go at it with the sander. So Rollie stood there, humming to himself and sanding and sanding the wood until Bridget's father took it away from him and held it up to the light. There and then he declared the overly sanded block of wood to be uncannily — one might say miraculously — representative of the Virgin holding the baby Jesus. He ran upstairs to show it to Bridget's mother and asked if she agreed, and Bridget's mother said that she supposed so, and so he hurried back down to the basement to varnish the new work and put it on display, stopping only to hand Rollie another piece of wood to get started on.

According to Bridget's mother, Rollie was becoming famous. Her father had a whole display of his religious carvings lined up on the shelf above the golfballs. Little cards in front of each announced what the wooden blobs were supposed to represent, from "Jesus Heals the Sick" to "Saint Paul on the Road to Damascus." Some people who visited the shop seemed initially dubious about the carvings until Mr. Murphy explained who had done them. He daringly set them at the same price as his carved golfballs, a great favourite among locals and tourists alike, and, in a flash of inspired business savvy, put up a bigger sign above them all which read:

Religious Wooden Statues.
Done by Retarded Man.
Twenty-five Dollars a Piece.

And now they were her father's number-one seller. Even more than the ducks. They were especially popular with Christmas being on its way. Bridget's father, in anticipation of the season, had glued sprigs of plastic holly to the occasional piece.

That, and the trial of Archie Shearer for murdering Jennifer MacDonnell in August, only now beginning. Now. At Christmas, people emphasized. Sad for the family, they said, meaning the MacDonnells. And the thought of sad families at Christmas inevitably brought to mind that of the self-slaughtered Kenneth MacEachern from down the street. The state of the local young people was freshly lamented around Bridget's kitchen table. So much unhappiness brought upon the families. Killing each other and killing themselves.

The visitors, coming round the house all through the holidays, said that. There was teensy Mrs. Boucher, Margaret P.'s old housekeeper, rasping between drags on her DuMauriers and kicking her dangling feet, which never reached the floor when she sat down. She always kicked them back and forth like an impatient six-year-old.

"It just make me sick," she would mourn, "all de deat." Mrs. Boucher was a mournful woman, sickly, with a sad life. She'd sip her tea, everybody aware of her fear for her married nineteen-year-old girl, in and out of the women's shelter every two or three months. Everyone in the house found themselves wanting to get things for Mrs. Boucher.

"I tell her, come home with me, Louise. No, Ma, I rather get the crap beaten out of me than live with my mudder like a little kid. Well, what do you do?"

Uncle Albert, down with Bernadette for the holidays, would nod soberly even though he wasn't. Bernadette reported that Albert was "back at it again," after thirty-three years. No one could really believe it. Apparently he had turned up with a bottle of Crown Royal one day last week and ecstatically poured himself three fingers in front of his wife.

("What in the lord's name are you about with that?" I said to him.

"To hell with it," he says. "It's Christmas, the kids are all gone, and I've been sober for thirty-three years. It's time to celebrate, Mommy!" And doesn't he gulp the Christly thing down in front of my eyes!)

Now, everyone sort of had the feeling the they should behave very disapprovingly and discouragingly toward Albert every time he came out from underneath the sink with his bottle shouting, "Who wants a snoutful?" — but with the exception of Bridget's father, no one could actually bring themselves to do it. He was too much fun. Except for putting him in perpetual good cheer and turning his cheeks and nose a welcoming pink, the liquor had no great effect on the man, certainly none of the adverse effects that everyone, for some reason, had been expecting. He was simply the same old Albert, spreader of good cheer, offering to replace poor Mrs. Boucher's tea with a hot buttered rum.

"No, it no good for my stomach, Ally."

"Ach, it's good for every goddamn piece a ya. A nice toddie then, Marianne?"

"No, Albert, no, I just have more tea."

Which meant Albert had to content himself with making a toddie for the priest, whom he did not approve of half as much as he did Mrs. Boucher, a woman who had spent six years of her life caring for Margaret P. in spite of her own hardships. Bridget could remember being small and sitting at the kitchen table at Margaret P.'s house with Mrs. Boucher, watching her smoke and listening to her ghastly stories about her no good brudder. Her no good brudder used to break into her apartment and steal the television set for booze. Her no good brudder would threaten to beat her if she didn't give him money. Mrs. Boucher said back then that she was so relieved to be working at Margaret P.'s, away from her no good brudder, that she was almost sick.

Bridget remembered trying to keep up by telling Mrs. Boucher about

Gerard, who always beat her up and spit in her hair and wouldn't play with her. He had gotten hold of her Wonder Woman doll and sawed the top of its head off with his pocket knife.

Albert was in a state that Bernadette cluckingly called "High Gear" — scuttling around to make toddies for himself and sleepy, pink Father Stewart, another harmless and uninteresting drunk, and then darting down the hall to check on Margaret P.'s cheer, which lately hadn't been too bad. Margaret P. had taken to singing the song about the three Marys since Bridget got home, and, despite the depressing lyrics, the singing seemed to keep her content and less likely to succumb to her usual macabre hallucinations. When Bridget first showed up, Margaret P. had been convinced that Bridget herself was one of these spectres, having returned from the dead after being shot by a boy. Margaret P. thought Bridget was Jennifer MacDonnell. Or else thought Jennifer MacDonnell had been Bridget. But this notion didn't seem to frighten Margaret P. in the least. She said, "Hello, dear. Are you still in purgatory?" and began to say a rosary. Since then, every time Bridget stopped into Margaret P.'s room, the ancient thing would say nothing beyond holding up the rosary, shaking it encouragingly and calling — as though Bridget were far away — "It won't be long now, dear! You just hold on a bit longer."

"I'm not in purgatory, Gramma."

"We'll get you up there, dear. I've lived a good life and they'll listen to me."

But now Margaret P. had forgotten about the continual rosaries and taken to singing "Mary Hamilton" all day long. She sat, rocking back and forth and singing about the three Marys over and over again, a smile nestled somewhere in the folds of her face. She only remembered the one verse.

> Yesterday e'en there were four Marys.
> This night there will be but three.
> There was Mary Beaton and Mary Seaton.
> And Mary Carmichael and me.

Albert and Bridget's father were pleased to hear the old lady singing after so long, but only Bridget seemed to recognize that Margaret P. had confused it for the rosary, that in her cobwebby mind she was still busy praying for Bridget's unworthy soul. And she must have considered it pretty unworthy because she hadn't stopped since Bridget got back.

Albert had been explaining all this to the priest and Mrs. Boucher — how Margaret P. had gotten it into her head that Bridget had been shot instead of Jennifer MacDonnell and as yet no one was able to convince her otherwise — and this was what set them off on the subject of the dead, bemoaning particularly the young people, and all the dying and killing they did.

"It's the parents!" Albert pronounced recklessly. High Gear had the effect of causing Albert to make several reckless pronunciations throughout the day. Ideas he might otherwise have made every effort to suppress in front of Bridget's father.

"It's not the goddamn parents," the latter countered at once. "I've never bought into that psychiatric free-love save-the-seals horseshit and I'm not about to now. Blame everything on the parents, forget about personal responsibility. I say if some little bastard is gonna be a weirdo goon and pick up a rifle to shoot some young girl stupid enough to get tangled up with him, then that's what he's gonna do. And people encourage that now, anyway. They think its cool to be wanting to do away with themselves or the young girls. It's in the videos they watch. Well I say let them kill themselves if they want to, but if they start aiming those guns at anyone else, by God, I'll hold the door to hell open for them and kick their arses through."

Bridget's mother said: "Well, I didn't know Archie Shearer, but Kenneth MacEachern was in my religion class and he was just a lovely lad. He told me he wanted to be a priest."

"Oh, yes, but the sons of bitches change once they hit their teens," Bridget's father said, happy to be angry and deliberately not checking his language in front of Father Stewart. "They get arrogant and start thinking they know everything, and you can't tell them a goddamn thing after that."

All the proof he needed of this was, Bridget supposed, sitting at the table with him. He had made his disgust at both her and Gerard's respective betrayals known since the first day they had ever disagreed with him. Gerard had been about thirteen, Bridget a couple of years older, and their father had been so offended that he hadn't bothered to try and tell them anything since. Now if he ever wanted to express displeasure at something they did, he pretended to agree with it, not speaking to them, but to the air. "Yes, that's what he wants to do," he would say. "He figures it's the right thing. Well by the Jesus, why doesn't he do just that? Why the hell not? Goddamn, if that isn't just a dandy one." Gerard could imitate their father at this with uncanny accuracy.

Bridget had to reacclimatize herself to all the chaos she'd forgotten about, especially now that she had the empty, echoing ward to contrast it against. She had read somewhere that people who are colour-blind all their lives find it too overwhelming, once their eyes are operated on, to experience the world in colour. They lose all perspective and are terrified and lost and sometimes get physically sick. That's what coming home was like, even though Bridget had spent all her life there and only four months on the ward. Coming out was a far greater adjustment than going in had been.

She would sit and drink tea until about three in the afternoon and then switch to rum and eggnog before dinner, wine during, and anything else went for the remainder of the evening. She could get away with this because it was Christmas and because everyone wanted her to be happy. She was genuinely pleased at how much easier it was to get drunk after four months' abstinence, although it was not the same kind of drunk as before. It made her serene, content to be doing whatever thing it was she happened to be doing. If she was baking cookies with her mother, she was content to be doing that. If she was helping Margaret P. to the toilet, she was content to be doing that. Because her feeling was that really she wasn't doing that. This was a relief. She didn't get edgy and excited like she used to, and have to leave the house at two in the morning.

LYNN COADY

And nobody chastised her, about anything. Her father did not even confide his displeasure to the air.

"What about you, Bridget? Didn't you know Kenneth? Or was it Archie Shearer you knew?"

Her mother had always been one to forget about unspoken household rules. Her father said she did it on purpose. Once when he had decided a few years back that he was going to disown Uncle Albert, and made it understood that no one in their family was to have any contact with him, Joan had forgotten all about this edict in the second week and ruined the effect by calling up Bernadette to make plans for a day of shopping at the Mic Mac Mall. So Bridget shouldn't have been surprised, really, that her mother would conformingly tiptoe around her for the first couple of days, clearing away teacups, before absently letting drop a question about killing and dying.

"Bridey's one of the good ones, goddammit!" Albert interjected, pink-faced and reckless. She could hear the recklessness in his voice as he stood at the counter behind her, and she could feel everyone willing him to sit down and have a piece of bannock or something.

"God only knows she could have taken the easy way out, or done something foolish or what-have-you," he came up behind her chair and Bridget could hear him swallow. She looked up at Gerard, who sort of smiled. He was leaning on his hand, fingers tapping against his head as if they were feeling for a trap door.

"We should just thank the lord she had enough sense to do the right thing!" Albert finished in an even louder voice than he started with.

"Yes, Bridget, you're a wise girl," Father Stewart agreed, being priestly in his attempt to save Albert from awkwardness.

"Goddamn right!" Albert barked, repaying the father with blasphemy. He gave Bridget a pat on the head which was too hard.

Bridget's father looked at Albert for a little while to make sure he was finished speaking. "That isn't really what we were talking about, now, is it?" he said, at length. "That's not what I would call the issue at hand. I believe what we were talking about was a lot of jeezless punks who should all be sent to military school. That'd straighten them all out pretty damn quick. They'd take that heavy-metal horseshit, the army would, and all those big ideas about the world and how they should all kill the parents who feed them and grow their hair to their arseholes and be a bunch of faggots who don't have children but want to adopt normal people's and eventually kill off the whole goddamn human race, the army would sew all that horseshit up into a tight little ball, stick it in a rifle and fire it straight up their arse, that's what a little discipline would do for those sons of whores."

"Oh, now," said Father Stewart, rousing himself a little. "My."

Between four and six in the morning, Bridget would dream she was still on the ward, packing to go home. She was feeling around in the ceiling tiles, where she used to hide money and Mars bars and the like from the staff, looking for her stuff, but none of it was there. Instead she kept pulling out handfuls of all these nonsensical items, all this crap. Car alarms, even though she wasn't really sure what a car alarm would look like. Plain doughnuts. The filter out of her mother's clothes dryer. The head off a Barbie. And one morning at about eleven o'clock Bridget came downstairs to pour herself a cup of tea and her mother told her she had already come down, four hours earlier. Bridget didn't believe her. Joan had said that Bridget had looked her straight in the eye and demanded: "Where the hell is it?"

"It's up in bed, dear," Joan had supplied without batting an eye. Maternal telepathy.

"Up in bed? Are you sure?"

"Yes, it's up in bed, dear, go on up."

"All right then!" Bridget supposedly had said, stomping back up the stairs.

LYNN COADY

Bridget's father had given her a couple of Rollie's statues. One blob was supposed to represent the Virgin and another was the Virgin and Child. It was ironic, but she knew he didn't mean it to be. When she and Gerard were children, her father always made sure that there were one or two religious pictures hanging on both their walls. Bridget always got the Virgin, the Baby, or the Virgin with the Baby, whereas Gerard always got a grown-up Jesus doing stuff — cleansing the temple, showing Thomas the holes in his hands and whatnot. Her father had this idea that girls liked Mary and boys liked Jesus, just as girls liked Barbies and boys liked GI Joes. So he had picked out the Madonna blobs for Bridget merely on the assumption that they were the most appropriate choices. Gerard got "Jesus Heals the Sick."

"There," he said. "You two go upstairs and pray to those for a little while, see if that doesn't do ya any good."

Bridget put them on her night stand, which was where he would be looking for them, and prayed vaguely for no dreams. Then she had as nightmare about the Christmas turkey, the first frightening dream she'd had since, probably, the first trimester, when she went around punching herself in the gut and doing sit-up after sit-up after sit-up. Her father had just cut into the bird when it leaped off the table, still hot and crackling from the oven, screaming, "Don't you dare! Don't you dare!" Trailing stuffing across the kitchen floor.

Santa Claus

TED RUSSELL

With Christmas gettin' closer every day, there's one thing I think I ought to mention. It's this argument we hear sometimes over the radio about whether Christmas nowadays is what it used to be. Some people think it's turned into a money-makin' affair, what they call bein' "commercialized." Others don't agree. Naturally the newspapers and radio stations that make money off advertisin' and the merchants with a lot of Christmas goods to sell and the companies that want to lend people money to buy 'em with, they don't see anything wrong with the way things are goin'. But other people seem to think it's a bad thing, and that Christmas is not what it used to be years ago.

Of course it's all away over our heads down here in Pigeon Inlet and to tell the truth, up till lately, we figgered 'twas none of our business. What other people did with their Christmas in places like St. John's or Toronto, well, there wasn't much we could do to stop 'em, and in any case, it couldn't affect how we regarded our Christmas in Pigeon Inlet. That's what we used to think. Now I'm not so sure. Look what happened to me about four weeks ago.

Little Judy Briggs is Pete Briggs's youngest. She can't be more than four or five years old, not started school yet. She come to my door this day to bring me back a screw-driver I'd loaned Pete the day before. So I asked her to come in while I hunted around to see if I could find her a candy and my radio was turned on and she happened to hear what was on it. 'Twas all about this big Santa Claus parade somewhere up on the mainland, and this only the early part of November. After I found the candy, I almost had to wake her up to give it to her, she was so much interested in the radio. She looked so sad, I thought she was goin' to cry.

"Uncle Mose," she said, "is that really Santa Claus up there in that place on the radio?"

What are you goin' to tell a youngster that age? So I said to her, "Well, Judy," said I, "what do you think?"

"Oh, I think it must be," said she, "cause they say it is. And they wouldn't tell lies like that over the radio, would they, Uncle Mose?"

And again, what could I say? There's a lot she's got to learn, but five years old is perhaps a poor time to learn it. But then she said, "Is he comin' here this year?" So I said, "Yes, he never failed to come to Pigeon Inlet yet, and he'll be here again, just wait and see."

But she wasn't satisfied. If he was comin' Christmas, what was he doin' visitin' other places almost two months before Christmas? Did that mean he was goin' to visit these places twice and Pigeon Inlet only once, or worse still, did it mean that he'd give up Christmas and was visitin' these big places now while navigation was open and perhaps wouldn't come here at all? Anyhow, if he was up there in Toronto now, and he must be, the radio said so, how could he be up at the North Pole where he was supposed to be, gettin' ready for his Christmas Eve visit to places like Pigeon Inlet?

Now what could I tell her? I'd like to have told the radio something. How if they wanted to pretend that Christmas came in October or November instead of in December, the least they could do was keep it to theirselves instead of blarin' their nonsense all over the world where little people like Judy could get upset by it. And I couldn't tell her the radio was tellin' lies. But I had to tell her something. So I scratched my head a bit and done the best I could.

"Judy," said I, "you know when Santa's birthday is?"

"Yes," she said, "Christmas Day, isn't it?"

"Right," said I, "and Christmas Day is a special day with Santa on account of it bein' his birthday. Now," I said, "Judy, take your own birthday. That's a special day with you, isn't it?"

"Oh, yes," she said.

"And what do you do on your birthday?" said I. "Do you go away to places like Rumble Cove or Hartley's Harbour?"

"Oh, no," she said, "cause it's my birthday. I stay home with Mommy and Daddy and have my really best friends in with me for a party. But," she said, "I go one place on my birthday. I always go up and visit Grandma every birthday."

"Why?" said I.

"Oh, because," she said, "now that Grandma is not able to get out of doors any more and come down to see me like she used to, I've promised her I'll come and see her every year on my birthday. I love Grandma."

"But," said I, "you do go to Rumble Cove sometimes?"

"Oh, yes," she said, "but not on my birthday. Birthday is for being home with Mommy and Daddy and my friends and visiting Grandma."

"And Judy," said I, "that's just how it is with Santa Claus on his birthday. That's the day he visits the people he loves, like you visitin' your grandma. Other days of the year you mustn't mind him visitin' other places like on the radio. (I almost called it Rumble Cove, which never would have done because actually 'twas a big place.) So if you hear of him bein' in these places in October or November or even June or July — the way things are goin' — don't get upset or worried about it. Don't forget Santa got a birthday and he's savin' that special day for a special purpose, same as you do, to visit the people he loves."

And do you know it cheered her up. Only she said she couldn't help feelin' a little bit sorry for the places that Santa Claus had to visit on other days besides his own special day, the day he visits Pigeon Inlet, his birthday.

And come to think of it, I can't help feelin' a bit sorry for 'em, too.

TED RUSSELL

The Brother Who Failed

LUCY MAUD MONTGOMERY

The Monroe family were holding a Christmas reunion at the old Prince Edward Island homestead at White Sands. It was the first time they had all been together under one roof since the death of their mother, thirty years before. The idea of this Christmas reunion had originated with Edith Monroe the preceding spring, during her tedious convalescence from a bad attack of pneumonia among strangers in an American city, where she had not been able to fill her concert engagements and had more spare time in which to feel the tug of old ties and the homesick longing for her own people than she had had for years. As a result, when she recovered, she wrote to her second brother, James Monroe, who lived on the homestead; and the consequence was this gathering of the Monroes under the old roof-tree. Ralph Monroe for once laid aside the cares of his railroads and the deceitfulness of his millions in Toronto and took the long-promised, long-deferred trip to the homeland. Malcolm Monroe journeyed from the far western university of which he was president. Edith came, flushed with the triumph of her latest and most successful concert tour. Mrs. Woodburn, who had been Margaret Monroe, came from the Nova Scotia town where she lived a busy, happy life as the wife of a rising young lawyer. James, prosperous and hearty, greeted them warmly at the old homestead whose fertile acres had well repaid his skilful management.

They were a merry party, casting aside their cares and years and harking back to joyous boyhood and girlhood once more. James had a family of rosy lads and lasses; Margaret brought her two blue-eyed little girls; Ralph's dark, clever-looking son accompanied him, and Malcolm brought his, a young man with a resolute face, in which there was less of boyishness than in his father's and the eye of a keen, perhaps a hard bargainer. The two cousins were the same age to a day, and it was a family joke among the Monroes that the stork must have mixed the babies, since Ralph's son was like Malcolm in face and brain, while Malcolm's boy was a second edition of his Uncle Ralph.

To crown all, Aunt Isabel came, too — a talkative, clever, shrewd old lady, as young at eighty-five as she had been at thirty, thinking the Monroe stock the best in the world and beamingly proud of her nephews and nieces, who had gone out from this humble, little farm to destinies of such brilliance and influence in the world beyond.

I have forgotten Robert. Robert Monroe was apt to be forgotten. Although he was the oldest of the family, White Sands people, in naming over the various members of the Monroe family, would add, "and Robert," in a tone of surprise over the remembrance of his existence.

He lived on a poor, sandy little farm down by the shore, but he had come up to James' place on the evening when the guests arrived; they had all greeted him warmly and joyously and then did not think about him again in their laughter and conversation. Robert sat back in a corner and listened with a smile, but he never spoke. Afterwards he had slipped noiselessly away and gone home, and nobody noticed his going. They were all gaily busy recalling what had happened in the old times and telling what had happened in the new.

Edith recounted the successes of her concert tours; Malcolm expatiated proudly on his plans for developing his beloved college; Ralph described the country through which his new railroad ran and the difficulties he had had to overcome in connection with it. James, aside, discussed his orchard and his crops with Margaret, who had not been long enough away from the farm to lose touch with its interests. Aunt Isabel knitted and smiled complacently on all, talking now with one, now with the other, secretly quite proud of herself that she, an old woman of eighty-five, who had seldom been out of White Sands

LUCY MAUD MONTGOMERY

in her life, could discuss high finance with Ralph and higher education with Malcolm and hold her own with James in an argument on drainage.

The White Sands school teacher, an arch-eyed, red-mouthed bit of a girl — a Bell from Avonlea — who boarded with the James Monroes, amused herself with the boys. All were enjoying themselves hugely, so it was not to be wondered at that they did not miss Robert, who had gone home early because his old housekeeper was nervous if left alone at night.

He came again the next afternoon. From James, in the barnyard, he learned that Malcolm and Ralph had driven to the harbour, that Margaret and Mrs. James had gone to call on friends in Avonlea and that Edith was walking somewhere in the woods on the hill. There was nobody in the house except Aunt Isabel and the teacher.

"You'd better wait and stay the evening," said James indifferently. "They'll all be back soon."

Robert went across the yard and sat down on the rustic bench in the angle of the front porch. It was a fine December evening, as mild as autumn; there had been no snow, and the long fields, sloping down from the homestead, were brown and mellow. A weird, dreamy stillness had fallen upon the purple earth, the windless woods, the rain of the valleys, the sere meadows. Nature seemed to have folded satisfied hands to rest, knowing that her long, wintry slumber was coming upon her. Out to sea, a dull, red sunset faded out into sombre clouds, and the ceaseless voice of many waters came up from the tawny shore.

Robert rested his chin on his hand and looked across the vales and hills, where the feathery grey of leafless hardwoods was mingled with the sturdy, unfailing green of the cone-bearers. He was a tall, bent man, with thin grey hair, a lined face and deeply-set, gentle brown eyes — the eyes of one who, looking through pain, sees rapture beyond.

He felt very happy. He loved his family clannishly, and he was rejoiced that they were all again near to him. He was proud of their success and fame. He was glad that James had prospered so well of late years. There was no canker of envy or discontent in his soul.

He heard absently indistinct voices at the open hall window above the porch, where Aunt Isabel was talking to Kathleen Bell. Presently Aunt Isabel moved nearer to the window, and her words came down to Robert with startling clearness.

"Yes, I can assure you, Miss Bell, that I'm real proud of my nephews and nieces. They're a smart family. They've almost all done well, and they hadn't any of them much to begin with. Ralph had absolutely nothing and today he is a millionaire. Their father met with so many losses, what with his ill-health and the bank failing, that he couldn't help them any. But they've all succeeded, except poor Robert — and I must admit that he's a total failure."

"Oh, no, no," said the little teacher deprecatingly.

"A total failure!" Aunt Isabel repeated her words emphatically. She was not going to be contradicted by anybody, least of all a Bell from Avonlea. "He has been a failure since the time he was born. He is the first Monroe to disgrace the old stock that way. I'm sure his brothers and sisters must be dreadfully ashamed of him. He has lived sixty years and he hasn't done a thing worth while. He can't even make his farm pay. If he's kept out of debt it's as much as he's ever managed to do."

"Some men can't even do that," murmured the little school teacher. She was really so much in awe of this imperious, clever old Aunt Isabel that it was positive heroism on her part to venture even this faint protest.

"More is expected of a Monroe," said Aunt Isabel majestically. "Robert Monroe is a failure, and that is the only name for him."

Robert Monroe stood up below the window in a dizzy, uncertain fashion. Aunt Isabel had been speaking of him! He, Robert, was a failure, a disgrace to his blood, of whom his nearest and dearest were ashamed! Yes, it was true; he had never realized it before; he had known that he could never win power or accumulate riches, but he had not thought that mattered much. Now, through Aunt Isabel's scornful eyes, he saw himself as the world saw him — as his brothers and sisters must see him. *There* lay the sting. What the world thought of him did not matter; but that his own should think him a failure and disgrace was agony. He moaned as he started to walk across the yard, only anxious to hide his pain and shame away from all human sight, and in his eyes was the look

LUCY MAUD MONTGOMERY

of a gentle animal which had been stricken by a cruel and unexpected blow.

Edith Monroe, who, unaware of Robert's proximity, had been standing at the other side of the porch, saw that look, as he hurried past her, unseeing. A moment before her dark eyes had been flashing with anger at Aunt Isabel's words; now the anger was drowned in a sudden rush of tears.

She took a quick step after Robert, but checked the impulse. Not then — and not by her alone — could that deadly hurt be healed. Nay, more, Robert must never suspect that she knew of any hurt. She stood and watched him through her tears as he went away across the low-lying fields to hide his broken heart under his own humble roof. She yearned to hurry after him and comfort him, but she knew that comfort was not what Robert needed now. Justice, and justice only, could pluck out the sting, which otherwise must rankle to the death.

Ralph and Malcolm were driving into the yard. Edith went over to them.

"Boys," she said resolutely, "I want to have a talk with you."

The Christmas dinner at the homestead was a merry one. Mrs. James spread a feast that was fit for the halls of Lucullus. Laughter, jest, and repartee flew from lip to lip. Nobody appeared to notice that Robert ate little, said nothing, and sat with his form shrinking in his shabby "best" suit, his grey head bent even lower than usual, as if desirous of avoiding all observation. When the others spoke to him he answered deprecatingly and shrank still further into himself.

Finally all had eaten all they could, and the remainder of the plum pudding was carried out. Robert gave a low sigh of relief. It was almost over. Soon he would be able to escape and hide himself and his shame away from the mirthful eyes of these men and women who had earned the right to laugh at the world in which their success gave them power and influence. He — he — only — was a failure.

He wondered impatiently why Mrs. James did not rise. Mrs. James merely leaned comfortably back in her chair, with the righteous expression of one who had done her duty by her fellow creatures' palates and looked at Malcolm.

Malcolm rose in his place. Silence fell on the company; everybody looked suddenly alert and expectant, except Robert. He still sat with bowed head, wrapped in his own bitterness.

"I have been told that I must lead off," said Malcolm, "because I am supposed to possess the gift of gab. But, if I do, I am not going to use it for any rhetorical effect today. Simple, earnest words must express the deepest feelings of the heart in doing justice to its own. Brothers and sisters, we meet today under our own roof-tree, surrounded by the benedictions of the past years. Perhaps invisible guests are here — the spirits of those who founded this home and whose work on earth has long been finished. It is not amiss to hope that this is so and our family circle made indeed complete. To each one of us who are here in visible bodily presence some measure of success has fallen; but only one of us has been supremely successful in the only things that really count — the things that count for eternity as well as time — sympathy and unselfishness and self-sacrifice.

"I shall tell you my own story for the benefit of those who have not heard it. When I was a lad of sixteen I started to work out my own education. Some of you will remember that old Mr. Blair of Avonlea offered me a place in his store for the summer, at wages which would go far towards paying my expenses at the county academy the next winter. I went to work, eager and hopeful. All summer I tried to do my faithful best for my employer. In September the blow fell. A sum of money was missing from Mr. Blair's till. I was suspected and discharged in disgrace. All my neighbours believed me guilty; even some of my own family looked upon me with suspicion — nor could I blame them, for the circumstantial evidence was strongly against me."

Ralph and James looked ashamed; Edith and Margaret, who had not been born at the time referred to, lifted their faces innocently. Robert did not move or glance up. He hardly seemed to be listening.

"I was crushed in an agony of shame and despair," continued Malcolm. "I believed my career was ruined. I was bent on casting all my ambitions behind me and going west to some place where nobody knew me or my disgrace. But there was one person who believed in my innocence, who said to me, 'You shall not give up — you shall not behave as if you were guilty. You are innocent, and in time your innocence will be proved. Meanwhile show yourself a man. You have nearly enough money to pay your way next winter at the Academy. I have a little I can give to help you out. Don't give in — never give in when you have done no wrong.'

"I listened and took his advice. I went to the Academy. My story was there as soon as I was, and I found myself sneered at and shunned. Many a time I would have given up in despair, had it not been for the encouragement of my counsellor. He furnished the backbone for me. I was determined that his belief in me should be justified. I studied hard and came out at the head of my class. Then there seemed to be no chance of my earning any more money that summer. But a farmer at Newbridge, who cared nothing about the character of his help, if he could get the work out of them, offered to hire me. The prospect was distasteful but, urged by the man who believed in me, I took the place and endured the hardships. Another winter of lonely work passed at the Academy. I won the Farrell Scholarship the last year it was offered, and that meant an Arts course for me. I went to Redmond College. My story was not openly known there, but something of it got abroad, enough to taint my life there also with its suspicion. But the year I graduated, Mr. Blair's nephew, who, as you know, was the real culprit, confessed his guilt, and I was cleared before the world. Since then my career has been what is called a brilliant one. But," — Malcolm turned and laid his hand on Robert's thin shoulder — "all my success I owe to my brother Robert. It is his success — not mine — and here today, since we have agreed to say what is too often left to be said over a coffin lid, I thank him for all he did for me and tell him that there is nothing I am more proud of and thankful for than such a brother."

Robert had looked up at last, amazed, bewildered, incredulous. His face crimsoned as Malcolm sat down. But now Ralph was getting up.

"I am no orator as Malcolm is," he quoted gaily, "but I've got a story to tell, too, which only one of you knows. Forty years ago, when I started in life as a business man, money wasn't so plentiful with me as it may be today. And I needed it badly. A chance came my way to make a pile of it. It wasn't a clean chance. It was a dirty chance. It looked square on the surface; but, underneath, it meant trickery and roguery. I hadn't enough perception to see that, though — I was fool enough to think it was all right. I told Robert what I meant to do. And Robert saw clear through the outward sham to the real, hideous thing underneath. He showed me what it meant and he gave me a preachment about a few Monroe Traditions of truth and honour. I saw what I had been about to do as he saw it — as all good men and true must see it. And I vowed then and there that I'd never go into anything that I wasn't sure was fair and square and clean through and through. I've kept that vow. I am a rich man, and not a dollar of my money is 'tainted' money. But I didn't make it. Robert really made every cent of my money. If it hadn't been for him I'd have been a poor man today, or behind prison bars, as are the other men who went into that deal when I backed out. I've got a son here. I hope he'll be as clever as his Uncle Malcolm; but I hope, still more earnestly, that he'll be as good and honourable a man as his Uncle Robert."

By this time Robert's head was bent again and his face buried in his hands.

"My turn next," said James. "I haven't much to say — only this. After mother died I took typhoid fever. Here I was with no one to wait on me. Robert came and nursed me. He was the most faithful, tender, gentle nurse ever a man had. The doctor said Robert saved my life. I don't suppose any of the rest of us here can say we have saved a life."

Edith wiped away her tears and sprang up impulsively.

"Years ago," she said, "there was a poor, ambitious girl who had a voice. She wanted a musical education and her only apparent chance of obtaining it was to get a teacher's certificate and earn money enough to have her voice trained. She studied hard, but her brains, in mathematics at least, weren't as good as her voice, and the time was short. She failed. She was lost in disappointment and despair, for that was the last year in which it was possible to obtain a teacher's certificate without attending Queen's Academy, and she could not afford that. Then her oldest brother came to her and told her he could spare enough money to send her to the conservatory of music in Halifax for a year. He made her take it. She never knew till long afterwards that he had sold the beautiful horse which he loved like a human creature, to get the money. She went to the Halifax conservatory. She won a musical scholarship. She has had a happy life and a successful career. And she owes it all to her brother Robert —"

But Edith could go no further. Her voice failed her and she sat down in tears. Margaret did not try to stand up.

"I was only five when my mother died," she sobbed. "Robert was both father and mother to me. Never had child or girl so wise and loving a guardian as he was to me. I have never forgotten the lessons he taught me. Whatever there is of good in my life or character I owe to him. I was often headstrong and wilful, but he never lost patience with me. I owe everything to Robert."

Suddenly the little teacher rose with wet eyes and crimson cheeks.

"I have something to say, too," she said resolutely. "You have spoken for yourselves. I speak for the people of White Sands. There is a man in this settlement whom everybody loves. I shall tell you some of the things he has done.

"Last fall, in an October storm, the harbour lighthouse flew a flag of distress. Only one man was brave enough to face the danger of sailing to the lighthouse to find out what the trouble was. That was Robert Monroe. He found the keeper alone with a broken leg; and he sailed back and made — yes, *made* the unwilling and terrified doctor go with him to the lighthouse. I saw him when he told the doctor he must go; and I tell you that no man living could have set his will against Robert Monroe's at that moment.

"Four years ago old Sarah Cooper was to be taken to the poorhouse. She was broken-hearted. One man took the poor, bed-ridden, fretful old creature into his home, paid for medical attendance and waited on her himself when his housekeeper couldn't endure her tantrums and temper. Sarah Cooper died two years afterwards, and her latest breath was a benediction on Robert Monroe — the best man God ever made.

"Eight years ago Jack Blewett wanted a place. Nobody would hire him because his father was in the penitentiary, and some people thought Jack ought to be there, too. Robert Monroe hired him — and helped him and kept him straight and got him started right — and Jack Blewett is a hard-working, respected young man today, with every prospect of a useful and honourable life. There is hardly a man, woman, or child in White Sands who doesn't owe something to Robert Monroe!"

As Kathleen Bell sat down, Malcolm sprang up and held out his hands.

"Every one of us stand up and sing 'Auld Lang Syne,'" he cried.

Everybody stood up and joined hands, but one did not sing. Robert Monroe stood erect, with a great radiance on his face and in his eyes. His reproach had been taken away; he was crowned among his kindred with the beauty and blessing of sacred yesterdays.

When the singing ceased Malcolm's stern-faced son reached over and shook Robert's hands.

"Uncle Rob," he said heartily, "I hope that when I'm sixty I'll be as successful a man as you."

"I guess," said Aunt Isabel, aside to the little school teacher, as she wiped the tears from her keen old eyes, "that there's a kind of failure that's the best success."

LUCY MAUD MONTGOMERY

From Santa with Love

EPHIE CARRIER

A few puffy clouds chased each other in the cold blue sky. My breath steamed as I sat on the log and watched my father loading firewood in the red sled with the high sides. It had iron under the wood runners which were turned up in the front and went real easy on the hard snow when the horses pulled. All good hardwood, maple and yellow birch, stacked piece by piece until the box was full.

"There! A whole cord for him," Pa said as he pulled the ropes tight between the posts. When my father said there was a cord, everybody believed him. He leaped to the ground, spoke to Bill and King, the horses, grabbed me by the arms and tossed me up on his shoulder as we went to the house. He was strong for his size they said, whatever that meant.

Mother had decorated the house with green branches and some red ribbons hung from the walls. She said Christmas was coming soon, but I heard her tell Pa that we didn't have any money for store presents. He laughed and said even if we couldn't buy presents, we had lots of food, because we could always eat all those potatoes we couldn't sell. Ma laughed with him and said she had plenty to cook at Christmas, and a big chicken, too.

But I remembered last year, when we had home made presents. I had got a new pair of mitts with strings. I wondered what store-bought presents would be like.

Pa put on his good cap with the ear pieces and his new mackinaw, then told me to stay in the house. He went out again walking quickly, his feet crunching in the icy snow. He climbed up on top of the wood and took up the reins. He looked real good. The horses were pounding their big paws in the snow, anxious to go. They snorted steam, and Pa was breathing white through his red whiskers.

"Giddyap," I heard him holler, and the team jerked the heavy load toward Grand Falls. The sled picked up speed down the small hill, and soon they were on the highway towards town. I watched his red mackinaw until it disappeared over the hill.

"Mom, is Pa selling the wood?" I asked

"Yes, he is."

I knew there was no sense asking for anything else. Mom had used that tone. So off I went in the cold bright sunshine to adventures in the barn. I had to re-set my rat traps and check the pigs snorting in their pens and the cows steaming in their stalls, munching straw and small amounts of hay. It smelled good around the cows. Sometimes Pa would feed them potatoes, but first he cut them. He said round potatoes could choke them. For the pigs, Pa always cooked the potatoes in the black pot, outside behind the machine shed. The chickens were clucking in their cold house, and I was looking for eggs when I heard Mother calling. Must be time to eat again.

After the food came the nap. I didn't want to nap because at six years I was old enough not to, but Mom said it was time.

The sun was nearly over old George's house when I opened my eyes. Then I heard them, the horses pounding up the hill in the driveway with their quick step. They knew they were headed for the stables and the hay. I got up and looked out the window.

Father was standing in the big box on the sled holding the reins in both hands, and the wood pieces were all gone. He drove straight to the stables, and I started to dress up and leave the kitchen to help him with the harnesses. But Mom said no, it was too cold, and I had to stay in the house. I didn't feel cold when I was out before my nap, and I told her. She didn't reply.

Soon father came in, looked at Mom, and picked me up even before he took off his cap. He smelled the good smell of horses.

EPHIE CARRIER

The next day we put up a nice tree. We had lots of trees but not much to put on the branches. Mother had strips of coloured paper, balls made with old Christmas cards, painted eggshells and an angel for the top of the tree. Mother said the rich folks bought all their ornaments, and their houses had electricity. Sometimes they had lights in the trees. She said she saw these things when she worked as a maid for the engineer. Electric lights in the Christmas tree? That was hard to believe, but my Mom didn't lie.

Next morning was Christmas, and it was still dark and cold when I woke up my younger brother Al. We both crept downstairs past the big bedroom. Mom and Pa weren't up yet, but they had been to midnight mass in Grand Falls and stayed for something called "reveillon." Boy, they got home late.

I lit the oil lamp. There were hot coals in the big stove, so I put in two pieces of wood. It got warm quickly in the kitchen.

We thought we should check our stockings to see what Santa had brought. Last year I had an orange. Mom always said if I was bad I would get a potato. I tried not to be bad, but sometimes I slipped, just a little.

As we walked toward the tree I saw it. "Look," I gasped. We both reached the tree at the same time and stood in awe. My hands were shaking and I could hardly breathe. I tried to move forward quickly but my legs wouldn't move fast enough.

Under the tree was a bright red sled, just like the big horse sled. The runners were carved with the upright pieces in place, just like the big one, and there was a piece of metal under each runner. The front of the sled had a frame with holes and a rope. The top of the sled was made with nice boards, even better than the big sled. Wow! My heart soared as I sat in the sled and held the rope, imagining the wind in my face as I slid down the hill very, very fast.

Al was dancing around the sled, touching the runners and the rope. He was giggling all the time, and I thought he would wake Pa and Mom. He was so excited he climbed in the sled just behind me. Then I laughed, too. So this was how a store-bought present felt.

We forgot to check our Christmas stockings.

The Christmas Chair

JESS BOND

Annie polished the old mahogany table with all the energy she could transfer from her skinny frame to the old towel dampened with lemon oil. Of all of her sister's furniture, this dining-room table was her very favourite piece. Annie polished and prayed that Sarah would be pleased with the job she was doing. The table had to look especially good because Christmas was only a few days away. When Harry, Sarah's husband, died, Sarah invited Annie to move in with her. There wasn't anything Annie wouldn't do to please Sarah.

When she and Sarah were kids, they ate their meals in the old Birch Grove farm kitchen on a long, wooden harvest table covered with oilcloth, the oilcloth held down with tacks, its yellow roses faded to a pale beige.

A dining room with real mahogany furniture, like the furniture in Eaton's Department store, was something Annie had dreamed about, like the way she used to dream about getting away from the drudgery of the farm and her father and two older brothers. She had Sarah to thank for her deliverance from that bleak existence. There wasn't a day of life that she didn't thank God for her sister Sarah.

Annie rubbed the lemon oil into the mahogany with intense pleasure. She rubbed and rubbed and thought about what her life would be like if she had been the sister who had married old widower Harry Bates. Sarah's move from Birch Grove into Sydney when she married Harry put Annie in charge of the farm kitchen. She hated that. She hated cooking.

The smell of fresh brewed coffee interrupted her daydreaming. She put down the polishing cloth and headed for the kitchen. Sarah passed her a steaming mug and nodded toward a plate of hot cinnamon rolls. Sarah could be cross and was often difficult to live with, but she sure wasn't mean with food.

Annie reached into her apron pocket for a small gift-wrapped box. It felt good to be the one giving for a change. She passed the box to Sarah. "Happy Birthday," she said loudly.

Sarah had been deaf for years but wouldn't own up to the fact. She just about had a fit the time Annie suggested a hearing aid. She acted so upset, Annie decided never to mention Sarah's hearing again.

Sarah looked at the box in her hands. "What foolishness have you been up to now?"

"It's a pin to wear on your good dress, Sarah. It's a sprig of holly. You can wear it on Christmas day. I saw it in a gift shop weeks ago and decided it was just the thing to get you." Annie felt badly that Sarah's birthday was so close to Christmas, so she bought a little gift to mark the day.

"Likely paid too much for it," growled Sarah. She had a low, raspy voice. "You're a great one for paying too much for things."

Annie had to watch her pension money like a hawk to save the twelve ninety-five for the pin. She ignored Sarah's remarks.

"How does it feel to be seventy-five years old, Sarah?"

Sarah's round, plump face looked startled for a moment. "No different than being seventy-four years old," she said. She stood up and began to line up her baking bowls and pans.

Cooking and baking were the most important things in Sarah's life. A week didn't go by that she didn't try a new dish. Sarah refused to share recipes with anyone but her best friend, Alma Stokes. Annie glanced at Sarah's notebook of Christmas recipes and thought, "I know several old biddies who would love to get their hands on that note-book."

"Alma is going to have supper with us tonight," Sarah announced.

"That's nice, Sarah." Annie drained her coffee mug and rinsed it out.

Sarah cleared her throat. "I thought you might like to ask Flo to join us."

Annie stared at her sister. She couldn't believe her ears. Sarah never had a good word to say about Flo; in fact, she was downright mean the way she poked fun at Flo's silly ways.

"I'm trying out a new cake recipe," Sarah said. "It's a gum drop cake. It's two layers, and we could never get it eaten up by ourselves."

She passed Annie a grocery list. "If you plan to drop in on Flo while you're out, don't stay too long. I need the cherries and coconut before noon."

"I'll get these things right away," Annie said. "I'll have my visit with Flo later. She's invited me to lunch, and she's going to give me a manicure."

When Sarah scowled Annie asked quickly, "Do you need me to help you this afternoon, Sarah?"

"You know I can't stand you underfoot when I'm baking. Stay over at Flo's the whole afternoon if you want to."

She banged a couple of pans on the counter, mumbling to herself about sixty-five-year-old women and manicures and people who didn't have the sense that God gave geese.

When Annie returned with the groceries she got a dressing down because she had bought the wrong brand of maraschino cherries. Sarah was also cross at her because she didn't put things away in a certain order.

Annie escaped upstairs. She put an extra measure of bubble bath in the tub and decided she was going to wear her very best dress. It was a red silk print with a frilly neckline and a full skirt. She thought it made her look not so skinny.

Annie had made the dress herself, copying the style from a magazine. Sarah said it was the most ridiculous dress she had ever seen, but Annie loved it.

Annie put on her coat and slipped out the front door without saying goodbye to Sarah. She had enough of Sarah's scolding for one day, and she didn't want to have to endure another run of Sarah's tongue.

Flo was a short, heavy woman with bright eyes and a fresh, unlined face. She was all smiles, standing in the doorway waiting for Annie. "Come in, Annie. Come in. Wait till you see the lovely lunch I've made for us. Chicken salad, tea biscuits and an apricot meringue that turned out just perfect."

"We better not have seconds today, Flo," Annie told her. "Sarah is cooking a special meal for her birthday and you're invited."

Flo looked surprised. "That's right. It's the old dragon's birthday today, isn't it? And she's seventy-five. Right?"

Annie smiled at her friend's name for Sarah. "That's right, the old dragon is seventy-five today."

"Too bad she's not turning ninety. You'd be closer to having that house to yourself."

"Don't say things like that, Flo. It upsets me when you say things like that. Besides, I have no idea what will happen to the house when Sarah dies. Harry had two sons and some grandchildren, you know."

"Okay, dear, I won't say anything about the house again. Now let's have lunch. Then I'll do your manicure, and then I have a surprise for you."

Flo was always giving her surprises. Sometimes it was a piece of jewellery she was tired of, or some hand lotion, or tickets to a movie. When Annie protested about Flo giving her gifts, Flo said, "Ducks, when my husband was living he was so tight he squeaked, and now that I don't have to check every cent I spend with the old skinflint, I buy and give as I please."

Then she grabbed Annie by the arm and led her to the back sun porch, which she had turned into a sewing room. "I can't wait until after lunch for you to see your surprise. It's your Christmas gift. Come on." She pointed to the chair in the middle of the room.

"Well, do you like it?"

It was a small bedroom chair with a dark rose velvet seat. Annie stroked the back of the chair trying to take it in that the chair was hers.

"I remember you saying once that you'd like a bedroom chair. This was packed away with stuff I don't use anymore, so I decided to clean it up and recover the seat for you."

Later that day, when Annie and Flo arrived at Sarah's, carrying the chair, Annie called out, "Sarah, come see the lovely chair Flo has given me for my bedroom!"

Sarah and Alma joined them in the hall.

"That's a very pretty chair, Annie," Alma said in the loud voice she always used around Sarah.

Sarah glanced at the chair and then gave Flo a blank, polite look. She didn't welcome her or greet her in any way.

Alma offered to help Annie upstairs with the chair.

Sarah placed herself between the chair and her guests. "I'll help Annie." She motioned to the dining room. "Please help yourselves to the cheese and olives on the sideboard."

When they were in Annie's room with the door closed, Sarah turned on her. Her face was red and her mouth was opening and closing as if she didn't know what to say.

Annie felt terrible. "Sarah, dear, why are you so upset?"

Sarah exploded. "Bringing cast-offs into my home!"

"But the chair is for my room. You don't have to look at it."

"I don't want that chair in my house. Now let's get downstairs before my meal is ruined. We'll finish this conversation later."

Flo and Alma tackled Sarah's excellent roast beef dinner with relish. Sarah ate silently and methodically. Annie pushed the food around on her plate, every bite tasting like cardboard.

Annie was grateful that Alma and Flo were old friends. They kept up a stream of chatter during the meal. Finally the meal was over, the table cleared. Sarah announced she was going to serve the cake and coffee in the living room. The gum drop cake was a masterpiece. The safe topic of cake recipes was pounced upon. Annie, who had no talent for baking, sat there sipping coffee and marvelling at how three women could talk with such animation and at such length about the art of cake-making.

When the guests had gone, Annie and Sarah cleaned up the kitchen in silence. Annie welcomed the silence. She was feeling too hurt about how Sarah had acted about her new chair to carry on any kind of a

JESS BOND

conversation. She hurried through her share of the cleaning so she could go upstairs to bed.

Annie climbed into her warm, comfortable bed. She whispered the same thing she whispered every night. "Thank you, God for this wonderful bed, and for my sister, Sarah."

From the tiny bit of light shed from her baseboard night light, she could see the outline of the chair. How could a chair that made her so happy make Sarah so cross?

Annie thought about her life with Sarah. In the past ten years, not a day passed that she didn't remind herself of her good fortune in having Sarah for a sister. She was used to Sarah's crankiness. Sarah wouldn't be Sarah without that sharp tongue of hers. Annie loved Sarah with all her heart, and she loved the comfort and safety of Sarah's home.

When they were young, Sarah had been the older, protective sister. She had been bossy and strict with Annie but always fair and generous, the very opposite of the two older brothers. The brothers and Sarah were close in age. Annie had come along ten years later. Everyone in the family except Sarah had treated her like the family pest.

When Annie was in her teens and twenties she had lots of boyfriends, went to lots of parties and dances with the girls she worked with at the Birch Grove General Store.

Sarah had to take on the running of the house after their mother's death. She used to warn Annie, "You better marry one of those boy-friends of yours or you'll be stuck in this house forever, like me."

It seemed to Annie that one year just melted into the next, and suddenly she was thirty-five and Sarah forty-five, both still unmarried.

Then Harry Bates came along. Sixty years old, recently widowed and looking for a wife. When he made his first overture to Annie, she told him there was someone else. Annie had been in love with another man at the time. She hadn't been the least bit interested in becoming Harry's housekeeper and bed warmer.

With a one's-as-good-as-the-other attitude, Harry started to court Sarah. It wasn't much of a courtship, but for Sarah it meant her own home and her escape from working her fingers to the bone for her father and two brothers.

Annie had never told Sarah about Harry's proposal to her.

Annie's bedroom door opened suddenly, letting in the hall light. Sarah was standing in the doorway. "I can't sleep. I went downstairs and put on the kettle for tea. Will you come down and have a cup with me?"

When they were settled at the kitchen table, Sarah poured the tea. She said, "Annie, why didn't you mention that you wanted a bedroom chair? I would have bought you a chair." She pushed the cake plate across the table.

This was the first time Sarah had ever made tea late at night. Somehow, sitting there at the kitchen table, past eleven o'clock, it seemed a good time for Annie to ask Sarah something she had always wanted to ask her.

"Sarah, did you ask me to come and live with you after Harry died because you felt sorry for me, or did you truly want for the two of us to live together?"

Sarah didn't answer. She just sat there sipping her tea.

Annie spoke again. "The very day of Harry's funeral you told me to pack my things and move in with you. I'll never forget that moment if I live to be a hundred. You knew how I hated it in Birch Grove, especially after the boys brought wives home. The wives expected me to cater to them just as I had to cater to Father and the boys. I hated that."

Sarah's voice was so low when she spoke that Annie had to lean forward to hear her. "I felt I owed you a home, Annie. I always felt Harry wanted you first. But it was more than that. I knew what it was like at the farm for you. I wanted you to have a better life than that."

Annie stared at her. "What are you talking about, Harry wanted me first?"

"Harry never came right out and said so, but he often hinted at it when he had one drink too many."

"For God's sake, Sarah, how could you believe anything that came out of a bottle?"

"Wasn't it the truth, Annie?"

"No, it wasn't the truth," Annie lied. She spoke louder than was necessary. God, how she wished she had told that man what she never had the nerve to tell him when he was alive, that he was a pompous old ass and that Sarah was far too good for him.

Sarah leaned back in her chair, her hands folded over her round stomach. "I behaved badly today, Annie. I get jealous feelings when Flo does something nice for you."

Annie held out her tea cup. She knew what an effort it was for Sarah to admit to bad behaviour. In her whole life, Annie had never heard Sarah say the word "sorry." She supposed that "I behaved badly" was as good as "sorry." It was likely the best Sarah could manage.

"Flo is a good friend to me, just like Alma is a good friend to you. But Flo isn't my sister, Sarah."

Sarah didn't look up from pouring more tea. When she put the teapot down, she held out the cake plate to Annie. "The next time Flo is here I'll tell her that she did a fine job on fixing that chair up for you."

"Thank you, Sarah." There was something else Annie wanted to say. She felt if she didn't say it that very minute, it would never get said, that they would go to their graves with the words unspoken.

Annie took a deep breath. Her voice was shaky as she said the words she had never in her whole life said to another living soul. "I love you, Sarah."

She was almost relieved when Sarah snapped at her. "Don't you think I know that, you silly goose? Now, let's wash these tea cups and get to bed. We have a lot of Christmas chores that have to be done."

Little Arthur's Christmas

PATRICK O'FLAHERTY

"Yes, sir, the hardest Christmas ever I'll spend, that's what I got ahead of me," Little Arthur Cooney said as he carried the gasoline can and grub bag down the lane from his house to the beach. He stopped now and then to shift the heavy can to the other hand, moving the grub bag with care because in it, along with the bread and bottle of water, was his compass, wrapped in an old wool sweater.

He could have brought his gear down in the pickup; but Arthur didn't like leaving his pickup near the beach, out of sight, where someone might damage it.

The swish of his turned-down long rubbers as he trudged along, and his own mutterings, were the only sounds of the morning.

But then the swishing startled a crow, which flew up, cawing, in front of him. Arthur laid down the can, made the sign of the cross, and began walking again, looking east over the dark ocean and seeing the familiar grey light of pre-dawn. Though he knew the moon was full, overhead he could see neither moon nor stars. To the south, the light on Cape St. Francis, on the other side of the bay, was not visible; fog, maybe, far out, or low-lying clouds. It was so warm he found he was sweating. It shouldn't be this warm, not in December, he thought. Something's wrong with the weather. I've never seen weather like it.

Then, out loud: "Yes, my sonny boy, the hardest Christmas ever, that's what I got facing me. I never had to do the likes of this before. That is, if I do it."

So there was a big if; this made him feel better. He talked to himself a lot because he fished alone, as he'd done since his son Aidan went to university. Aidan lived in Toronto now: a teacher. Arthur got the phone in so he'd be able to call Toronto now and then.

"Dad," Aidan said in their last call, "Why don't you give up the fishing, you got enough money; it's too hard a life."

"I'll stick at it for another year or two," Arthur said.

"Well, at least put your skiff up in Arnold's Bight; they got a wharf there."

"I'll think about it."

Aidan persisted. "Come and stay with me and Jan this winter. Noddy's Cove is too cold and you only got that old woodstove. We got a spare room in the basement hooked up to the furnace. You're not young anymore."

It was true: he was fifty-six. But Aidan had his own life: family, house, big job. It was enough for him to send socks and a card Christmastime. As for himself, Little Arthur didn't like gift-giving. Poor Nell used to get a box of chocolates every Christmas. Aidan got a money order: forty dollars. A lot, but Arthur wasn't stuck for a dollar.

Arnold's Bight wharf? All the young fishermen had their boats up there; it was only ten miles away by road, next to Morey's fishplant. But Arthur held back, wanting to keep using his father's fishing room, thinking it wasn't good to be so far away from his skiff. As long as Morey's truck picked up his fish, he was staying put.

Basement room? Likely! He snorted. No city uptear for him. He still had a house to take care of. His father's house, really; but now his. And he had graves to tend. His father's and mother's. Nell's.

When Nell died of stomach cancer nine years ago, Little Arthur, having taken care of her himself for a year and two days after she came out of St. Clare's — he wasn't having any snippy nurse come to look after his woman, no sir! — having done his duty by Nell and then buried her in a good coffin as she should be buried and put up a headstone with room left on it for his name — having done that, he'd settled back to punch it on his own.

And now this.

It was hard, all right. Hard as dogs. His own father, Art Senior, as he was called, didn't have it any harder.

Damn Molly Cumby anyway, what the hell did she come back for, he thought. Then, reconsidering: no, not damn her. Not that. It's Christmas Eve. I don't want that on my conscience to have to tell Father George in the confession box.

He walked down the government road to Sandy Beach, laid down his gear and looked over his dory, which for safety was tied onto a beam in the winch-frame. Nothing wrong. No rainwater in her, so he wouldn't have to tip her up. No thole-pins cracked off. No paddle robbed. No stave loose in the bait-tub. Plug in place.

He was a watchful man and knew that some fishermen might resent him for what he was doing. They might think he was showing them up, and so he was, in a way, but he didn't mean to. The few men who still fished from Sandy Beach had pulled their skiffs and dories up on the bank for the winter in mid-November, the usual time; but it had been a peaceful mild fall, no storms, no bad weather really, hardly any frost or snow; and Little Arthur kept his boat in the water because fish were still getting on his trawls and there was money to be made and work to be done.

He'd never fished this late before. December sixteenth had been the limit; that was one year before the War when Small Madeira was going for $13.50 a quintal and every fish counted.

But he knew he was at the end of it. His boat had to come ashore. He'd pushed his luck far enough. Three of his five fleets of trawl-lines were already in his fishhouse, along with his herring net. The other trawls were coming in today.

At six o'clock there was no one around to help him launch his dory. He lifted the stern a foot and kicked one of the ways well in under so the dory would roll on it. He put another way a few feet beyond the first, and a third beyond that, as his father had shown him. Then he went to the bow and pushed with all his strength, inching the heavy boat, water-logged after the long season, towards the water. At last she was half in. He sat on a rock to catch his breath.

Then he put his can and grub bag in the dory and pushed off. As he shoved the paddles out, he felt a stab of pain in his right shoulder. It's nothing, he thought, rheumatism; I had it in my hip years ago.

He rowed slowly towards the skiff moored on the collars a few hundred yards offshore, finding his way by instinct, thinking again of Molly. Thinking of her as a girl thirty-five years ago. The belle of Noddy's Cove, she was. As a Cumby, she had everything she wanted; Silas, her father, made sure of that. She went off to Canada to school in the winters, and even in the summer holidays her mother brought her to St. John's on weekends to take music and speech lessons. Whenever Arthur saw her up close, he'd look at his stumpy fingers, rough from spreading and lifting fish, and note how long and slender hers were. Tall, fair-skinned, dark-haired, she glittered above him. He was short, thick, with red hair and pimples.

And yet, he screwed up his courage at the Job's Cove garden party and asked her to go walking to Peg's Tolt. She answered, "I'm afraid that's not possible today."

Today, she said. That wasn't final. One rejection was nothing. "Chin up!" his father told him over and over. "The working man's day is coming." Art Senior had studied the Bolsheviks: the same thing would happen here, he said, we'd wake up one morning and the government would be toppled, and people like him would be in charge.

The next day Arthur waited behind the bush at the foot of Duncan's Lane, but heard her giggling with other girls: "Foxy Art's trying to get with me," she said.

He stayed hidden and reddened with shame. Foxy Art. So that was what she and her friends called him behind his back.

Her remark still stung, after so many years.

She'd trained as a nurse in St. John's, but a lawyer's son from Harbour Grace swept her off her feet and took her to a place called the Eastern Townships, where he had a practice. As Little Arthur's own life took shape, he heard rumours about hers. The lawyer's son turned out to be a drinker and womanizer. Molly fell on hard times.

The Cumby shop fell on hard times too. It was long gone, together with the premises near the water where Arthur's father drove in his horse-and-boxcar to sell his fish. Too often it was put in the lowest cull, West Indie. "The merchant's cull," Art Senior called it. He hated lots of people, but merchants were at the top of the list, just ahead of priests.

Of all the property the Cumbys had owned, only the house was left standing. Molly came back to it in early July and spent the summer fixing it up. As men worked at the clapboard and roof, she lay out in the front garden on a blanket, getting a suntan. It was the first time anyone her age was seen in a bathing suit. If she wasn't tanning herself she was planting flowers, and before long the property was in bloom. Old men walked by to have a look at her. Timothy Foley, a sixty-five-year-old bachelor who hadn't had a shirt and tie on in twenty years, was seen going into the house dressed to the nines, carrying a posy.

She told everyone she was staying for good. Everyone, except Little Arthur, who kept his distance. Damned if he was going to lift a finger on the Cumby house, anyway. His father would turn over in his grave.

And on August fifteenth, Lady Day, too blustery for him to go fishing, she came and knocked at his door.

The dory knocked roughly against the skiff lying at anchor. Arthur stowed the paddles, jumped to the bow, placed his good arm over the gunwale of the skiff near the engine room, took the gear out of the dory and stepped aboard the bigger boat. There was a bit of a rolling sea on; nothing to hurt. He walked to the stem over the deck, untied the skiff's mooring and fastened it to the dory's painter; then let the skiff go adrift, trusting the engine but knowing his sculling oar would get him back to the dory if the engine didn't start.

He poured gas in the tank, primed the piston, checked the spark. All well. He gave the flywheel a sharp turn, using his left arm; then another, using the right one this time, though he wanted to spare it in case of trouble on the fishing grounds. The 6-Atlantic hissed, caught, roared; there was no finer engine, in Arthur's view.

He took the tiller-stick, sat on the side of the engine-house opposite the muffler and turned the skiff out towards Little Bank. Glancing back, he lined up the church with Peg's Tolt on the hill behind it. Art Senior called the church the opiate of the people. "Get Peg's Tolt between the spires of the opiate," he'd say, "and go straight out."

Yes, she'd come straight up to his door. By the time she got to the platform and knocked, he'd ducked into the parlour.

He hid from her!

She knocked twice more, then left. Arthur feared his hiding away would become known. His pickup was in the front yard: if he wasn't on the water, this was the sign he was home. "Boys, oh boys," he said, as the engine banged and the skiff cut smoothly through the water, "what will people think of me at all?"

He found his buoy on Little Bank and hauled it into the midship-room. Since the whole trawl was coming aboard, he pulled the outside mooring in and the twenty-pound rock fastened to it. The sea rolled gently under him. The water was deadly calm, and there was no tide. He could see the rock coming straight up from ten fathoms. Most of the men cut their trawl rocks off every fall and looked for new ones in the spring, but Arthur kept his. He stowed the rock and mooring in the midship-room, feeling again the pain in his arm.

Back in the fore-cuddy, he hauled the trawl itself, seeing the glitter of one or two fish well down. The first ten hooks came aboard, hanging off the trawl line on white seds; he pinched off the old bait for the gulls and hung the hooks neatly along the top of the staves of the bait-tub at his feet, circling the trawl line in the tub's bottom.

In came a sculpin, stone dead. Overboard it went. Two small codfish, thrown back in the midship-room. A hook missing, twisted off: dogfish teeth. Six more baited hooks. Sea-cat. Live rock. Two more cod, bigger than the first two. A bare hook. Then: a big, thrashing maiden-ray.

His father had hated rays, claiming they gave off electric shocks. Arthur took his gaff, stuck it in the mouth of the huge flopping fish and hauled it aboard. As it was coming over the gunwale, it gave a savage lurch, somehow tearing the gaff and baited hook from its mouth. Arthur slipped, fell back, reached out to save himself and drove the bare hook that was hanging off the trawl line behind him into his right hand, between his second and third fingers, between the knuckles.

He swore, and three gulls that were keeping him company, picking up fish scraps, took off and pitched farther away. Remembering Father George, Arthur took back the oath and asked for forgiveness. It's Christmas, he thought again; no time to take the good Lord's name in vain. I swear too much. But it's not that big a sin. I won't have to pay for it.

He straightened up, hitched the trawl line over the stem of the skiff and cut the sed fastened to the hook stuck in his hand, using his pocket knife. Placing one foot on the thrashing ray to keep it quiet, he gaffed it with his left hand and tossed it in the midship-room.

The hook had gone deep into his palm but the barb hadn't pierced through to the other side. There was no way to get it out until it went all the way; Arthur pushed it through at once, past the bones of his knuckles, then sat back on the deck and considered his hooked, bleeding hand.

"By gum," he said, "the fish got you this time, Arthur."

This was a pickle! He had pliers in the fore-cuddy, but they weren't the kind to cut wire. He made a mental note to get the right kind the next time he was in Arnold's Bight. Perhaps, using the pliers, he could straighten out the eye of the hook. He tried this, but couldn't get it done with his left hand. Aware of time passing, he applied the pliers to the other end of the hook, flattening the barb as well as he could. Then, with the fingers of the wounded hand stiffly apart, he tried to pull the barbed end through the flesh, hitting bone, getting stuck. He relaxed the fingers and tried again. The hook came out, but shreds of flesh were torn away by the still-lifted barb. He looked at the hook. At least it wasn't rusty.

Arthur leaned over the gunwale and washed his bleeding hand in the water. He took out his shirt tail, used his pocket knife to cut off a piece and put the cloth between the sore fingers, pressing hard to try and stop the blood. In five minutes it slowed to a seep. He put his two cotton gloves on the hand to hold the piece of shirt tail in place and went back to work.

The ray was noisily flopping among the codfish. Arthur figured it took the bait just as he started to haul in. "I'll deal with you later, mister," he said, knowing the wings of a ray made good eating.

The water was still fairly calm, but it was turning cold. He dug his sweater out of the grub bag and, as he put it on, looked around to get his bearings. The cloud cover was low, as it had been for a week or more. There was no bad weather in the forecast. But he knew forecasts could be wrong. He resolved to work fast.

In Noddy's Cove a mile or so NNE, smoke was going straight up from Timothy Foley's house on the Point. That old bugger! Arthur thought. Just getting out of bed, and the day half gone. He'll probably be over chopping wood for her later on. Or putting up her tree.

Back to the trawl he went. By the time he reached the last of the hundred and fifty hooks, he had twenty-seven more codfish, some big enough to be culled Large Madeira in the old days.

With the inside rock aboard and stowed with the other one in the midship-room, Arthur took a spell to have his bread and water. A light breeze was now blowing; the sea turned choppy. He took out his pocket-watch. Late. Morey's truck would be on the beach an hour early today.

He started the 6-Atlantic again and headed out to Nelly's Ledge, twenty minutes' steam away.

Nell Foley from Island Cove, six miles down the shore, had been his woman, and a fine woman she was. She was four years older than him but, to many who knew her, she seemed younger. He made a list of her virtues: a hard worker, sensible in most things, religious, a good mother, careful with his money, a good cook, nice to his father. His father said he couldn't stand women, but for some reason he didn't mind Nell. "Fine piece of stock, you got there, son," he'd say, clapping him on the shoulder. Hitting him hard.

But not as hard as he'd hit ...

The skiff beat her way through the seas, as Little Arthur remembered his mother, Sarah, cringing from his father's blows. He was only nine when she died of TB in the St. John's Sanatorium. He remembered only one beating; he'd come down the staircase on a cold night after waking to the noise of a racket below and opened the kitchen door, terrified. He saw his father strike her across the face twice with the flat of his hand; then stand over her, flushed with anger.

"Tell me no more about him!" he shouted. "Never mention his name in this house again, do y' hear?"

"I do hear you, Art," she sobbed. "I hear you."

She was on the floor, her slight form writhing on the boards, her long black hair spread over her face.

Art Senior lowered his hand when he saw his son. He sat in the rocking chair by the stove and slumped forward, his head bowed as if in prayer.

Little Arthur went back to bed and listened. Low moaning sounds came up to him as he fell asleep.

Who was never to be mentioned again? For a while, Little Arthur fancied it was Sarah's father, a blowhard who sometimes came to visit. But when his heart went out to Molly Cumby and stirred with anguish as he saw her walking with the bucko from Harbour Grace, he knew he was wrong. It was another he that was never to be mentioned in the house: a man unknown to this day, whose name would never be known.

He stood up in the engine room and shook himself, seeing his buoy just ahead. He stopped the engine, ran forward and picked up the buoy with his boathook. It had gotten even colder. Looking back, Arthur couldn't see the shoreline. Fog. Or a snow shower. Nothing to worry about. He knew where he was, and he had the compass.

Fog and snow weren't much bother, but now there was a tide, the water was stirred up in a rising wind, and he had a tough haul-up ahead of him. He set to it, getting the outside rock with no trouble and pulling back to the trawl. His left arm and hand did most of the hauling, but the right one had to be in on it too. The cut reopened; more blood dripped from the gloves. His arm ached. Two more rays came aboard; eighteen big codfish, one more than twenty pounds, maybe twenty-five, hauled in with difficulty; a dozen or so sculpins; and seven dogfish. The trawl came in slowly as he pulled against the tide; the skiff lurched in what was becoming a heavy sea. A few snowflakes fell: just what I need, Arthur thought.

At last he had the trawl aboard, inside rock and all. He left the two rocks from the outer trawl in the bow for ballast. Tired now, Arthur put his gaff in its place and went aft. It was after two o'clock, late to be out on Nelly's Ledge; but he still had some daylight left. Time to take the skiff ashore if he really hurried; but then he thought, no, I'll leave the skiff out tonight, I'll get it later. I don't want to miss Morey's truck. And I've got a big thing to do this evening.

"That is, if I do it," he said yet again.

He started the engine once more, got his compass from the grub bag, took a bearing and headed home. He'd been out with his father in weather like this, learned from him how to handle a skiff in a following sea. Art Senior laughed at weather. "God damn it, if you're going to blow at me, blow a good stiff one," he'd shout at the sky, "don't give me a piss-warm wind, this is Art Cooney you're dealing with, Mister." He had rackets even with the weather.

Yes, his father wasn't tough just with merchants and priests. No man on the North Shore could stand up to him. He'd take on the devil himself, Art Senior would. Or shout down a politician.

Or run down women. All of them, except Nell.

Arthur thought long and hard about Nell as the engine hammered in his ear.

She was a fine, decent woman, but he'd never liked the way she talked. Something about it grated on him. She talked too much, with a down-the-shore accent he couldn't get used to; and, worst of all, there was nothing that interested him in what she said, though others seemed to like it well enough, or at least said they did. She'd talk at him for hours. Over nothing.

And everything was "sweet" to her. Children were sweet. A bird-song was sweet. Sunset was sweet. The first snowfall was sweet. Arthur could make sense of all this, but there was hardly anything in Noddy's Cove that wasn't sweet, damn it. Old Father Moakler preached tough sermons; he was sweet. Dandy, a horse, nothing more, was sweet. Piss-a-beds were sweet. Crab apples. It drove him crazy.

Her talking made him quieter and made him seek quiet. He lingered in the woods, trouting where no trout were to be caught. Some days he spent hours in his fishhouse sitting on a keg rather than face the tedium of the kitchen.

It wasn't a big fault. There were things about her that made up for the endless gab. He again listed her virtues. He'd never spoken a rough word to her. Yet at times he felt like saying, For Christ's sake, woman, shut your mouth, and give me a bit of peace.

Once or twice he'd looked down and seen his fists clenched in rage. He could have hit her, as his father hit Sarah. He hadn't. Not in deed; in thought only. Still, inside, where it counted, he'd struck her.

Nell might have been better off with someone else, he thought now, Mick Power from Bay de Verde, for instance, or Joe Oliver from Gull Pond, both of whom had come courting, so she said; and both, of course, were sweet. Mick had gone all out to get her. But Arthur won her. Spent twenty long years with her. And buried her.

He saw water falling on his sore hand. Then he realized the water was tears. He was crying! And he knew why. "Ellen Catherine Cooney (1903-1954). Beloved wife of Arthur Cooney. R.I.P." One word in that was a lie, and he'd been wrong to have it chiselled above her bones.

He asked for forgiveness again, for what he knew was a bigger sin than swearing. "I am heartily sorry for having offended Thee," he said in the familiar words of contrition, "I detest my sins most sincerely." It was Christmas. He might be let off. It was a time for letting sinners off.

He felt he wouldn't be let off; he'd have to pay.

He looked at his hand and his boat and the thought came to him that he'd already been paying. But the sin was a big one.

He didn't know what his mother had done with the unnamed man; he wasn't prepared to say. It might have been only a passing fancy, a look, a smile, any of which would have maddened his father. It might have been nothing at all, the accidental mention of a name. But he asked forgiveness for any sins she might have committed. "Not that I'm sure, mind," he said out loud.

He asked the same for the many sins he knew for sure his cantankerous old sonofabitch of a father had certainly committed. Yet he said: "Let them fall on my head, let the old man have peace." He paused. "Let me stand in for him, I'm all he has left. Wipe the slate clean."

Snow was falling steadily into the darkening ocean. The engine sputtered, coughed, roared along, lifting the bow of the skiff, which then fell as into an abyss, slapping the water hard, driving spray up and over her deck. At times the propeller came out of the water and the skiff seemed to stall atop a wave; but she settled down in the curve of the one behind, lurching sideways, then straightening up, under Arthur's firm grasp, to face the next challenge. The trawl-rocks bounced on the floor-boards. He should have thrown them overboard. Too late now. It wasn't possible to spare his right hand. Arthur held the tiller with it and bailed water from the engine room with the other. Now and then he took the compass out of the bag and adjusted his course.

The 6-Atlantic. No finer engine.

He'd just sighted his dory through the blowing snow when the engine gave a half dozen fast strokes, shrieked, then stopped, dead. The dory's shape dwindled to a shadow and vanished.

If he took time to try and start the engine, he'd forget where he'd seen the dory. Arthur grabbed the sculling oar, stuck it out through the hole in the stern, held the end with his sore right hand and the pin with his left, and sculled toward the place the dory had been. It was his right hand and arm that had to work harder.

After a few minutes the dory reappeared, tossed in breaking seas. Pushing hard, he got closer. Then he pulled in the oar and ran forward, catching the dory's painter with the boat hook and hauling it over the stem of the skiff. He put the skiff back on her mooring. He hove the fish in the dory, leaving the bait-tub behind, lashed down, with the gasoline can packed securely in it. He rolled himself into the dory, shoved away from the skiff and made it to the beach. Morey's truck was waiting for him, along with a dozen men and boys.

"Bit on the rough side out there today," Morey's driver said after the dory was winched up and the fish boxed safely in the truck.

"Allan Morris's taxi dropped something off on your platform," Will Woodfine said.

Arthur headed home. "I'm not doin' it," he said, halfway up the lane.

At eight o'clock Arthur left his house, locking the door in case some of the youngsters went janneying early. The box Allan Morris brought was under his left arm. He had his suit on. Anyone who looked at his right hand might have noticed an iodine-stained bandage.

The squall of wind was now little more than a breeze and it had stopped snowing, though it was damp underfoot because of the wet weather earlier. The full moon lit up the cove.

He saw Will Woodfine coming toward him. Will was on his way to nine o'clock mass; it would take him an hour to walk the two hundred yards to the church, Arthur knew, since on Christmas Eve his habit was to drop in on neighbours along the way to have a glass or two of malt beer.

Arthur thought of darting up Foley's Lane to avoid him. But decided not to.

"Evenin', Arthur," Will said, stopping.

"Evenin', Will." Arthur slowed down.

"Fine evenin' now."

"Fine evenin'."

"Weather passed off."

"Yeah, passed off."

"Still a bit windy."

"Bit windy."

"How's the hand?"

"Good."

"Goin' t' mass?"

"I think I'll go tomorra'."

"Goin' over t' Timothy's?"

"No, Will. Maybe tomorra'."

"Goin' . . . ?"

But Arthur had slipped by.

He got to the gate, opened it, walked slowly to the platform. He took the brown paper off the parcel so that what was inside could be seen through the cellophane, and tucked the paper between the edge of the platform and the clapboard. The board was loose; it needed a nail or two. The platform, too, should be fixed up; he ran his expert eye over it.

The light was on over the porch door. The door had a silver star on it. Tinsel, neatly cut.

"Damnedest thing I ever did," he said.

He knocked.

She came out. "Why, Arthur Cooney," she said. "Well, if this isn't . . ."

"I brought you something," he said, handing her the box of four red roses with his left hand. He held his right hand behind his back, as far as the arm would take it. "Merry Christmas to you."

"Well, I never . . ." she stammered, holding the door open. "How nice of you."

"I heard you like flowers, so . . ."

"It's very nice of you to think of me, Arthur," she said. "Very sweet. Merry Christmas to you, too. Won't you come in?"

Arthur said nothing. He paused for a second, thinking, two nices, one sweet, I can live with that. If that's . . .

"Coming, Arthur?" she asked.

He glanced furtively skyward.

Then he cleaned the mud off his shoes on the mat, followed her inside and shut the door tight behind them.

Charlie and the Paper Boy

DAVID WEALE

He grew up poor, in a large family of brothers on the Miramichi. When he was old enough to work he became a lumberjack, and with his thick tree-trunk of a body and large powerful hands, he looked every inch the part. But as a young man he gave up the life of the woods for another vocation. He became an entertainer, and by the time his life was over, his rich baritone voice, gregarious disposition and mischievous stage antics had established him as one of the country's best known and most beloved troubadours.

His name was Charlie Chamberlain, and during the 1950s and 1960s he became famous across the country as the lead male vocalist in the downeast band Don Messer and the Islanders. Charlie was always a show-stopper. Whether at a one-night stand in some small Maritime community, on-stage in Hamilton or Calgary, or in front of the CBC television cameras, he could take a song to the hearts of his audience in a way that was the envy of other performers. "He was a good-hearted, great fella," recalled an acquaintance, "and the sadder the song the better he liked it. He'd make himself cry and make everyone else cry, too."

Charlie was, perhaps more than anything else, a master of musical nostalgia. His sincere, even maudlin renditions of traditional Irish folksongs, favourite hymns or popular ballads were delivered with such unabashed sentimentality that his listeners felt somehow comforted and reassured. He touched them in deeply familiar places, and they loved him for it.

In 1953 Charlie and the rest of the band were living on the Island. Charlie had a house in Charlottetown, on Churchill Avenue, and on the afternoon of the day before Christmas he put in a call to his long-time friend, Russell Downe, inviting him to his place for a little talk and a few tunes. Russell was happy to oblige. He grabbed his guitar and went over, and before long the two men were seated on the edge of two chairs in the living room, one on either side of the Christmas tree, having their own little Christmas concert. They sang some carols as well as other favourites and were right in the middle of "Down in the Little Green Valley" when the doorbell rang.

It was a little fellow from up the street, the paper boy, who had come to collect his paper money. "Come on in," Charlie invited, and began to fumble in his pockets for the right change. While this was happening the boy, wide-eyed, was staring at the tree. Charlie noticed his look of wonderment and asked, "Do you like my tree?"

"Yes, sir," said the boy.

"Do you have a tree like that at your house?" Charlie asked off-handedly.

"No, sir," was the soft, flat reply.

"You don't have a Christmas tree!" Charlie exclaimed incredulously.

"No."

"Do you have a turkey?"

"No."

"Any presents?"

"No."

By this point in the conversation, Charlie, guitar in hand, was looking quite disconcerted by the boy's replies.

"Why haven't you got anything for Christmas?" he queried.

"My father's not workin'. He told us we're gonna have Christmas next year," was the boy's answer.

"Do you have any brothers or sisters?"

"Yes."

"Well!" stated Charlie emphatically, "You must have a tree! That's all there is to it!"

With that he laid his guitar on the couch and walked over to the tree. His friend Russell watched in amazement as Charlie proceeded on a course of action that was so unexpected and so impulsively generous that, after all these years, it stands out vividly in his memory. "I will remember it as long as I live," he told me.

Charlie unplugged the Christmas tree lights, then reached through the branches and, with his big right hand, picked the tree off the floor — lights, ornaments, tinsel and all. Tree in hand, he marched out to the kitchen where a turkey was lying in the sink, the neck flopped out over the side. With his left hand he grabbed the turkey. "Open the door, Russell," he ordered. "We're going to make a little call."

"Show me where you live, young fella," he said, as he stepped outside, pulling the tree through the door behind him.

"It was quite a procession," recalled Russell. "The boy was ahead, and behind him came Charlie carrying the turkey and the tree, with the cord from the lights dragging in the snow. I was bringing up the rear, shaking my head in amazement and laughing at the look of Charlie heading off up the street."

When they arrived at the paper boy's house his mother came out on the porch. "Open your door wide," shouted Charlie.

The woman, taken completely by surprise, blurted out, "Oh, my Lord! Mr. Chamberlain! I don't believe it."

"Well, we're here anyway," retorted Charlie as he swooshed by her into the house. He proceeded to set the tree in a corner, and then he strode out to the kitchen, at the back of the house, where he deposited the massive Christmas bird in the sink.

"Merry Christmas," he called out, as he exited the house as abruptly and flamboyantly as he had entered.

As they walked back, Russell reminded Charlie that he now had neither a tree nor a turkey at his own place and that the stores were closing in just a few minutes. "You're right, Russell," replied Charlie, a triumphant grin on his face. "I don't have a turkey and I don't have a tree. But I made someone happy. I've got that."

It was the kind of episode someone could write a song about — the kind of song Charlie Chamberlain would have loved to sing.

Seasonings

ROBERT GIBBS

My dad was our link to the Victorians. He was past twenty when the old queen died in 1901. His parents, immigrants from England, had a shop on Sydney Street in Saint John. It was mainly a candy store; my grandfather was a candymaker. My Uncle Syd inherited the house and shop, which he turned into a post office and music store. He was a maker, repairer, and player of stringed instruments. He also sold school supplies and candy, the pink, white and brown-striped rock he forged on the marble slab his father had used. The shop, just up the street from our very old school, Victoria, was a favourite with kids.

Only when I went to England did I realized how English my uncle's shop was. Even today there are small shops and local post offices with the same plain furnishings, high ceilings and wire-cage partitions that I remember from my childhood.

My dad and his brother grew up on annuals sent from England of the *Boys' Own Paper*. They were massive books from the 1880s and 1890s, which we inherited, which we pored over until they fell apart, and which sometimes had us believing we were English schoolboys of that era. Like many English families, Dad's had a set of Dickens, and he kept a copy of *Oliver Twist* in his shop — workshop we'd call it now — on King Square. The Cruikshank illustrations, so dark and gothic and strong, took me into a world that seemed to be to be continuous with my own — the dark alleys and hovels and white-faced slum children we lived a step or two away from. When I first walked out of Liverpool Street

Station in London, I felt the kinship of a familiar home place. The smells, particularly that of coal gas, were especially haunting.

My father's jewellery repair shop, up two flights in a little wooden building squeezed between larger ones, was one of our Christmas centres. In early fall, Dad would secure from my mother some available tins, Magic Baking Powder, Coleman's Mustard or Baker's Cocoa; he would cut slits in the lids, which he would then solder on tight. These Christmas banks we'd open in December and find maybe a dollar or more in nickels and coppers, depending on how diligently we'd saved what we earned for chores. My mother once paid my two brothers each a quarter for keeping silent for an hour. Needless to say, I didn't qualify, being the mouth of the family.

Christmas shopping didn't take us long, and the rest of the afternoon, singly or with my brothers, I'd spend in Dad's shop, rummaging through boxes of scrap jewellery or doing simple tasks like drawing silver or brass through the graduated holes of a wire-plate. Sometimes there would be an orange-crate from Eaton's groceteria stock-room, which was on the ground floor of Dad's building. Dad used the dark South American wood of the ends for making doorplate supports and burned the rest. The soft pinkish tissues he'd have us smooth out and string on a circle of wire for use in the communal toilet downstairs.

Dad used a blowpipe and charcoal for melting precious metals. His shop had gas, coal gas extracted in the old works on Carmarthen Street, installed. You'd smell it as soon as you entered the building. Mr. Cowie used it, too, in his jeweller's workshop downstairs. He was English, as was Mrs. C., a formidable woman with a fishwife's tongue, who always referred to me as "poor little devil." The gas smell, common in Saint John only to workshops like my father's, I later recognized as an English smell, a London smell. Though the gas laid on now in English houses and businesses is natural and odourless, that smell lingers in some older premises, particularly if you're climbing creaky stairs.

On December nights, when we'd walk home with our dad, we'd go through the Square. Christmas-tree lots, farmers and woodsmen, horses and sleds, with their attendant smells would have taken over. Large woollen mitts would slap together, heavy feet, men's and horses', would stomp, and steams from breath and manure would rise against the cold.

Sometimes we'd turn the other way and enter the old City Market. It was not too unlike what it is today, especially in smells — raw poultry; fish, salt and fresh; dulse; bunched sage and savory; sprays and wreaths of pine, fir and spruce. Dad loved old cheddar, head cheese and English brawn, all of which my mother abhorred, though she put up with his offerings, especially in the good-will season. Only once do I remember her hanging a package of especially old cheese out on the clothesline. Sometimes, in the pre-war days when they were still available, he'd buy chestnuts to roast in the oven or on the grate. Our old house on Pitt Street had no central heating, but it had three fireplaces, besides kitchen and hall stoves.

Our mother's kitchen was our other chief Christmas centre. The season would start in early fall, as soon as the pickles and preserves were done and stored away in pantries as cold as ice-boxes. Mum would dig out her once-a-year towering tin steamers and concoct her three dark cakes, one large, one middle-size and one small, but all richly loaded with raisins, nuts, dates, candied citron and peel. I loved to sniff the empty packs for smells unique to the season. Then, out would come our largest stew pot and the meat grinder for the making of mince meat, an ample supply, not just for Christmas but for much of the winter. Mum would explain that hers, though good, was never as good as her mother's, made with genuine deer meat.

In the week before the big day, Mum would get at her doughnuts and cookies, date-filled and ice-box, piling the plates high to cool, then storing the goodies in square biscuit tins. The kitchen would fill with, and spill into the whole house, cinnamon and yeast smells of her huge loaves of plum bread, the plums being those large seeded raisins she preferred to cook with. Finally, she would stuff dates and roll them in sugar, a confection to be set out in glass dishes in the parlour, the cold, cold parlour. We used to sneak in early and purloin those goodies to munch in bed.

Our tree would come down from the Kingston Peninsula with Mr.

Bradley, a long-time friend of Dad's, whose sister had been one of his old flames. (She sent him withered violets when she learned of his marriage to Mum.) He would bring, too, our Christmas poultry, two very amply fed chickens. The tree was always a foot or so taller than our twelve-foot ceiling would accommodate, so Mum would have the sawed-off part from which to take branches. She would get Dad to drill holes in the bald places and fill them in, all the time scolding Mr. Bradley for his bare-assed trees, perhaps recalling those withered violets.

Once up, the tree would remain untrimmed until Christmas Eve after we kids were in bed. Mum would recall for us Christmases in Turtle Creek, her home in Albert County: how once her brother had got only coal in his sock for debunking Santa by calling him "old muddy Claws." We always wanted to hear again about the time she and her sisters had almost burned the house down by lighting the sparklers on their tree while their parents were out. We, who were familiar with sparklers as firecracker-day treats, couldn't imagine the brilliance of a tree lit with them, we with our strings of Japanese lights in series, which would all go out at once if there were one bum bulb among them. Grandma would link us to an earlier age with her songs and endless rhymes. She always came down for Christmas and the winter, bringing dried summer savory in bunches, as well as her liniments and soothing syrup, bought from an itinerant Rawleigh man.

The war years were good to us. Privations were slight, though often complained of. Our mother managed to maintain her traditional cooking by trading tea coupons for sugar with two of her sisters, who were working women and tea addicts. None of us kids drank tea; so Mum, while equally addicted, had coupons enough and to spare. It wasn't until I went off to England that I saw what scars and raw wounds the war had left — whole streets turned into scooped-out bomb-sites and Wren churches gutted and windowless.

London was for me a dream place. The first time I set foot on its rain-slicked pavements in the autumn of 1952, I was at home. Its air was raw and smelly; its bulky public buildings, soot blackened; its inhabitants, war-weary and much of the time queued up for one scarce item or another. But I loved it on sight (and smell and hearing) and still do, changed and unchanged as it is.

I had friends from home living there, in Bloomsbury, in a flat left over by the bombers from what had been a handsome terrace, Georgian, on Mecklenburg Square where Virginia Woolf had lived and her Hogarth Press. I managed to contact my friends, and they suggested I occupy their place for a couple of weeks over the holidays. It would be my first Christmas alone and away from home.

Arriving at King's Cross Station in early December, I decided, since I had only my club bag, I'd walk from there to Bloomsbury. It didn't look far in the *London A-Z* guide. On the train, coming through the fens, a heavier than usual mist had hung over the land, but I wasn't alarmed, for the pale December sun had a way of breaking through before it set between three and four o'clock. In the station, the mist strangely persisted; it caught in my throat and burned. Outside, I literally had to feel my way from lamp-post to lamp-post down Gray's Inn Road. This fog was a decisive visitation.

Cinemas and theatres were closed. The fog screened screens and veiled footlights. People were advised to stay indoors. Some with breathing problems choked and died. This last great poisonous shrouding stirred the government to legislate against coal-burning, industrial and domestic. So began the transformation I wasn't there to witness to the bright white London of today.

The fog cleared a few days before Christmas. I roamed and revelled, seeking out Dickensian pockets that had survived the raids and visiting the more ominous sites of Eliot's *The Waste Land*. I still love to walk from Charing Cross up the Strand and Fleet Street to St. Paul's, then on via Cheapside to the Tower and the Thames. I still on winter visits to my sister (who lives now in Harrow) like to pick up a bag of too-hot-to-handle chestnuts from a brazier in Trafalgar Square and savour their sweet, smoky mealiness. But then, my friends having departed for Scotland, I had to think about my own domestic arrangements.

My aim in preparing for my solitary feast was to make it as much like ours at home as I could. Some of the means — chow-chow, high-bush cranberry jelly, nuts, chocolates and parcels wrapped in green or red tissue with plenty of stickers — I had on hand from the huge box that had come from home. The chief item I had to purchase was the bird. Poultry was not rationed, so I had a free hand, but I decided on a modest-sized chicken. I walked out and blundered onto a poulterer's with all his birds — geese, turkeys and chickens — hung up by their feet with long necks, heads and eyes intact, dangling down. Overcoming my qualms about coping with such a specimen, I made my purchase, which the butcher obligingly decapitated. I brought it back in triumph, only to find it undrawn, and I spent the best part of an afternoon eviscerating it and scouring out its cavity for the stuffing. My one complaint was that I wasn't able to find summer savory, essential seasoning to our kind of homemade dressing. So I settled for a package of the prepared kind (which turned out to be surprisingly good).

I timed my Christmas Day to coincide with events at home, my overriding concern being to keep in as close touch with the family as feasible. (Long-distance calls, especially from overseas, were too rare in those days to have occurred to me, especially since even local London connections were notoriously difficult.) The BBC with its rich musical offerings kept me company all day. On Boxing Day I sallied out and wandered down to the West End, where I was happy to join a meagre audience at Drury Lane Theatre for a matinée of *South Pacific*, not the most Christmasy of shows but its brassy Americanness somehow a touch of home.

My first absence from Christmas at home marked a break with the feasts of childhood, but it was not the first such nor the most crucial one. No, it was not the war, though that sombred our holidays, nor was it our passing from schooldays into the army, the work world, and college. It happened two years after the war ended, the Christmas Eve my father died.

The season was always my father's busiest, and we were used to his working late, often well into Christmas Eve, to engrave a last-minute bracelet or watch. That year was not an exception, even though he was weak from flu and had suffered recurrent chest pains. (Our doctor had expressed no alarm and had prescribed a blood tonic only, Beef Iron and Wine.) My mother got Dad to bed as early in the evening as possible, while we continued with our usual preparations.

That night and the days that followed are a blur. I do recall us kids assembling in the kitchen to pray for Dad as his cries of pain sounded from upstairs. The doctor came after midnight with his needle and went. Then Mum called us. I realized, I think, at that time that a breach had opened, not to be closed, in our togetherness as a family.

It was seventeen years later that I was able to face that night and write about it.

ROBERT GIBBS

The Death of My Father

ROBERT GIBBS

My father died Christmas Eve in
the middle of the night and
the green breath of the big tree
in our front room mixed with
the dark smell of death upstairs.
My mother called us in and said
"I think he's gone, your father's gone," and
seeing the slack black gape
of his mouth, I thought of the cold
bluebodied turkey in the fridge downstairs.

A praiseworthy man, on Sundays out to meeting
with praise of God in his eyes, and not
a pigeon missed with breadcrumbs nor
a dickybird in the gutter, and not
a tomcat passed with his ruff
unruffled or his rough purr unpurred.
A man simple enough, in love with sunsets
and butter-and-eggs by the railways tracks
where we took our Sunday walks around
the waterfronts, and afterwards reformed
baptist hymns, which his thick fingers pressed
from the thick strings of his cello.

I see you Dad on your high stool in
your shop, eyeglass wrenched into play and
fine curly gold turning up and off from
your keen graver as you cut "Love for
always and always" on the inside circus
of a secondhand wedding ring.
And how we hoarded the dust from
every sweeping in a tall black can and
shipped it away to the refiner to have
your gold and silver letters, all
your days' cuttings from coffin plates
and baby spoons   cradled out
in his white secret fire and
sent back   sent back.

ROBERT GIBBS

The Consolation of Pastry

PAUL BOWDRING

Mother discovered the croissant late in life — I remember it was on her sixty-fifth birthday, when my sister, Ruth, and I took her down to the Newfoundland Hotel for brunch. And after a lifelong loyalty to the lemon cream cracker, brief affairs with the bagel and the English muffin, and an abiding, if intermittent, affection for the jam jam, the tea bun and the apricot square, the croissant was now her absolute favourite. As Ruth said, it was nice to see her being enthusiastic about something, even if it was only a piece of pastry. After Dad's death just before Christmas the year before, she had lost interest in just about everything and for a while seemed to live only on tea and toast.

After I'd started high school, Dad had taken me aside one day and asked me if I'd like to call him "Des." Without giving it any thought, I said yes, but after a few attempts, the bald and unfamiliar diminutive had (if you'll forgive me) desiccated on my tongue. Like distances at sea, from "Dad" to "Des" had been much farther than I thought.

I'd settled on "Desmond," which was what Mother had always called him, though the rest of the world knew him only as Des. Before that I had experimented with "Father Des" and "Father Desmond." Being a lapsed Catholic, he'd got a great kick out of that. I spoke his name, however, only when I had to, and always found it hard to avoid a comic and ironically formal tone.

"Desmond obviously deplores the present government's tendency toward largesse," I would intone in response to one of his occasional but loud anti-welfare barks, from which the bite of conviction was so obviously lacking. Despite the relative prosperity — admittedly hard won — of his later years, he had grown up too poor himself to be able to deny a few crumbs of subsistence to anyone else.

"What's he on about now?" he would reply, addressing my mother.

"Eat your food, dear," was all she would ever say.

Ruth had continued to call him "Daddy," though we were just a year apart and she had received the same invitation. For a while, though, during a brief but intense love affair with the noble and handsome Adam of *Bonanza* fame, she had taken to calling him "Pa." Although I had expected him to flare up at this, he had shown only the slightest hint of distaste, looking at her sometimes and moving his mouth as if he had just licked a postage stamp or had something stuck between his teeth. Nor was he much bothered by "Sugar Daddy," which she had adopted for a time during our university years.

But he had never been that sweet, and now that he was gone, the formality of "Desmond" sometimes felt just right. Once in a while, however, "Father Des" would slip from my tongue, perhaps because it recalled the smile that had sweetened his face whenever I had used it. It wasn't often that I'd seen my father smile.

After Mr. Jackman's space heater had exploded early one cold fall morning and almost burned his house to the ground, Mother, whose row house was attached to his, decided to move out of the downtown. Mr. Jackman had escaped through a hatch onto the roof. He hadn't been outside his house in years, and a fireman found him hiding behind a chimney with his arms around his head, perhaps more in fear of that blinding ball of fire rising in the eastern sky than the smoke and flames that were rising through the open hatch.

"Just a skeleton in a singlet" was how Mother had described him, having watched a fireman carry him down a ladder. She used to rap on his door and leave plates of food on his step, but he was almost deaf, and most of the time it had been left there only to be eaten by dogs or cats.

She was now living in an apartment on the outskirts of town, and on Christmas Day the taxi driver entertained me en route with a half-baked history of the croissant delivered in a St. John's brogue so well preserved it might have been buried in a peat bog for the past two hundred years, like half the artifacts in the museums of his ancestral homeland. He'd been inspired by the large plastic bag of croissants sitting on my lap, beneath which was Mother's Christmas present, a copy of Bing Crosby's *White Christmas* that I'd found in a Woolco record bin downtown. It was her all-time favourite album, and if the mood struck her, she might play it at any season of the year. During the Terrible Two's our daughter Anna had remoulded the original record into a serviceable concave kitchen platter by inserting it into an electric heater, and Kate had been unable to find a replacement.

We drove through the suburban wasteland of northeast St. John's, through Centennial Meadows, Eastmeadows and the perversely named Spruce Meadows, where trees, it seemed, had been feared more than triffids, and had been just as heartlessly dispatched. To replace them, fortress-like fences had been erected as buffers against the heavy traffic on the main streets. I imagined wary suburbanites stationed behind them with anti-triffid weapons: flame-throwers and mortar-bombs.

Between two sections of a strip mall, a fluorescent OPEN sign shone optimistically in one of the drably curtained windows of the forlorn facade of a Chinese restaurant and take-out. There seemed to be one like it in almost every part of town, a mythical chain whose links were only in your head. It was probably the area's original eatery, but was surrounded now by gleaming and gilded competitors.

In a car that didn't seem to have a single shock remaining, we negotiated the frost heaves and hollows, the ruts and potholes, in the winter pavement. The cab driver informed me that the croissant was Austrian, not French, as most people believed, and had been invented in the seventeenth century during the Turkish siege of Vienna to strengthen the people's resolve. Turkey, he reminded me, had a crescent on its flag, so every time a loyal Viennese citizen ate a croissant with his coffee, he was symbolically gobbling up another Turk. He had once worked under a pastry chef in a Montreal hotel. He had very cold hands, he said. Perfect for pastry.

The driver was still talking as we pulled up in front of Mother's apartment building in Vinland Villa, a seniors' complex of dreary brick blocks whose aging exteriors matched the facades of their residents. In the fading afternoon light a rusting replica of a Viking longboat was listing to starboard in the common courtyard. It sat upon a crumbling concrete pedestal floodlit by high-intensity lamps.

This man knew more about pastry than I had the inclination or cash to find out. With the meter running, I waited patiently while he licked the last few flakes of his story from his perfectly cold fingers and then finally got out of the car to open the door to let me out, as there wasn't a single door or window handle on either side of the back seat.

I laid the croissants and the record on top of the cab as I searched through my pockets for my wallet.

"A little on the dark side," he said, peering through his dark glasses at the pastry in the plastic bag. In the eerie blue light of the mercury-vapour lamps, the croissants gleamed Dali-esque.

"Merry Christmas," I said, handing him two tens.

He smiled and nodded his black watch cap at me, which had a dreadlock tassel in Rastafarian red, yellow and green.

"You're not dressed properly," Mother said predictably, having given me the once-over through the security eye in her apartment door. "The radio said it's five below."

And the gifts I had come bearing were no distraction. She took them without acknowledgement and stared severely at my bare hands and head, my raglaned body, my sneakered feet. I removed the coat and sat down on the wooden bench in the hallway to take off what she always called my sad excuse for boots.

"Why are you still wearing this get-up in the middle of winter?" she said, hanging the offending piece of khaki in the closet, out of her sight.

"It's not that cold, Mother," I said, in my useless defence. "Anyway, I didn't walk way out here. I came in a cab."

I pictured myself hobbling in here at seventy-five, when Mother would be one hundred and four, and having this very same conversation.

What seemed fanciful, even absurd, at twenty seemed merely inevitable at forty.

There were three clocks in Mother's apartment, but none of them were working. They hadn't been working for a long time.

"What does it matter to me what time it is," she'd said to me the last time I mentioned them.

Under a glass dome on the dinette sideboard, an ornate brass-tone clock with black spade hands and a pendulum of rotating carousel horses said eleven-fifteen. Dad had given it to her on their fortieth anniversary. The carousel wasn't rotating now because the battery probably hadn't been replaced for years. Beside the clock, in a gilt-wood frame, was an out-of-focus photograph of Ruth and me that Mother had taken at Ruth's university graduation.

On the wall in the living room, a large electric clock with radiating wooden arms alternating with metal spokes — a stylized sun — said twenty to seven. When it was plugged in, it made a sound like a fast-moving locomotive, but the hands of the clock didn't move at all.

On the kitchen wall a clock with a red plastic frame, a miniature hula hoop, said half past four. It too was unplugged, but in ten minutes it would be right for the second time that day.

There seemed to be some minor profundity here, some soft philosophical currency that my mind tried hard to negotiate as Mother and I sat at the chrome table beneath this clock in the windowless kitchen of her one-bedroom apartment, drinking King Cole tea and eating Purity partridgeberry jam and croissants.

She said she didn't want to eat too much because she was going over to Aunt May's for Christmas dinner. But as I hadn't had any lunch, and as this was probably going to be my Christmas dinner, I ate, as Mother remarked frankly, like a horse. Or perhaps like a loyal Viennese. I might have been trying to rally my own resolve.

The croissants were a sensational distraction, so to speak, and before you could say thesis-antithesis-synthesis, my philosophical fog had dissolved into dew. The pleasure, the power, the consolation of pastry was not something to be taken lightly.

Mother's problem, however, was getting her hands on it. Mr. Bowman, the downtown grocer with whom she had dealt all her life and who still delivered, free of charge, her meagre carton of groceries once a week, did not carry the croissant. And in the outrageously expensive deli in the strip mall across from her apartment building, the only source of pastry in the neighbourhood, the owner, who was also the baker and the cashier, was in the habit of intimidating his customers by correctively echoing their requests and then repeating them audibly over and over to himself as he filled them.

Mother had enough trouble with the pronunciation of the word as it was, having little flair for foreign tongues, but this man's repetitive hissing of the word "croissant" had so unnerved her on her first visit to this deli that she had never gone back again. She had refused to settle for more pronounceable but more pedestrian alternatives, though I had armed her with "puff pastry" and "crescent roll."

And so it was that I became her lifeline for these unobtainable delicacies, which she savoured almost as much as Antonio Salieri his Nipples of Venus. They were no small solace to her in her later years, when she was besieged by sorrows I could hardly name. And whenever I called her to see how she was getting on, she would always request a fresh supply — a large secure fresh supply — enough, indeed, for a sizeable hoard. She stored them in her refrigerator in wide-mouth Masons.

Mother had always been a big fan of the Mason jar, and her kitchen cupboards were chock-full of them — the wide-mouth Mason being her favourite. Up until a few years ago, she had used them only for homemade jams and pickles, but she didn't bother with that any more, for, as she said, "Who's going to eat them?" Now she was using her large stock of jars to store her entire food supply, meagre as it was, and into them went everything from lemon creams to kippers — and, of course, when she could get them, her entire cache of fresh croissants.

After finishing our tea, we went into the living room and sat side by side on the sofa to open our Christmas presents. On the coffee table was a miniature Christmas tree in a green plastic pot covered in cheery red tinfoil, a present from Ruth via one of the local florists. Three Styrofoam ornaments hung from its cilia-like branches — a Little Drummer Boy's tiny white drum with drumsticks attached, a red bell with a green ribbon and a child's alphabet block with coloured letters. Between the tinfoil and the plastic pot was a small rectangular card that said, "All my love, Ruthie." Sticking out of the soil was a narrow plastic strip on which was stamped "Norfolk Island Pine."

Besides the few greeting cards on the sideboard, this was the only sign of Christmas in Mother's apartment. Next to the tree were copies of the *Sacred Heart Messenger* and the *Fatima Times*, which her childhood friend, Sister Perpetua, had been sending her faithfully every month since I was a child. Beneath these was a large and official-looking *Reader's Digest* Super Grand Prize Sweepstakes Certificate with Mother's name inscribed on it in computer-generated, inch-high bold capitals. It informed her that it had been "duly recorded" that she had passed through the first two stages in a selection process and that her further participation was "herewith requested" — a prompt reply and a sub- scription renewal cheque for twenty-five dollars, which would make her eligible for Stage Three, a chance to win ONE MILLION DOLLARS.

I had given Mother a one-year subscription to the *Reader's Digest* as a birthday present about five years ago, but she had let it lapse, probably because Ruth had done me one better — given her a three-year subscription to the *Catholic Digest*. The secular digest, however, had not lost faith in her; after five years they were still trying to persuade her to renew her subscription. Unfortunately, the effect of this most recent and impressive-looking solicitation was undermined by a hot rose plastic packet stuck conspicuously to the back of Mother's Sweepstakes Certificate. Labelled, appropriately, CONFIDENTIAL, it looked exactly like a condom. If Mother had noticed that, she would have made a special trip to the garbage chute. Inside was a Prize Validation stamp to be stuck to the postage-paid envelope enclosed for her prompt reply.

Mother, who was a sock artist of some renown with a broad and unusual palette, had somewhat surprisingly knit me two identical pairs of grey wool stockings. Upon this conservative canvas, however, she had designed a colourful configuration of three intersecting diamonds to be displayed by the outer ankles. Two smaller diamonds, formed by the intersection of the blue figures with the central yellow one, appeared to be a shade of green, but the colour kept blurring in and out, and I couldn't tell if it was in the wool or in my eye. She was borrow-ing tricks from the Impressionists, juxtaposing primary colours instead of mixing them, and letting the eye of the beholder blend them itself.

Inside one sock was a small rectangular tin of Erinmore pipe tobacco, the brand Dad had always used in his Peterson pipe. I didn't bother to tell her that I'd given up pipe smoking. The Christmas before he died he had given me an identical briar and a soft brown leather pouch filled with Erinmore tobacco. He had also given me duplicates of all his pipe-smoker's paraphernalia: beechwood filters and hemp pipe cleaners, scoops and picks for scraping dottle out of the bowl, a tamper for pressing fresh tobacco in, a clip-on perforated damper for windy days and a lighter whose flame shot out the side instead of the top, so that you didn't scorch your fingers while lighting up. You almost needed a small suitcase to cart all this stuff around.

That, and the fact that I could never keep the thing lit, damper or no damper, had discouraged me from becoming even an irregular pipe-smoker. Not to mention my chronic self-consciousness about having that Sherlock Holmes sheep-crook hanging from my lip. And being a heavy cigarette smoker at the time, I didn't have the meditative temperament required to go through the smoking equivalent of the tea ceremony every time I needed an infusion of nicotine.

Crowned with the traditional Santa Claus cap, Bing Crosby's disembodied head was prominently displayed on the cover of his *White Christmas* platter. Set in an eternally youthful face, a pair of unnaturally blue eyes and teeth whiter than any white Christmas shone upon Mother, his loyal and adoring fan of forty years. His face was artificially tanned with make-up for the flash bulbs and the TV lights. Beneath his chin was a bow tie made of holly leaves and berries attached to a white fur collar that matched the trim and tassel on his cap.

Mother beamed back at this boyish face for several minutes. At one time she used to call him Harry, having discovered his real name in a movie magazine. It was beyond her, she said, why anyone would want to call himself Bing.

She struggled in vain with the tight plastic wrapping before handing the record to me to open. As I laid it on the turntable of her tiny record player and lifted the tone arm to remove a belly-button bushel of lint from the needle, it struck me that I didn't know whether or not Harry was still alive.

"Is Bing dead?" I ventured, but Mother had quietly left the room.

Bing himself replied unequivocally, or unequi-vocally, with a sprightly rendition of "It's Beginning to Look a Lot Like Christmas," but followed that with a somewhat solemn "God Rest Ye Merry, Gentlemen."

To put it mildly, he had never been one of my musical favourites. Perhaps it was simply because my parents liked him. At a certain age you stop listening not only to your parents but also to whatever they're listening to. At any rate, the song arrangements certainly didn't help, the thin, tinny-sounding orchestras that always backed him up, the bloodless mixed choruses and chorales, and especially the chirrupy chipmunk sister trios that seemed to pop up out of the holes of every song. But when Bing himself got a chance to sing . . . well . . . on this Christmas day I began to warm to him, I had to admit.

He was singing a very silvery "Silver Bells" when Mother came back into the living room. She had taken off her sweater and slacks and put on a semi-festive plum red dress with a white belt and matching orthopaedic shoes. She sat down in the rocker and put her feet up on the humpty.

"Why don't you come on over to May's with me," she said. "You know how much they love to see you."

"I don't think so, Mother," I said. "You go on, I'll just sit around here for a while."

"They like to eat a bit early. May's always asking about Anna. 'Baby Anna,' she still calls her. I says, 'May, she's almost seven years old.' 'She was a baby the last time I saw her,' she says. It's too bad that woman never had a child of her own."

Mother's face darkened, and she picked up several magazines from the end table.

"I don't suppose you heard Silas Keough died," she said.

"No."

"Poor Elsie, I should call her up. I didn't know about it until he was buried. May saw the notice in the paper but that was about a week after the funeral. She's got papers lying around for weeks before she reads them. She got on the phone to Mrs. Kenny, my God that woman knows a terrible lot of things. She was talking to Elsie on the phone and she told her she was in the hospital when Silas died. She'd been phoning home all morning to tell Silas they were letting her out and when he didn't answer she said she was afraid to go back home. They took her home in the ambulance and she asked them to go in ahead of her and check. They found him on the bathroom floor.

"They brought him home to bury him but she went right back after the funeral. I don't think I seen them since they went away. That must have been twenty years ago."

Her voice trailed away and she began browsing distractedly through copies of the *Sacred Heart Messenger*, the *Catholic Digest*, and the *Fatima Times*. And as I sat watching her and listening to Bing begin a spooky but seductive rendition of "I'll Be Home for Christmas," I had a sudden fantastic thought.

In *The Secret Life of the Unborn Child*, one of the many baby books I had read before Anna's birth, there was a story about a man who had been a musical prodigy. He had become a conductor at the tender age of thirty-five, mere infancy for conductors, many of whom are still waving the wand well into their nineties, and though he had received his musical training on the violin, he discovered to his surprise that he knew the cello parts of certain scores by heart, sight unseen. The mystery was solved when he informed his mother about his strange gift. She herself had studied the cello and played with an amateur orchestra in her younger years. It turned out that the pieces he knew by heart were the very ones she had been learning to play when she had been pregnant with him — and, I suddenly realized, Mother had been playing Bing over and over when she had been pregnant with me.

Jesus, Mary and Joseph, as Mother would say. Bing by osmosis? Insidious croonings rippling through the amniotic fluid as I floated innocent and inert? A biological programming that I was no longer able to resist? And it was a sad measure of my present emotional state that by the time he had reached the end of "I'll Be Home for Christmas," the syrupy old crooner had me by the heartstrings. My secret life was no secret anymore, but thank God it was osmotic and not aesthetic.

For Mother, though, it was a different story. Hers was a real emotional bond. She had first heard "White Christmas" in the fall of 1942, in the middle of the war, and she and Dad had danced to it at their wedding. He had been home on leave, and they got married on Christmas Day, not the whitest, but the coldest, Christmas in memory.

He gave her the record, along with a phonograph, as a combined Christmas and wedding present. On the flip side, appropriately enough, Bing sang "Let's Start the New Year Right." It was a new 78 rpm single that he'd bought from a soldier at Fort Pepperrell, the American forces base in the east end of St. John's and, as Mother had told me many times, she had listened to it all through the following year while she waited for him to come home for good.

Not that he was very far away. He had enlisted in the Newfoundland Militia in 1939 and was stationed about twelve miles away on Bell Island, manning the guns of the 1st Coast Defence Battery on the cliffs overlooking Conception Bay. He came home on leave just about every month.

From "overseas," his brother-in-law, Joe Kelly, used to say, tormenting him incessantly during his visits to the house after he'd retired and come back home from BC. He'd gone there to work as a logger in 1949. Joe spent most of his visiting time at loggerheads with Dad. They seemed to be prolonging some lifelong dispute that they had never been able to iron out.

Joe himself had actually served overseas, with a sort of paramilitary unit called the Newfoundland Foresters. "Logger" Joe, as Dad had always referred to the man whom Ruth and I liked to call "Uncle Mary" (but that's another story), had cut trees for the war effort on one of the great estates in Scotland, or, as Dad liked to describe it in defending himself against Joe's merciless needling, lounging on his arse in the heather while he and his comrades back home fought off German U-boats in Conception Bay. Joe would counter by characterizing this heroic activity as merely terrorizing the farmers in Broad Cove, on the other side of the bay, who, he claimed, used to harvest more shrapnel balls every September than turnips or carrots or Broad Cove blues.

Overseas or not, every time Dad left home Mother was convinced he would never come back. And her fears were not unfounded, for in September of 1942, and again in November, just a few weeks before their marriage, German submarines had sunk ore carriers anchored off the loading pier on Bell Island — ships that were loaded with iron ore for the Allies. They also torpedoed the pier itself, shocking the islanders from their sleep in the early hours of the morning and sending an aftershock of rumour that a German invasion was imminent. Though this, of course, had never occurred, Bell Island had been the only place in North America to have been attacked by the Germans during the war. The torpedoes had claimed four ships and sixty-nine lives. And it was a post-war sore spot with the old man, and additional ammunition for his tormentor, that the commander of one of those German submarines, Captain Friedrich Wilhelm Wissmann, had what Joe called the "Kraut version" of our family name. And not only that: Joe once wondered aloud if I had been named after him.

I had drifted into a dreamy and languorous repose due to the extreme thermostat settings in Mother's apartment. When I opened my eyes, I saw her standing at the window in her coat and scarf. She was waiting for May's husband, Ewart, to come and pick her up. Her hands were folded across her stomach, and her white purse hung from the crook of her arm. The purplish black fingers of a leather glove protruded from the open mouth of the purse like a multi-forked tongue from the jaws of a serpent.

PAUL BOWDRING

Large shadowy flakes of snow were falling through haloes of bluish light in the courtyard. Bing had almost reached the end of side two and was well into his signature tune, "White Christmas," when Mother put her hands up to her face and her shoulders began to shake with silent sobbing.

"What's wrong, Mother?" I said, sitting up, but knowing full well what was the matter.

She shook her head and exhaled a long sigh. Just then Bing began a foolish little whistle. Though I'd heard this tune a hundred times, I couldn't recall ever hearing that.

"Oh, Will," she said, right in the middle of it, "why did you have to go and leave that lovely girl . . . and what's going to become of Anna?"

I hadn't expected that and said, wearily, "Now, Mom, please don't start on that. It's Christmas," I added, with cheerless conviction.

She stopped crying, but continued to stand with her back to me, looking silently through the window at the snow falling before her eyes, upon the listing ship, upon the empty courtyard, upon the dead who were never really dead, and upon the useless grief of the living.

Candylights

CLARISSA HURLEY

Glasses would have been better on a night like that. Contacts were never quite as clear and mine had been in too long, fused to my eyes like plastic tics. But I hate looking into frames, as if the world is one more picture I have to watch from outside.

I tried the brakes and felt the rear end fishtail gently, like hips flouncing in stilettos. Greasy, as the meteorologists like to say.

Waterloo Row was festooned with bright chrome tears. Tiny bulbs outlined windows and spattered the dark green trees, icicle lights dangled from eavestroughs like running sap electrocuted into stillness, frayed edges whispering the violence of heat. So many are colourless now, a glaring metallic transparency called "white" by Martha Stewart and Wal-Mart. Where colour featured it was in carefully balanced, contrasting patterns.

I had just one stop to make before the Eve-Eve party at France's grandparents' place. The long, diffused frenzy of preparation was drawing to a close. Anticipation was creeping into present tense. I had gathered — gradually, painstakingly — now I would deliver.

"Eve-Eve" was the Langley's annual At Home on the twenty-third. It would be another tastefully silly evening — scotch and cigars, fine claret, smoked salmon, lobster and foie gras, all carefully accessorized. Someone would play the piano so that France and I could do our red-mini-skirts-and-stay-ups rendition of "Blue Christmas." There would be crackers, paper hats and candy canes for the children. At an appropriate point in the quiet revelry, Charlie "Chief" Langley would ask for our attention so that he could remind us what Christmas was really about and how lucky we all were. He would still do this tonight, with only a slight catch in his fluid baritone. It would be as other years; occasions should neutralize the past through replication, close the circle of time. There would be just one aberration: no eggnog this year. France's grandmother had always made that. The family had agreed that no one would be able to match Edie's nog; better let it be the stuff of sweet memory, like her.

The flat, shimmering green box lay beside me on the CD holder. I stroked the gold ribbon through my gloved finger. A hot cadence of blood erupted inside me.

"That time of year again," the cashier groaned amiably, taking my credit card as I dropped the red lace thong panty beside the "Please give generously to Kids with Cancer" cardboard box.

"Yes," I smiled back. Her remark reminded me of "that time of the month." It was important, I suppose, to euphemize references to occasions associated with birth.

"Wrapped up?" she asked, raising a high-plucked brow and twirling the stretchy V around a polished fingernail. "Or did you want to wear it out?" she giggled conspiratorially.

"No, this one's a wrap," I giggled back, as Jose Feliciano crooned "Feliz Navidad" somewhere above me.

Elm Street was perpendicular to Waterloo Row. I peered through the clear rectangle in the middle of my windshield, trimmed around the perimeter by two ragged inches of sticky snow.

Yves had bought and bought boldly. With the exception of an Acadian premier, few if any francophones had ever lived in this neighbourhood. I wondered if he knew he would always be *arriviste*. This was home to the FOFFs, Fine Old Fredericton Families, daintily, enigmatically pronounced "foofs." The riverfront runway nestling in the curve of the Saint John River guillotined the town: north/south. A nineteenth-century home here, a Foffdom, once required at least a three-generation indigenous dynasty. France's grandfather had been

Chief Justice of the Court of Appeal, sound credentials for the Row, in spite of the suspicion that he'd been an American early on. My mother's friendship with his daughters was bequeathed to France and me, so I had become a favoured intruder, a privileged poor relation, an Edward the Bastard. I had grown up with — if not on — the Row.

We would be sent outside at the parties to play in the snow, amidst a chorus of stern warnings not to go beyond the end of the garden. This stopped the year they found a snowman on the front lawn with carefully sculpted breasts and bright red nipples, frozen cranberries fished from the vodka punch, modelled on the tender purpley welts swelling on our own chests.

Edie figured we were old enough to learn to cook after that. She showed us how to crack and separate eggs for the eggnog and told us stories of her friend, the doctor's wife who had fallen from the train bridge backwards and gone through the ice one Christmas. A tortoiseshell sling-back sandal was found on the bridge, but she didn't show up until the next spring, amongst the fiddleheads near the Loyalist cemetery. Torn by bloated flesh, her black cocktail dress clung to her neck by a single strap, wafting like a bridal train behind her through the ferns. "Damned fishy" was what most people thought. It was said she had been having an affair with a local lawyer, a friend of her husband, and what kind of woman goes off to kill herself in heels and a short dress but no pantyhose? Fishy.

But Edie said no one would ever know now, so why tell tales about it?

"Only the future is there for sure, girls, the past melts like lipstick in a leather purse on a hot car seat. You can't wear it any more after that, so you might as well throw it out and try a new colour. If something is worth forgetting, then don't bother to remember it."

The next Eve-Eve, I gulped and gargled cranberry vodka to anaesthetize the bitter prickle of smoked, probing tongue in my mouth. I ran beyond the garden, heels puncturing the crusted snow on the riverbank, and penguin-dove onto the powder-dusted ice. The balm of cold against my breasts whitened the blotches left by hungry, sausage-plump nicotine fingers. My breath cleared a window on the frigid surface, and I prayed to see a frozen ghost, swimming to find a shoe. In the morning, France and I breathed into our coffee steam, brittle as spun sugar, "Absolutely overhung, darling." Last summer, after Edie's funeral, we sipped crantinis on the veranda and watched the river.

I skidded onto Elm Street, breathing deeply through the open window. Air warms even in this weather by the time it reaches your bronchi, but the suggestion of cool quelled the simmering beneath my breasts. It might be better to drop off Yves's present on the way home, well after midnight, but it seemed long overdue already. He had asked for it this time last year and I hadn't let him have it then. It would be most effective to get onto the roof somehow and drop it down the chimney, but I was wearing stay-ups, and besides, those old houses often boarded up their fireplaces now — too expensive, too inefficient. My gift could be entombed in a stone chimney, discovered one day by a real estate agent with beautifully blunt-filed fingernails and a horsey Chardonnay voice who would write up the discovery in her file on the house's historic lore. No. Yves must receive it. Propped up against the door would have to do. I'd make a discreet phone call from Langley's house; if his wife should answer, I would be pleasant and professional, advising her of a delivery. My explanations were well-rehearsed if I should be seen; people would talk otherwise. Talk is precious here; talk is the economy of a town like this.

It was this time last year that I had first met Yves. I didn't notice him until I stopped at the Second Cup, where a crab-shaped hand with tufted knuckles slid a fifty-dollar bill onto the counter in front of me to pay for my decaf caramel moccacino. Coffee with adjectives — bad habit. Plain coffee would have demanded merely a thank-you, but "European Beverages" weren't cheap, especially not the North American ones — worth about ten minutes of my time, by my calculations. So I listened to his stories about Montreal, and we rolled our eyes about life in small towns, he asked for my number, I said I'm in the book, told him my last name and went to buy cashmere socks for my boyfriend. That's Yves with a Y, like St. Laurent, the has-been designer.

His voice was throatier on the phone. He said he had seen the outline of my thong through the back of my pants when I had bent over to observe the muffin display. No one had heard of Monica Lewinsky then. He loved my "accent" — I said I didn't have one, just enunciated my consonants. He said we were meant to be together because of our names.

"Sam and Yves," he said. "Sounds like . . . Biblical, almost."

He said I was the best Christmas present he'd ever had, so I didn't give him one. We dined on Bollinger and whoopee pies; we dropped tiny marshmallows from his ninth floor condo balcony onto the white-lit tree on top of Tim Horton's. He gave me a gold necklace, some incense and a little ornate box. "The gift of the Magi, babe," he said.

"So what's with the box?"

"I didn't know what myrrh was. I thought maybe it's like *mur*, so I gave you four walls — that's how I want to keep you, inside my four walls forever."

"You're as cliché as Christmas, Yves."

"I know."

"That's why I love you," I tried to say, but his tongue muffled my words, and I felt the delicious comfort of repetition, revisiting, memory. I owed him a present, that was all. No damage desired or intended.

The car drifted to a snow-squeaking stop in front of the fenced garden. I stared at the decorations, sprawled in unruly contrast to the miniature monochromatic order of his neighbours' creations. Yves had the old lights, primary colours, randomly strung. Candlelights. *Daddy, Father Christmas is coming. Are you going to put up the candylights?* My father always reminded me that they were not the kind of candies you could eat. The explanation stayed the same as years went by. *Don't put them in your mouth, darling. They grow on trees once a year, but they aren't meant to be tasted. You don't need to know what they taste like, there are things you don't need to know.* Yves was putting up lights for his child now.

The car door thudded dully like distant cannon fire, then tingling silence under the wet, plummeting flakes. I approached the house tentatively, with the toe-heel toddler gait that works well on snow. If I fell and broke an ankle at this point, none of my explanations would stick. I'd never keep my stories straight.

The house was well lit, curtains open and welcoming. The door had a brass newspaper rack — the parcel would fit nicely. It was a simple act of trespassing. I needed to see Yves's house, to get into his frozen garden — the garden he had gated against me when he had grown tired of temptation.

The tree stood in the large bay window, girdled with gold ribbon, baubles hooked and dangling like exotic fat fishes poached from an aquarium. Yves stood terrifyingly close to the window talking to someone I couldn't see, pointing and laughing at something on the tree. The child, wrapped in a red and green blanket, clung to him, a tiny fistful of his shirt in her mouth. I wiggled my numbing toes and stepped carefully into the shadow of the entry way. Mouths move more slowly behind glass and under water. His body was larger, darker, proportions had altered. This was and was not Yves.

I backed slowly away from the window and walked a few steps onto the bed of pristine snow. It really must be a beautiful garden in the summer, I thought, as I faced the house and fell gently backwards onto the soft whiteness and made an angel beneath the coloured lights. Easter would be a better time to settle things with Yves, or Canada Day, perhaps. There would be fireworks then.

The frozen Saint John made a scimitar-arc in my rear-view mirror, gunmetal grey in the moonglow. I flicked drops of water from the little green box on the seat beside me.

It was late for Eve-Eve now, but France would get a kick out of the thong.

The New Sled

JOHN STEFFLER

The new sled
which the boy insists on calling
the GT Snowracer
and is no mere sled in his opinion
(the very word *sled* makes him laugh with brief
contempt as he pulls his woollen helmet on)
can swoop like an osprey
down the valley's white throat

can veer out of sight in the afternoon
which is only sky

and the boy, from a far speck,
against regrettable gravity, comes
wrestling his hawk-hearted companion back
to the father-held earth,
flame-faced and loud with something of what a hawk
must know.

The Christmas Kiss

WAYNE JOHNSTON

That fall, we practiced for the Christmas concert. There was to be a play within a play, the nativity story, as told by a young married couple to their children on Christmas Eve. The play would open in modern times, the family sitting round the fire. In this introductory scene, the father would begin to tell the Christmas story and then the curtain would fall. Minutes later, it would come up again on Joseph and Mary in the manger. At the end, an epilogue would bring us back to modern times.

My teacher that year was Sister Haymond, and she was in charge of the play. Assigning parts, she made every possible unpopular choice, except in making me Joseph. I was generally acknowledged to be perfect for the part. Mary, Sister Haymond said, must be played by someone with that name. Not counting Ambrosia, whom no one but the members of her family called Mary, there were two Marys in my grade eight class: Mary Smythe, a pretty, uppity blonde, and Mary Hart, a big girl who had a wart on the side of her nose and hands as grey as old rope. As luck would have it, Mary Hart was chosen to play the Blessed Virgin. Mary Smythe, Sister Haymond said, would play "the modern mother." I was by no means indifferent to these choices because, as St. Joseph, I would have to kiss the Virgin's cheek, and I would much rather have kissed Mary Smythe's cheek than Mary Hart's. Kissing Mary Hart's cheek, I would come perilously close to the wart. (Mary Hart was Mary Wart to people who didn't like her, and that was almost everyone.) To top it off, Sister Haymond revealed that the boy playing "the modern father" would get to kiss Mary Smythe full on the lips. A good-looking fellow named Tony McGillivray was chosen for that most coveted part.

The play, Sister Haymond said, would centre around the kisses. "The kiss of Joseph and Mary, chastely on the cheek. The somewhat less chaste kiss of father and mother, lightly on the lips. Chastely on the cheek, lightly on the lips, opposing ever so neatly the saintly purity of the Holy Family and the restrained, respectful passion of the modern Catholic family." Unfortunately, not everyone shared Sister Haymond's enthusiasm. Mary Smythe's father, for instance, wanted to know how lightly was the lightly his daughter would be kissed. And it was generally acknowledged that "full frontal kissing" was a bit much for grade eight boys and girls. In an editorial, Kellies monthly paper allowed that, "perhaps in this, the bard's advice is best: 'If it were done when 'tis done, then 'twere well it were done quickly.'"

Bowing to pressure, Sister Haymond announced that the "modern kiss" would not be rehearsed and would be left out altogether at the matinée for the younger children. "Instead of kissing," Sister Haymond said, "father and mother will smile affectionately." So as not to "unbalance the drama," the chaste kiss, too, would neither be rehearsed nor included in the matinée. There would be but one kiss of each kind, "chastely on the cheek," and "lightly on the lips," during the main performance. This seemed to satisfy most people. Tony McGillivray was disappointed, of course, and went around saying that, if there was only to be one kiss, he would make the most of it. It was hoped among the boys that Tony's kiss would bring Mary Smythe down to earth, "melt her snows," as my father put it. Mary herself was said to be dreading the kiss. She was said to have a boyfriend on the mainland, where her family vacationed every summer. Having a boyfriend on the mainland was about as stuck-up as you could get.

My father referred to the upcoming kiss as "the ravishment." He would not, he said, for anything in the world, miss the ravishment of Mary Smythe. He wondered if it could be arranged to have this sort of thing done on stage once or twice a week in Kellies. My mother, on the other hand, was the only person in Kellies who opposed even the chaste kiss. "My concerns, I assure you, are purely hygienic," she said. She had long believed that people were contagious, "not just when they're sick, but all the time." She said the body was a breeding-ground; it was a little-known fact that each of us carries around inside us at least one of every kind of disease-causing germ known to man. "Our own germs can't hurt us," she said. "Disease occurs when people start exchanging germs." She said we had to keep a proper distance between ourselves and others. We must imagine ourselves encased in a sterile bubble and let no one come inside it. "Remember the bubble, remember the bubble," my mother liked to say. "If someone comes too close, step back." What about married couples and families, I wondered. My mother said that, by the grace of God, a man and a woman became "immune" to one another at marriage. "I'm immune to your father, and he's immune to me." It worked with children, too. "We're immune to you, and you're immune to us. Isn't that wonderful?"

The problem with Mary Hart, my father said, was that her germs were bigger than mine. Her germs were "bully germs" that had been lifting weights and jumping rope since birth. My mother denied this, saying that Mary's germs were not bigger, "just more numerous." People said I was so holy that, when I kissed Mary Hart, her warts would disappear, then reappear on me. I didn't believe any of this, of course, but it made me think a lot about warts, and I was by no means opposed when my mother came home one day with something called Wart Guard and, every morning afterwards, rubbed it on my face and hands. It was a white cream that, when applied to the skin, vanished. My mother said it was best to start using it right away so that, by the time of the concert, a good resistance would have formed. She said that, on the night of the concert, I was to kiss Mary Hart with my mouth closed tightly. And afterwards, my father said, I must douse my head with disinfectant or pour boiling water down my throat. Or better yet, why not hose down Mary Hart before the play or get an exterminator to give her a good going over?

My mother, of course, could have refused to let me take part in the play. Indeed, it was originally intended that, at the end of the play, the

Christ child would rise in gown and golden halo and say, "God bless us, every one," and my mother had hoped that I would get that part. But as it turned out, it was decided that a doll and not a live Christ child would be used. As Sister Haymond said, any child old enough to stand and speak would not make a credible baby. "Anyway," my mother said, "it's not every day a person gets to be St. Joseph." My father reminded me that I was playing the part of the most uncomplaining cuckold who ever lived. My mother read from her *St. Joseph Daily Missal*: "Jesus, Mary and Joseph exemplify the proper relations that should exist between husband and wife and parents and children. We should often ask them to sanctify our families by their example and intercession." And she had me learn by heart the Litany of St. Joseph. Once, when my mother was not there to hear, my father pointed out the strangeness of using, as an exemplary family, one made up of a man and a woman who never made love and a boy who grew up to be God.

We practised three times a week throughout November. We had to make our own costumes and, as she was afraid that we would damage or lose them, Sister Haymond decided there would be no dress rehearsal. My parents did not make my costume until the day of the concert, a Saturday. My mother borrowed a wig from one of the St. Stephen's Sisters and decided to make me a beard from the box of hair under her bed. I said I didn't need a beard, but my mother said St. Joseph had to have one. She went to her room and, locking the door, made the beard by pasting bits of hair onto a piece of cloth. When she was done, it was big enough to cover half my face, and it had what my father called a wizard's whisker that hung down to my chest. She put it on me right away, using glue and string that looped about my ears. Then she put the wig on and then a robe she made from a blanket by cutting holes for my head and arms. To complete the costume, my father lent me a pair of his sandals. There was still an hour before we left, but it was decided that I would leave the costume on and wear it to the concert. My mother was afraid the beard, if taken off, would fall apart. She said I could take off the wig if I liked, but, as my father pointed out, I would look even weirder without it. My father sized me

WAYNE JOHNSTON

up and said that, unfortunately, I looked, with my complexion, more like a bearded lady than a man. We sat and watched television, and he kept asking my mother, who was in her room getting ready, if she had noticed that lately I'd been looking old. Was it, he wondered, altogether normal for a thirteen-year-old to have a beard, or to wear a blanket for that matter? He knew what it was, he said. It was the new biblical look that was all the rage at school. I tried to ignore him, but he kept at it. I was about at the end of my rope when, to make matters worse, Rennie and Dola and the girls dropped in. Ambrosia had her costume in a bag, but, when she saw that I was wearing mine, begged Dola to let her put hers on. Dola relented, and Ambrosia went to the bathroom, from which she emerged, minutes later, wearing a snowsuit inside out. It was lined with wool, and she did, indeed, look like the lamb she was supposed to be. Her black boots looked like hooves, as did the baby shoes into which she'd halfway forced her fingers. At rehearsals, her bleating had been rated exceptional. She had been chosen to be, not just a lamb, but the lamb that had to bleat and move the most, "the prime lamb," my father said. She got to crawl around and look at the baby Jesus and didn't just have to lie there sleeping, like all the other lambs. "Show them the head, Mary," Rennie said. Ambrosia reached into her bag and took out the head of an oversized toy panda bear. Emptied of its stuffing, it hung limp on her hand, like a puppet. "It was her favourite Teddy bear when she was little," Dola said. "We found him in the attic today." Ambrosia nodded, sadly it seemed, then put the head on. Where the bear's big eyes had been plucked out, spaces were left too large for Ambrosia's eyes, so a lot of her face was visible on either side of the plastic nose. "The only hard part," Dola said, "was the ears. We had to take the old ones off and put some new ones on." The new ears were made from hollow slips and were too large. Cheryl said they made Ambrosia look like an Easter bunny.

"Bobby looks nice, doesn't he, girls?" Dola said. It was generally agreed that, though I looked nice, I looked more like Moses than St. Joseph. My mother said that was all right, just as long as I looked like *someone* holy.

Our play, which ran only twenty minutes, came on after the Glee
Club and the tap-dancers. We waited off-stage in one of the dressing-
rooms, cramped and warm. Ambrosia, to the mortification of the lady
in charge of the Glee Club, practised her bleating quite loudly. "Baaa-
aaa, baaa-aaa." My beard smelled of mothballs. It got in my nose and
made me sneeze. Mary Hart and I tried not to look at one another.
She was wearing bed sheets, blue and white, and holding a plastic baby
Jesus in her arms. When we finally did go on, the play went well, up
to the point where Mary, sitting, holding the baby Jesus, turned to me
and said, "Kiss me Joseph, so that, for a moment, we three may be one."
I was standing beside her, and she was to lean a little toward me, so
as to seem, Sister Haymond said, "not just kissed but kissing." To the
audience, it must have seemed that Mary Hart, holding the baby Jesus
with one hand, grabbed me by the beard with the other and, pulling
my face down to hers, kissed me, not chastely on the cheek, but deeply,
passionately, on the lips. (As my father said, "You wouldn't think Joseph
and Mary, married this two thousand years, would still carry on like
that.") But what actually happened was that, extending her cheek, Mary
leaned too far and started to fall and grabbed me by the beard to save
herself. Consequently, I missed her cheek and got her on the mouth.
It was my misplaced kiss that kept her from going over, because the
beard, though it held at first, came off in her hand the moment her
lips met mine. And what, to the audience, must have seemed passion,
was both of us pushing to get her back into the chair. We had to push,
lest our faces slip apart. Not wanting to let on that anything was wrong,
I did not use my hands but, to keep my footing, held my arms out like
a surfer. And Mary did not use her hands, because she dared not drop
the baby Jesus nor acknowledge the beard by dropping *it*. Nothing
touched except our lips. We might have been two acrobats performing
some rare feat of balance. My arms out straight, my face shoved her
face back until she rolled into the chair.

While this was going on, the only sound in all the hall was that of

Ambrosia bleating — and, in the bleating, there was an undercurrent of giggles, which she was trying to suppress. So infectiously risible was this combination of bleats and giggles, there was, very soon, a tremendous release of laughter, as from people who'd been holding back for years. It started at the back and moved like a wave to the front, like an avalanche of forbidden fruit. It came roaring, not in giggles but great guffaws, and broke upon the stage. Even the nuns and the priests in the front row laughed. My mother would have it, later, that my father was one of only a few people who found it funny. But according to him, she, too, laughed loudly. "Outrageous," was the word she used. She said the reaction of the audience was "outrageously disrespectful." "Go on," my father said, "everyone laughed except Mary and Bobby and the baby Jesus." We, he said, seemed stunned and looked out at the audience as if *its* drawers had dropped, not ours.

We managed to finish the play. The audience settled down when, at a signal from Sister Haymond, Ambrosia stopped bleating. It was the birth of Christ, slapstick style. My father said that later, when the Wise Men came on stage, he expected them to pull out pies and cream the Holy Family. For Tony McGillivray and Mary Smythe, it was a hard act to follow. It was generally agreed that their kiss was nothing next to ours. It was done, in that final scene, so lightly on the lips, no one batted an eye. Afterwards, Sister Haymond went out and bravely announced that the play had ended. No one got blamed for the fiasco. Concerning Mary Hart and me, my father said it was "hard to know who ravished who." My mother got her beard back, and, to her relief and mine, I did not develop warts.

Whisper to the Wind

MARY JANE LOSIER

Not all children are happy at Christmas, and ten year old Lina was one of those who could find little joy in the season. She lived many years ago near Tracadie, New Brunswick, when the town was just a small village. Few families had electricity. A kerosene lamp stood in Lina's kitchen window. The flame flickered over the worn wooden table where Lina's mother was whipping batter in a large bowl. Lina could see her brush away the strands of dark hair that escaped from a tight bun she wore at the back of her neck, through the window's glow. Just once, Lina thought, I would like to see Maman smile like she did before . . . before everything changed.

"Dépêche-toi, hurry up with that wood," her brother Arthur shouted, shoving her so hard she skidded in the icy yard. "At the rate you're going, the fire will be out."

Lina regained her balance and adjusted her load. Nothing about this evening made her think it was la veille de Noël, Christmas Eve. There was no shiny sink in Lina's house, no freshly painted walls or cupboards full of china, or drawers of silver cutlery, or refrigerators full of food. Instead, the family sat at a long scarred wooden table in the kitchen of the one-floor, one-room home. They ate from pewter plates and drank from pewter mugs. They used wooden benches instead of chairs, and these slid against the walls when the meal was finished. Milk, cheese and eggs were stored in an ice chest. Home made jams and preserves were kept in a pantry, vegetables in a root cellar which they could reach from a trap door in the pantry floor.

The family drew water from an outside well into an oak bucket. It was so heavy water sloshed across the floor as Lina tried to carry it inside. When the well water froze, usually by late December, Lina took her turn, sometimes digging through the snow, sometimes breaking through ice, to bring water to the surface. Lina washed over a wash basin every morning, and once a week she bathed in a tin tub set behind a screen in the kitchen. The water was heated on the stove. On really bad weather days or at night, the family went to the toilet in chamber pots that were stored under the bed. Otherwise they had to go to an outside privy.

Lina never felt she was poor. Until the tragedy, her life was like that of most children in the village. She enjoyed going to school, even though it took her an hour to walk there each morning. She liked going to church and singing with her father in the church choir. She liked playing tag with her brothers and sisters, or hide and seek, or jumping in the hay. She liked strapping a pair of wooden skates to her boots and skating on the river in the winter time, or building snow forts, or leaping from the roof of their house into soft white snowbanks that drifted under the eaves.

Her dark eyes used to shine with happiness, but, alas, they were not shining now. Some months earlier, in the season of the year when the snow melts and bits of grass start turning green around the edge of the house, Lina's cher Papa became ill. The doctor's treatments were no help at all; every night, when they said their evening prayers, Lina asked Jésus, Marie, et Joseph, la Sainte Famille, to cure him. Père LaChance, their parish priest, even put her father's name on the list of special intentions so everyone in the village could pray for him. But her papa got weaker and weaker until he could no longer rise even to sip a little of her mother's fine nourishing bouillon. One day Père LaChance came to the house. Lina's mother and her older sister May met him. They carried two lit candles. No one spoke. They led Père

LaChance to a corner of the kitchen, where Lina's father rested on a cot so the warmth of the stove kept him from getting chilled. The priest set the candles on a nightstand beside a crucifix.

"Good afternoon, Père LaChance." Lina curtsied as she was taught when greeting members of the clergy.

"Shh," Arthur scolded. "He can't talk to you now. He has to talk to Papa and bless him and give him la Sainte Communion." Arthur was an altar boy and sometimes he went with the priest to visit the sick. "He can only talk to Papa."

"Why?" Asked Lina.

"Because, stupid, he is carrying the Holy Communion."

"You mean Jesus in the bread and wine."

"Yes," said Arthur.

Later, her mother called all the children together, and with Père LaChance they knelt and recited their chapelet, the rosary. Even Lina's little brother Willie who was only three, repeated the opening words: "Je vous salue Marie . . ." at each repetition of the prayer. Lina ran outside before it was over and knelt in the hayfield near the garden. "Please, please, please, God, make Papa well," she begged, "and I will never tease my brothers and sisters again, I promise." It was too late. No promise great or small could save him. Her papa died that night.

Lina's house was full of relatives and friends. Her grandfather and uncles made a coffin. Some stayed even after the funeral was over. They tilled the large garden making it ready for seeding. They planted the potatoes, carrots, corn and other vegetables. Lina, playing with the other children, occasionally forgot why they were there. Her aunts cooked and cleaned and stored the gifts of food. They sat with her mother and talked and made tea and sipped tea and talked some more. They shook and aired the bedding and put away the cot where her father had rested. Eventually, though, everyone had to return to their own work. "Winter will be here soon enough," Lina's mother said to them one morning, "I will need your help, if we are to get through it." Lina, putting her father's loss behind her, was determined to help her mother any way she could.

All summer they picked berries: wild strawberries and raspberries in July; blueberries in August; and cranberries in the fall. Her mother made fruit pies until late in the night-time and jars and jars of preserves. These she traded at the store for rations of molasses, flour, sugar, beans, oatmeal, or sometimes for a piece of fabric or a ball of wool. That September they brought in the vegetables from the garden, storing the potatoes, carrots, onions and turnips in le caveau, the root cellar, and loading the pantry with canned beans, peas and tomatoes. The house reeked of vinegar and onions, and mounds of cucumbers were stacked on the table, but that didn't stop the neighbours who came to buy her pickles before her mother could bring them to the store. Lina's uncle brought them a large side of pork, and Lina's mother salted it so it would not spoil. They salted cod and herring, too. The family would dine on these foods most of the winter.

Arthur, thirteen, and Lina's sister May, twelve, did not go to school that fall. They were needed at home. Lina knew there was more than enough work for her also, but that September, when school opened again, her mother said, "Lina, your father wanted you to have an education. He wanted you to be a teacher." She handed Lina the old lunch pail that belonged to her papa. It carried two thick slices of home made bread, cheese and a jar of milk. It was just after seven, so early the fields were still wrapped in a nipping predawn frost, and the grasses Lina walked through were imprinted with wet tracks trailing behind her.

"Anyway, in just a few weeks the school will close for the winter," May called to her. "We will still have lots of work for you."

Last year, her father, who was a buyer for a produce company, asked Lina to keep a record of the vegetables and fruit he purchased and sent in crates to Bathurst. Lina carefully copied into a black notebook the names of the people doing business with her dad, what they sold and how much her father paid them. She was so good at her work, he used to run his fingers through her hair and tell his customers she was "ma petite comptable." Lina swallowed hard to keep her lips from trembling. Papa was gone. She shut her eyes, but not before a few tears spilled down her cheeks.

May was right. The school closed in November because the trustees did not have enough money to buy fuel or to pay a teacher through the winter months. Lina helped the others cut branches from the fir and spruce trees. These they mixed with seaweed and mud and banked around the outside of their little house to keep out the winter wind and snow. Last year her father hired a man to help him and for a whole week they did nothing but saw logs, chop the wood, and stack it in a wood shed. That wood had aged and was ready to burn, but this year was the time to season the logs for future use. There was no money to hire a helper, so Arthur, May and Lina's mother did the work themselves, while Lina looked after five-year-old Médora and Willie. Lina was used to working hard but never without her father to shoulder the heaviest chores. Never without his gentle teasing which made her mother smile. Never without her father, and everyone else so cross and hurt.

This day started like any other winter day. While Lina peeled potatoes for their dinner and kept her eye on the younger ones, her mother and the other two milked and fed the cow, brought fresh hay to the horse, cleaned the barn stalls and gathered the eggs. Last year the house was filled with the aroma of fresh baked pâté au lièvre. The family, from the youngest to the oldest, went to la Messe de Minuit, and later they gathered with their cousins at her grandparents' house for a réveillon. There was no decorated Christmas tree, for it wasn't a custom, but every family brought something for the Christmas feast. "Your maman is the best cook in the village," Lina's grandmother whispered as she helped lay out the food on a long table.

The men brought in two heavy kegs of apple cider. There was lots of music. Lina's mother sang and played the accordion, two of her uncles were violonneux and played their fiddles, and Lina's brother Arthur played the harmonica as well as the violin. Lina danced and danced, and when she grew so tired her legs could not dance another step, she tapped the rhythms on her knee with a pair of spoons. Her papa held Willie and waltzed him high above the others.

Everyone dined on the patés. The meat was seasoned with onions and summer savory. The aroma coming from the oven as they baked

MARY JANE LOSIER

sent Lina rushing back and forth asking her mother over and over again, "Can we eat now? Please?" They ended the night singing carols and folk songs. Later, bundled in their wool coats and knitted scarves, they snuggled under the hay in the back of the wagon. Lina fell asleep listening to the sound of runners slicing the snow and her mother and father talking softly. When she woke she was covered in layers of quilts on the straw filled mattress she shared with Médora and May. It was le jour de Noël, Christmas Day, and their stocking caps, which usually hung on wooden pegs near the stove, were now on the table, each stuffed with a new pair of mittens and socks her grandmother knit for them, some barley toys and even an orange. Oranges were rare and very hard to get in Tracadie.

"Père Noël came, Père Noël came. Maman, Papa look what he brought us!" Lina shouted. Soon the family was up, for they all slept in the same room. The benches were opened and the children rolled up the straw tick mattresses and quilts that were stored in them. That afternoon they went coasting, using sleds her Papa made out of old wooden kegs.

"Non!" Willie shouted so loud it startled Lina from her thoughts. Médora began to cry.

"What are those two fighting about now?" her mother called in an exasperated voice.

"How should I know?" May shouted. "Where is Lina? She is supposed to look after them."

Her house, set far back in a field of snow and nestled against a stand of evergreens, seemed cold no matter how great the fire in the stove. Arthur shoved past her through the doorway. The flickering lamp in the window was not comforting at all. Instead of love and joy Lina felt sadness and anger. Why did her Papa leave them, anyway? It wasn't fair. She could contain herself no longer, "Will Père Noël come tonight?"

"Hush!" May said crossly.

"Not tonight," said Arthur, stacking the wood near the fire. "Not ever."

A heavy log fell from his arms and crashed on the floor. Lina adjusted her load. May, who was darning a sock, stopped pulling on the yarn; Médora let go of the tin whistle she and Willie were fighting over. They all looked first at Arthur, then at their mother. Lina's mother, not noticing the noise or how disappointed the children were, poured the mixture she was beating into a pan and set it in the oven. Wiping her hands on her apron, she said, "We are going outside."

"Again?" asked Lina who was still wearing her coat and shawl.

"Yes," said her mother. "You, too, Arthur, and May, put down your mending and help Médora. Come here, Willie." Willie blew a few piercing notes in his mother's ear before she pulled the whistle from his fingers long enough to put on his coat.

"Come closer, Lina, Arthur, everyone. We will keep each other warm." The little group bundled about their mother. "Papa did not want to leave us," she said. "It is not his fault. Do you understand?"

"It's my fault," said Lina sadly. "I promised God I would never tease Willie or Médora again, and then I told them ghost stories and made them cry."

"It was my fault, too," Arthur was trenching the snow with the heel of his boot. "I was really angry at Papa because he wouldn't take me hunting with him last winter."

"Hush," said Lina's mother. "It wasn't anyone's fault. God doesn't punish children by taking away their papas. He just got sick. We don't know why."

Millions of stars, sparkling like tiny candles, were shining on them. "Your Papa wanted us to be happy even if he couldn't be here."

"I'm cold." Médora squeezed herself under her mother's long shawl.

Lina's mother sat on the icy step, wrapped a thick wool blanket around Willie and Médora and held them on her knees. "After Papa died it seemed to me that all the love in our house went away, and I was so angry, so busy, so tired, I forgot . . ."

"Forgot what?" May asked.

"I forgot how much I love you all, or to thank God for giving me such beautiful children." For the first time in many weeks Lina began

MARY JANE LOSIER

to feel a little happier. "Do you remember what Papa told you before he died?" Lina didn't want to think about that now, but her mother said again, "You were gathered around him, and he touched each of you . . ."

"And he said he loved us and he would always be near even if we couldn't see him," said May, gazing up at the stars.

"If we were in trouble . . ." said Arthur.

"Or sad and lonely," interrupted May.

"We just had to whisper to the wind and Papa would come," said Lina. "He will come into our hearts and we will feel him there." Lina shut her eyes. The cold night air swished over her cheeks. "Cher Papa," she said, and paused. "What will I tell him?"

"Tell him you love him," her mother said.

"Je t'aime, Papa," Lina whispered to the wind. "And I miss you. I wish you were here with us tonight." Everyone, even Médora and Willie, looked and listened. The stars grew even brighter. Then the evergreens shivered in the darkness sending pine-scented breezes over her cheeks. Was that her father's love she felt, that filled her heart so she wanted to weep for the joy of it?

"I'm cold," said May.

"Me, too," said Willie.

"Me, too," said Lina's mother with a laugh. "And you, Willie, are heavy," she added, setting him down just inside the door.

"Come now, who wants a piece of gingerbread right out of the oven?"

"Gâteau à la mélasse avec crème et sirop d'érable?"

"Oui," their mother smiled.

Jingle, jingle, jingle. The children stopped eating to listen. Through the window they saw their grandparents, their uncle and aunt and several cousins.

"Come with us to la Messe de Minuit," the uncle shouted.

"Can we go! Please! Can we!" All the children clamoured at once.

"We can all go," Lina's mother laughed as she helped them into their clothes. "Keep still," she said, removing a bit of whipped cream from

Lina's scarf. They all snuggled deep into the warm hay that was piled on the back of the wagon. Lina's mother held Willie on her lap while Lina and Médora nestled next to her. "Look, children, look at the stars." A gentle wind, fresh as snow, blew against her cheek. "Papa is here with us," she called to the others.

As they drew closer to the church, they met families and friends from all over the region. Someone was playing "Sainte Nuit" on the church organ. Arthur started to sing, then May and Lina, even Médora and Willie, and finally Lina's mother, their pretty voices carrying the melody through the winter night.

Lina was crammed into a pew near the front, squeezed between Arthur and May, her mother, Médora and Willie. The church was full. Some men and boys were standing at the back. Père LaChance came in, led by the altar boys and followed by les soeurs de St-Joseph. Everyone was singing, "Il est né, le devine enfant," while a young girl from the orphanage placed le Bébé Jesus in a crèche that was set under some spruce boughs on the altar. "You were wrong, Arthur," Lina whispered. She felt a cool breeze like a gentle kiss caress her cheek. "Christmas is here."

It was very late by the time the service ended. Willie and Médora fell asleep, but Lina held her eyes open all the way home. Everyone came inside for the réveillon. Lina's mother stirred the fire in the grate, added more wood, and put the four meat pies she had prepared earlier and stored in the caveau, into the oven. Relatives, bringing pastries and other good things, spilled into the house. Arthur played the harmonica, and Lina gave her mother the accordion.

"Please play," she said. The room was soon filled with so much music, dancing and singing that scarcely anyone noticed when Lina slipped outside for a moment. "Je t'aime, Papa," she whispered to the wind. "Thank you for being with us tonight. Merci." The nearby ever-greens creaked, and a fresh breeze, like fingers, stirred through her hair.

The Authors

BRIAN BARTLETT, a native of Fredericton who now lives in Halifax, is the author of several books of poetry, most recently *Underwater Carpentry* and *Granite Erratics*. His fiction has appeared in *The Journey Prize Anthology* and *Best Canadian Stories*, and he is working on a book of essays, journals, columns, memoirs, and other prose pieces, *Living with Poetry*.

JESS BOND was born and raised in Glace Bay, Nova Scotia. A graduate of the University of New Brunswick and Fredericton Teachers' College, she taught elementary school in Fredericton for several years and then moved to Scarborough, Ontario, where she taught for twenty years. Now retired, she lives near Belleville, Ontario.

PAUL BOWDRING, a St. John's, Newfoundland, writer, editor, and teacher, is the author of two novels, *The Roncesvalles Pass* (1989) and *The Night Season* (1997). "The Consolation of Pastry" was first published in *The Fiddlehead* and subsequently included in *The Night Season*, which was broadcast on CBC Radio's *Between the Covers* in December, 1998.

HARRY BRUCE is an essayist, editor, journalist and freelance writer. Born in Toronto, he moved to Nova Scotia in the early 1970s. Well known for his contributions to magazines and his syndicated newspaper column "All About Words," he is the author of a dozen books, including *The Short Happy Walks of Max MacPherson*, *Movin' East*, and *Down Home: Notes of a Maritime Son*, the collection from which "Home for Christmas" is taken.

EPHIE CARRIER is retired and lives at Dumfries, New Brunswick. Born in Grand Falls, New Brunswick, he has lived in many parts of Canada and travelled all over the world. For the past several years he has been writing and telling stories for Storyfest New Brunswick. He is co-author with Jan Andrews of a children's book, *Harvest* (1999). His story "Just Pick Up the Sticks" appeared in *Echoes* (Maine).

LYNN COADY grew up in industrial Port Hawkesbury, Nova Scotia. After earning her BA from Carleton University, she lived for a year each in Malagash, Nova Scotia, and Saint John, Sackville, and Fredericton, New Brunswick. While in Fredericton she wrote her first play, *Cowboy Names*, and most of her novel, *Strange Heaven*, a finalist for a Governor General's Award, from which "The Three Marys" is adapted. Since 1996, she has lived in Vancouver.

KELLY COOPER, originally from Saskatchewan, lives on a dairy farm in Belleisle Creek, New Brunswick. Her work has been published in *The Fiddlehead, Pottersfield Portfolio, CV2* and *The New Brunswick Reader*. She is one of the authors featured in *Water Studies: New Voices in Maritime Fiction* (1998), and she won the 1999 New Brunswick Writers' Federation David Adams Richards award for fiction.

ANN COPELAND, a native of Connecticut, lived in Sackville, New Brunswick, for twenty-five years before moving to Salem, Oregon, in 1996. A popular fiction writing instructor at workshops in Canada, the US, and New Zealand, she is the author of *The ABCs of Writing Fiction* and six books of stories. *The Golden Thread*, linked stories about Sister Claire Delaney, was a finalist for a 1990 Governor General's Award; "Another Christmas," first published in *The Fiddlehead*, is part of *Strange Bodies on a Stranger Shore*, the sequel to *The Golden Thread*.

HERB CURTIS lives in Fredericton, but he grew up on the Miramichi and returns there at every opportunity. He is the author of three books of humour, a collection of yarns and tales, the 1999 story collection *Luther Corhern's Salmon Camp Chronicles*, and four novels, including *The Brennen Siding Trilogy*. "Hilda Porter's Christmas" is from *The Last Tasmanian*, the second volume of the trilogy.

ROBERT GIBBS grew up in Saint John, New Brunswick. After graduating from the University of New Brunswick, he spent two years at Cambridge University. He has taught in rural and urban schools in New Brunswick as well as in the Department of English at the University of New Brunswick, from which he retired in 1989 as Professor Emeritus. As poet, editor, book reviewer, he has had a long association with *The Fiddlehead*. He has published several collections of verse, a novel and two collections of short stories, the latest of which is *Angels Watch Do Keep* (1997).

RAY GUY was born in Come By Chance, Newfoundland, and now lives in St. John's. A journalist and playwright, he has published several books, most recently *Ray Guy's Best*, a collection of his columns from the magazine *Atlantic Insight*. "A Christmas Story" first appeared in *That Far Greater Bay*, for which he won the Stephen Leacock Award for humour in 1977.

SUSAN HALEY lives near Black River, Nova Scotia. *Blame It on the Spruce Budworm* (1998) is her latest novel. "Dene Christmas" was first published in *The Gaspereau Review* (1998).

DAVID HELWIG has written fifteen books of fiction (most recently the novella *Close to the Fire*) and numerous works of non-fiction, including poetry, documentary, translation, and memoir. A frequent contributor to major newspapers and magazines, he was a founder and the long-time editor of *Best Canadian Stories*. After living in Kingston, Ontario, for many years, he moved to Prince Edward Island in 1996.

MAUREEN HULL's poetry, short stories and non-fiction have been published in journals and magazines across the country; some of it has been anthologized. She is the author of a collection of stories, *Righteous Living* (1999), and a children's book, *Wild Cameron Women* (forthcoming). She lives on a small island in the Northumberland Strait, where, with her husband, she fishes lobster.

CLARISSA HURLEY, a writer and actor, lives in Fredericton. Her story "Women and Linen Look Best in the Dark" won first prize for short fiction in the 1998 New Brunswick Writer's Federation Competition.

WAYNE JOHNSTON, a native of Newfoundland, is the author of five novels, including *The Colony of Unrequited Dreams* (1999) and *The Divine Ryans*, winner of the Thomas Raddall Atlantic Fiction Award. His first novel, *The Story of Bobby*

O'Malley, from which "The Christmas Kiss" is excerpted, was his University of New Brunswick master's thesis and won the *Books in Canada* First Novel Award.

MARY JANE LOSIER wrote "Whisper to the Wind" in memory of her mother-in-law, Lina Robichaud. She is a co-author of *The Children of Lazarus: The Story of the Lazaretto at Tracadie* (1984) and the author of *Amanda Viger: Spiritual Healer to New Brunswick's Leprosy Victims* (1999). She is the Community Liaison Representative in Bathurst for the Department of Extension, University of New Brunswick, and she gives workshops on life writing to children and adults.

LUCY MAUD MONTGOMERY (1877-1942) is Prince Edward Island's most famous daughter and one of the world's favourite authors. "The Forgotten Brother" is from her story collection *The Further Chronicles of Avonlea* (1920).

BERNICE MORGAN, a resident of St. John's, Newfoundland, is the author of two highly praised novels, *Random Passage* and *Waiting for Time*. Her third book, *The Topography of Love*, will be published early in 2000.

PATRICK O'FLAHERTY, who lives in St. John's, Newfoundland, has written four works of fiction, the most recent of which is the novel *Benny's Island*. His latest book is *Old Newfoundland: A History to 1843* (1999).

ROBERT B. RICHARDS is a retired librarian living in Fredericton. He has been a New Brunswicker forever and an on-again off again contributor of poetry to different periodicals, notably *The Fiddlehead* and *The Cormorant*. His poetry chapbook *Unfolding Fern* was published by Spare Time Editions.

TED RUSSELL (1904-1977) was born in Coley's Point, a small community in Newfoundland. He was a teacher, a magistrate, a member of Joey Smallwood's cabinet (he resigned after two years), and an insurance salesman. He turned to writing when he was over fifty. "Santa Claus" is from *Tales from Pigeon Inlet* (1977).

SYR RUUS was born in Tallinn, Estonia, and educated in the United States, and she has lived in Nova Scotia ever since. Her juvenile novel *Edgar* took first prize in the 1994 Writers' Federation of Nova Scotia competition, and she is now concentrating on adult fiction. "Christmas in the Country" first appeared in the anthology *Taking Off the Tinsel* (1996).

ANNE SIMPSON is a writer and artist living in Antigonish, Nova Scotia. In 1997 she was one of two winners of the Journey Prize for her short story "Dreaming Snow," first published in *The Fiddlehead*. More recently she was a finalist for the Chapters/Robertson Davies award for *Canterbury Beach*, a novel manuscript.

SUE SINCLAIR has published both fiction and poetry in journals across Canada and has a master's degree in Creative Writing from the University of New Brunswick. Her thesis, *Bees and Keepers,* was a finalist for the Chapters/Robertson Davies Award. She currently resides in Toronto but hopes to move back to the east.

JOHN STEFFLER lives in Corner Brook, Newfoundland, where he teaches literature and creative writing at Sir Wilfred Grenfell College. His books of poems include the award-winning *That Night We Were Ravenous* and *The Wreckage of Play*, the source of "The New Sled." His novel *The Afterlife of George Cartwright* was shortlisted for a Governor General's Award and the Commonwealth First Novel Award and won the 1992 Smithbooks/Books in Canada First Novel Award and the Thomas Raddall Atlantic Fiction Award.

MARK TUNNEY is the editor of *The New Brunswick Reader*. Born in Toronto, he has lived in New Brunswick since 1982. Although he has been a journalist for many years, this is the first time his work has appeared in a book.

DAVID WEALE, a professor of history at the University of Prince Edward Island, is the author of *Them Times* (1992) and *A Long Way from the Road* (1998), collections of Prince Edward Island humour and wit; *The True Meaning of Crumbfest* (1999), a children's book and animated TV program; and *An Island Christmas Reader* (1994), the collection of PEI stories and memoirs from which "Charlie and the Paper Boy" is taken.

Acknowledgements

The editor and publisher thank the following for their kind permission to use their works in this anthology: "Cousin Gifts," from *Underwater Carpentry*, by Brian Bartlett, published by Goose Lane Editions. Reprinted by permission of the publisher. "The Christmas Chair," © Jess Bond. With permission of the author. "The Consolation of Pastry," from *The Night Season*, by Paul Bowdring, published by Killick Press. Reprinted by permission of the publisher. "Home for Christmas," from *Down Home*, by Harry Bruce, Key Porter Books, 1998. Used with permission of the publisher. "The Christmas Sled," © Ephrem Carrier. With permission of the author. "The Three Marys," copyright © by Lynn Coady 1998. Adapted from *Strange Heaven* (Goose Lane Editions, 1998). Reprinted by permission of the author and the publisher. "Waiting for Gabriel," © Kelly Cooper. With permission of the author. "Another Christmas," from *Strange Bodies on a Stranger Shore* by Ann Copeland, published by Goose Lane Editions. Reprinted by permission of the publisher. "Hilda Porter's Christmas," from *The Last Tasmanian* by Herb Curtis, published by Goose Lane Editions. Reprinted by permission of the publisher. "The Death of My Father," from *The Tongue Still Dances: Poems New and Selected* by Robert Gibbs, published by Goose Lane Editions. Reprinted by permission of the publisher. "Seasonings," © Robert Gibbs. With permission of the author. "A Christmas Story," © Ray Guy. With permission of the author. "Dene Christmas," © Susan Haley. With permission of the author. "One More Wise Man" and "The Feast of Flesh," © David Helwig. With permission of the author. "The Montreal Aunts," © Maureen Hull. With permission of the author. "Candylights," © Clarissa Hurley. With permission of the author. "The Christmas Kiss," an excerpt from *The Story of Bobby O'Malley*, by Wayne Johnston, is reprinted by permission of Oberon Press. "A Whisper in the Wind," © Mary Jane Losier. With permission of the author. "The Brother who Failed" is excerpted from *The Further Chronicles of Avonlea* by L.M. Montgomery, with the permission of Ruth MacDonald and David MacDonald, trustee, who are the heirs of L.M. Montgomery. *L.M. Montgomery* is a trademark of the Heirs of L.M. Montgomery Inc. *Avonlea* is an official mark of the Anne of Green Gables Licensing Authority Inc., which is located